Mon
Monroe, Steve,
'46, Chicago

$ 22.95

1st ed.

# '46, Chicago

STEVE MONROE

# '46, Chicago

TALK MIRAMAX BOOKS

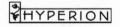

LIBRARY OF CONGRESS CATALOGING-IN-PUBLICATION DATA

ISBN: 0-7868-6731-0

FIRST EDITION

10      9      8      7      6      5      4      3      2      1

**FOR MY FATHER**

*A real American hero*

# '46, Chicago

## FRIDAY, MAY 10, 1946

COM ED RATIONING ELECTRICITY is like a hooker rationing the cooze, I thought, as the dishwater blonde worked for a tip.

Nine days into the dimout and the madam who ran the brothel followed the mayor's edict; the room was lit by lantern. I watched as my girl finished in the flickering light; our shadows played a skin flick on the wall. She left the room, came back with a wet rag, cleaned me up.

"Like your work?" I asked.

She ignored it: "That's three dollars."

"I'm a veteran," I said.

She didn't look up. "So am I, honey. All right, make it two."

I sat up on the side of the bed, grabbed my boxers off the end table, slipped them on. I grabbed two singles and a quarter, handed them to her.

"Hope you don't have to work nights to make up for that tip," she said as she wadded the bills and grabbed her housecoat off the floor.

"You want more coin, suck a mint," I said.

No laugh. She eyeballed me. "Want another one? On the house?"

I laughed. "You're no vet. New?"

She nodded. "Rita. Ask for me next time, huh?"

Chicago thunder roared.

"That sounded like a gunshot," she said. It roared again. She yelped, dove off the back of the bed. I grabbed my .38, cracked the door. The hallway was dark and narrow; I looked left, right. The candles on the

1

banister to my right flickered, cast a glow across the wall in front of me. Sudden motion to my left: A figure burst out of a room, two doors down. It ran my way. I got a quick make: a colored man—dark hands popped out of his coatsleeves, hat pulled down low, a gray scarf wrapped around his face. He held a .45.

He ran by our room, missed me in the doorway, headed for the stairs.

I stepped into the hall; the door creaked behind me. He heard the noise as he reached the stairs. He looked over his shoulder, saw me, turned and lifted the gun.

I raised my .38. "Drop it!" I yelled.

He fired—a bullet tore into the doorjamb above my head. I dove to the ground, hesitated. He lowered the gun, fired again. The bullet chewed up the floor in front of me. No choice: I squeezed two quick ones into his chest. He caught them, toppled down the stairs and came to rest in the foyer.

Screams from everywhere. Doors opened. Men popped eyebrows into the hall. I turned, ran down the hall, pushed the door open, prepped myself for the first dead body I'd see since the war. I got one and a half.

The man was sprawled on the bed, facedown: Two bullet holes in his back turned his birthday suit into a retirement suit. The girl had it worse: Underneath him, she'd taken the leftovers. She was still alive. Barely. Blood gurgled out of her mouth, bubbled as she moved her jaw, tried to talk. Her eyes registered shock. She wouldn't make it to the hospital. I felt the man's left wrist, nixed on a pulse, pulled him off her.

"Janey!" A young brunette in a housecoat pushed me out of the way, started for the girl. I grabbed her, held her back.

"Call an ambulance!" I pushed her out the door, stepped toward the girl. "We're getting help. Try to stay calm." Her head nodded in rhythm; blood spat out of her chest. I grabbed a pillow, placed it against her stomach, gently took the back of her head in my hand. Her head lolled onto my side, her breathing slowed.

Noises: loud footsteps down the hall, back stairs. The back door creaked open, slammed shut: Customers escaping i.d. Closer, wanton women gathered in the doorway, screaming, crying. The madam stepped into the room, hands on her cheeks, yelling at me. I stopped her with a hand in the air: "I'm a cop."

I turned back to the girl. Civilians fight it hard, too, I thought, as she died.

FIFTEEN MINUTES LATER, dressed, blood washed off in the kitchen sink. The ambulances were headed to the morgue. Cops questioned the women, burned that none of the johns stuck around to talk. I reached toward my shirt pocket for a cigarette as the kitchen suddenly filled with light. Startled, I turned toward the doorway. A heavyset man with a thick moustache moved his hand from the light switch, stepped into the room and doused the candles. His ease and weariness gave him away—he was as easy to i.d. as the prosties. He was a homicide dick.

"Dimout ended an hour ago," he muttered. "Another whore who thinks she did her civic duty."

"Every little bit helps," I said. "Guess the supply ain't really unlimited." I turned back toward the sink, turned on the faucet, threw my hands under the stream so he wouldn't see them shake.

"I hear you're a cop."

"Yeah." I dried my hands on an old dishtowel, told him my name, showed him my badge.

He motioned to the kitchen table, sat down. I sat down across from him. He leaned forward, pushed up the sleeves of his sport jacket. "Carl Jameson, homicide. Mind telling me what a cop is doing in a place like this, Officer Carson?"

I glared at him, he looked it: a choirboy with a pair of brass knuckles, a goon for God. Medium height, about forty extra pounds, thinning brown hair and a handlebar that hung too far over his lip.

I took the cigarette out of my shirt pocket, grabbed a book of matches off the table and lit it. "Making up for some time overseas."

"Navy?"

"Marines."

"No excuse. You shouldn't have been here. But you were. What happened?" He waved his hand in front of his face. "And you can leave out the details of your lewd behavior."

I gave him my story, told him I'd offered up a warning, stressed the gunshots. I didn't want to shoot him, but I'd had no choice.

He drummed his fingers on the table. "Bad break for the shine, you being here and all. Anyone know you were coming?"

"The dame."

"You schedule an appointment?"

"Skip it. Just kidding."

He leaned forward, plucked a crumb from his moustache. "Leave the yucks for someone else, Officer. Answer the question. Anyone know you were paying a visit?"

"No. Last-minute decision."

"Habit?"

"No."

"Been here before?"

I shrugged my shoulders, blew smoke. "Uh-huh."

"When?"

"Few years ago, maybe three times since my discharge."

"Anyone know you came here before?"

"No one. Sam Brody."

A grunt, surprise: "South Side Sam Brody?"

"One and the same."

"Figures. *He* couldn't tip anybody off."

"Long-distance call from Terre Haute."

"South Side Sam," he said. "Served him right. Dirtiest cop I ever met. Now how would a...?"

I cut him off. "Right. History. Let's get this over with."

Jameson looked at me, shook his head. "You queered this one, Officer. A young man like you shouldn't be in a place like this, and you sure as hell should've taken off after the shooting. You ain't no hero. All you did was kill a shine and make my job that much harder. You're a regular screwup, just like Brody."

I digested it, let it pass. "That all?"

"No, give your statement to Sergeant Anderson when he comes down. I'll call you if we need any more of your 'help.'"

I got up, started out. "Say, Casanova," said Jameson, stopping me in the doorway. "You know the deceased?"

"Which one?"

"The man, you idiot."

"Which one?"

"Very funny, wisenheimer. The white guy."

"No," I said. "Who was he?"

"Driver's license says 'Don Cordell.' Business card says, 'Attorney at Law.'"

I bit my lower lip. "How 'bout the other one?"

"The other one?"

"The colored man."

He picked at his nails with a match. "The shine? Who cares."

IT WAS NEARLY MIDNIGHT by the time they took my statement and gave me the scram. I guided my Olds south on Dearborn, turned east toward Rush Street, caught a glimpse of the bright lights and changed my mind. I pulled a quick U-turn, turned south down Toothpick Row, drove into the heart of the Loop, hit Madison and headed west. I parked in the rear of my apartment building and walked a couple of blocks to Harry's, my favorite gin mill.

Harry's was packed, a fact I didn't like but Harry probably did. Several booths sat to my right, filled with working-class stiffs dressed up for their big night out. Tables were scattered to my left, and a crowd in front of me gathered around the corner of the bar, watching a man challenge the dealer in a game of Bing. I watched just long enough to see the dealer spill a pair of sixes out of her cup—the player groaned when he realized he wouldn't get to roll. Frank, the bartender, caught my eye, motioned toward a stool at the end of the bar, near the jukebox. I pushed my way through the crowd and sat down.

"Figured you might like it back here better tonight, Gus," he said as he set a copper mug full of beer and a shot of whiskey in front of me. I polished off the shot, followed it with a slug of beer. He adjusted his bow tie, jerked his head toward a group of men in the front of the bar, "Construction workers, celebrating somebody's birthday."

I glanced their way. They'd pulled a group of tables together; a couple dozen empty beer bottles and countless shot glasses testified to their night. Two of them were arm-wrestling while the others urged them on with whoops and hollers.

"Harry 'round?" I asked Frank as I shifted two pennies from the right front pocket of my slacks to the left.

"'Course. Friday night. He's in the back room. Should be out in a minute." He took my shot glass and walked toward the sink.

I introduced myself to my beer again. We were getting better acquainted when I felt a tap on my shoulder.

"You gonna give all of your attention to that beer, Gus?"

I glanced at her over my shoulder. She was a broad redhead who would always look at home in her green waitress smock. I couldn't picture her in street clothes and didn't see the benefit in trying. "Evening, Mabel."

"You mean, 'Good morning, Mabel,'" she said. "As much as I'd love to hear you say that to me, this isn't exactly the spot I'd want to hear it."

I laughed. She grabbed it like it was on sale. "Big, blond and buff, just the way I like 'em. Wanna walk me home tonight, Officer?"

I shook my head. "Think I'll be here for a while."

"I will, too," she said as she set her tray down on the bar and wiped her hands on her apron. "I'm closing tonight."

"Your close and mine might not be the same."

"They will tonight. Harry's got a date, and me and Frank's closing up."

I threw my hands up in the air. "Another three hours 'til closing. We'll see what happens." I listened to the tune coming from the jukebox—it sounded like a drill sergeant screaming a lullabye. "What's with this garbage?"

"The worst, isn't it?" said Mabel. "Bix Bennett. Harry said to give it six plays every hour."

"Tell him to bring back the piano player."

A roar fell off the three tables in the front. A big, bearded man raised his fists in the air and growled, "Shots for the house!"

Mabel rolled her eyes and turned to the bar. The big man came over, ran his hand through the back of her hair and said, "Shots for the house, sister. Big Mike's won again."

He caught me out of the corner of his eye, slapped me on the back. "Order up, mister. Big Mike's buying for the house. I just won another two dollars."

I smelled the alcohol and onions on his breath, and I didn't turn toward him. "Nothing for me, thanks."

The man squared up, stepped closer. "I guess you didn't hear me. I said I'm buying a round for the house."

I eyed him in the mirror: a few years younger than me, say twenty-four, twenty-five, scuffed-up hands, coat and tie on their last legs. His hair, beard and 'stache were dark, and I figured him for black Irish. "I heard you. I just had a shot. I don't need another."

He rested a big arm on the bar. "Not even the frogs turned down a drink with a member of this man's army, and I'll be damned if it's gonna happen here."

I set my beer down, held onto the copper mug, turned to face him. One of his friends stepped up beside him, threw an arm around him and told him to go back to their tables.

"Oh," said Big Mike, "I'm just trying to buy the guy a drink. There ain't gonna be no trouble. C'mon, mister. Let me buy you a drink. You don't even have to drink it."

"Dogface," I said, "I appreciate the offer, but you'll just be throwing it away. Between you and Bix Bennett, I've decided that home might be a better place for me right now."

"Barkeep, give him another of what he's having," said Big Mike.

Frank shrugged, brought me another copper mug full of beer. I gave up, raised my glass to toast Big Mike and his friends. They played Mabel's game; they pulled up the "For Sale" sign and moved in next to me at the bar.

"Hell, I knew you couldn't resist a drink with this man's army," said Big Mike as he pulled a stool up next to me.

"Talk a little louder so I don't have to hear the jukebox, will you?" I said. I smiled to help wipe the confusion off his face.

"You're a funny one, Mac," he said.

His friends gathered around. They drank like there was no tomorrow—*that* I could understand. They took turns introducing themselves to me, thought it was a lark when I repeated all of their names, had me do it again.

"How the hell can you remember thirteen names that quick?" asked one.

"Lucky, I guess."

"Lucky, my ass. What kinda work you do?"

"Cop."

They burst into laughter. "And to think," said another, "Big Mike was getting on him. The guy's nearly as big as Big Mike *and* he's a cop!"

They roared. Big Mike decided to test me. "My grandmother's been married three times. Her name's Ellie Joan Fitzpatrick–Ryerson–Fitch."

Another chimed in: "My mom's maiden name is Glenker."

"My sister married a bohunk named Aramas Roscovitch."

"I know a gal named Alice Wharton–Grabowski."

The baker's dozen all got 'em in. I took a snort, set down my mug, turned to the group. Matter of fact: "Your name is Allen Adams, and your first-grade teacher was Henrietta Hall. You're Tim Bounds, and your first girlfriend was Tammy Peacock. Your barber's Bob Davidson, so you must be Hank Berman. You're James Baron, and your brother is Robert Jeffrey Baron. But he isn't related to Robert Weiss, because Robert Weiss's brother-in-law is right here—he's Dan Summerfield. This is another Robert, though; he's Robert Green, and his favorite pinup wasn't Betty Hutton, it was a girl from his high school named Elma Zileski. Ted Feeney here married Mary Baker. Scott Willard played baseball with Bill Cavaretta, but he's not related to the Cubs' Phil Cavaretta. You were too easy on me, there, Scott. Cletus Stemple here fought a man named Sean O'Reilly over a girl named Martha Dandridge. Fred Decker knows a gal named Alice Wharton–Grabowski. Titus Agnew's sister married a bohunk named Aramas Roscovitch, although that doesn't sound Bohemian to me. Ralph Barnes's mother's maiden name is Glenker, and Mike Fitzpatrick's grandmother was married three times and her name is...is..."

You could've heard a beer bubble pop.

"Well, goddamn it, you just gotta know this one!" yelled Titus Agnew.

I motioned to the bartender. "The next round is on the grandson of Ellie Joan Fitzpatrick–Ryerson–Fitch!"

The dam burst: Cheers filled the room. The men bellied up to the bar; Big Mike threw an arm around my shoulder, told me it was the damnedest thing he'd ever seen.

I didn't tell him that his hand on my shoulder felt like a tarantula. Didn't tell him that just a few years ago I'd have beaten him senseless for raising his voice to me. Didn't tell him that I remembered names because I wanted to stay close to those who'd died and that I'd killed a man just hours before. I didn't tell him I still had one foot in a watery grave. I told him I appreciated the beer, and I drank it like a sink draining tap water.

HARRY DIDN'T COME OUT of the back room until four. The place was near empty; Frank and Mabel had wiped down the bar and tables and left. Spilled booze had turned the floor into a skating rink; the Bix Bennett tune was scratched—he screamed at me over and over.

I forced my lids high, focused on Harry. Fatigue had chased me all night. It caught me.

"You look like you're down for the count," said Harry, peering down at me over his tiny accountant's glasses.

I smiled at him. He stood around five foot ten but probably only weighed a buck and a half, so I looked down on him like a heavyweight sizing up a lightweight. He wore a starched white shirt with a black vest and a thin, red tie. A pencil was tucked behind his right ear.

"Gonna sleep here tonight."

Harry ignored it. "I looked out earlier. Watched you play the crowd. Sure wasn't the old Gus."

"Men change."

"Thank God."

"Him too. Why're you playing that Bax Bennett shit?"

"Bix. I didn't know you were a music fan."

"Keep playing that garbage and I never will be."

"Why do you want to stay here tonight?"

I reached over the bar, grabbed a bottle, filled a glass. "I thought you had a date tonight."

"Girl up at the Garter. I called and told Tony to tell her I had a problem with the bar. Cubs game yesterday. Must've drank three dollars worth of beer myself. I still haven't recovered."

"Pity," I said as I tipped the glass.

He looked at me. "I agree," he said. He handed me the keys. "Don'll be here to open at ten. You leave before that, make sure you lock up. Cot's in the back. Try to keep track of your drinks. You owe me."

I jiggled the pennies in my pocket. "Don't worry, I'm keeping track."

Harry left. I took a long drink, checked out the guy in the bar mirror. Not bad in the looks department but aging fast. An old man in a young man's body. I closed my eyes, dropped my chin against my chest. Bix Bennett screamed "I love you" over and over.

I stumbled to the back room, fell onto the cot. Names ran through my head like a ticker tape. The colored man curled up on the foyer floor. I felt Sollie the Jew gently lift my head out of the water. "You're gonna make it, Gus," he said as I slipped into the deep, dark ocean.

## SATURDAY, MAY 11

I WOKE UP JUST BEFORE TEN. I locked up, left the key in the usual spot—a crack at the base of a street light. The pennies in my pocket crashed like cymbals as I walked the two blocks home.

My one-bedroom apartment: hardwood floors that warped in the summer, cracked in the winter; a front room that was only called "living" by custom, a kitchen the size of a kennel cage, a bathroom with a shower, sink and medicine cabinet and a small bedroom with one leaky window. But at least the walls were as thick as unleavened bread.

The furniture came from one of Sam's deadbeat tenants—a musty old couch, an end table and coffee table that looked like I used them for whittling, a radio and phonograph player. The phonograph player didn't work. The bedroom held a king-size mattress and box spring perched on an iron frame with no headboard. The dresser was the color of burned coffee, and the matching mirror was cracked in the lower left-hand corner and simply sat on the dresser and leaned against the wall. The only personal touch in the entire apartment was a photograph of my mother—it was a head shot from her attempt at becoming an actress, and it was faded and wrinkled. I'd put it inside a nice gold frame and turned it to face the bed.

I stripped out of my dirty clothes, turned the shower as hot as I could stand and washed away the night. I stepped out of the shower, filled the sink with water, brushed shaving cream over my face, dipped the straight razor into the water and shaved. The phone started to ring before I was done—I made the caller wait while I cleaned up my neck.

"Carson," I said as I picked up the phone, wrapped a towel around my waist. A post-booze effect: My baritone voice was even deeper. "Bullshit. It's my day off." My protest fell on ears paid to be deaf. "Figures. Give me an hour."

Not good. Captain Griffin wanted to see me, pronto. It didn't fly: Wrong place at the right time, but it was a clean shoot. I brought down a double murderer, the kind of action that warranted awards.

I walked across the hardwood floor, through the bedroom, reached into the closet and grabbed a clean pair of gray slacks. I dressed up for the captain: white dress shirt, hand-painted light blue tie. My shoes were shined the day before—they gleamed.

Coffee boiled on the stove; I filled a cup, waited for it to cool off. I could hear my upstairs neighbor's kids through the ceiling—Saturday; they'd make a racket all day. I'd have to find some way to kill time after my meeting. No rest for the weary.

I swallowed two cups of joe, threw on my shoulder holster, covered it with a dark blue sport jacket and a tan trench coat. I stepped out into the hall and smelled the boiling diapers.

"Hey, Mrs. Williams," I yelled up the stairs. "Shut the door when you're cleaning those diapers."

A heavyset woman stepped into the hall at the top of the stairs. Her thick black hair was dank, and sweat poured off her forehead. "Why the hell do you care? You're leaving."

"C'mon, Abbie. You know I'm his eyes and ears here. You got neighbors."

"Bastard," she muttered as she slammed the door. My eight-dollar-a-month break didn't feel like such a break—I still paid twenty a month to listen to that bull.

I let myself out the front door, walked around back and started up my machine. It coughed, belched, fired.

I drove through the Loop, caught Wabash, headed south. Not the quickest route, but I was in no hurry. I cracked the window, probably fifty degrees, colder by the lake. I drove slow, checked out the crowds. A block away, State Street looked packed. I passed a Wimpy's, thought about stopping in for a burger. The London Room's billboard said Louis Armstrong at nine o'clock, a seven-course meal at midnight.

I pulled into the station lot, parked my car and went in the front door. Activity hit me like a cloud of dust. Brother cops brushed by me.

"Welcome back, Carson!" yelled a uniformed—and he didn't mean the war. Another clapped me on the back, the desk sergeant tousled my hair. All foot soldiers—in the trenches together. Some good, some bad, but they'd all watch each other's back. Couldn't say the same for the brass and the dicks. They were like shitty house painters—one eye on the house, the other on the ladder.

Squad room noise: "I got a report on a burglary in progress, thirty-five-hundred block South Michigan."

"So I've got the dago cuffed to the car when his old lady comes running out, screaming bloody murder!"

"Hey, Gussie!" Tony Carvone stepped in front of me, poked me in the ribs. "What say, what say?"

"My meat's on the grill."

"Last night. I heard. Don't worry, your weight's so heavy they gotta move you around with a crane." He ran a hand through his wavy black hair, flipped his dark eyebrows like Groucho Marx.

"The mayor cut that a few years ago."

"But your Boy Scout act's got you moving up again. Watch, they'll slap you for being there, pat you on the back for taking down the perp."

"We'll see."

"Hey, whatcha doing tonight?" he asked. "I wanna go chase dames."

I saw Dan Summers beckoning me from the captain's office. "Gotta go. I'll buzz ya later this afternoon."

Tony looked over my shoulder. "Don't worry, brother. This ain't no lynching. You ain't Brody."

I could see Captain Griffin through his office window, but he was still talking to Dan Summers, so I knocked. Summers let me in, left.

The captain was seated behind his desk, looking through a file. A picture of him with the mayor sat to his left; a Bible was the only other thing on the desk. The desk mirrored his appearance—uncluttered, cold and impersonal. He wore horn-rimmed glasses that made his face seem even more colorless, and he didn't look up when I entered the room. "Sit down, Officer Carson."

I took off my trench coat, draped it over the arm of one chair, sat in the other.

He finally looked up. "That is a chair, Officer, not a coat rack," he said. "There is a coat rack just outside the door. Kindly hang up your coat, come back in here and sit down."

I complied. "Officer Carson," he said when I sat back down, "you've been back with us for a little less than a year now, and I thought you had started to change your ways. I haven't had a complaint against you since your return. No fights, no bribes, no extortion, not even a restaurant owner complaining that you demanded free doughnuts and coffee. But now, this."

He shook his head, pursed his lips. "I'm no prude, Officer. I know that many of the men don't share my faith or morality. But for God's sake—

no, for the department's sake—I expect them to use good judgment. Apparently you don't have that ability."

"Captain," I said, "if you chewed out every man that paid for his pleasure, your throat would be so sore you couldn't swallow soup. It was bad timing, but I did the right thing."

He looked me in the eye for the first time since I'd entered the room. He raised an eyebrow. "Prostitution is illegal!" he yelled. "Maybe my predecessors looked the other way at such indiscretions, but I won't. I wasn't here before you enlisted, but I was fully aware of you and Sam Brody, and I knew you were two problems with which I'd have to deal. Brody took care of himself. I'd hoped you would, too. I've had no problem with you since your return, but it's obvious you are no changed man."

"You don't know me, Captain."

"I know your kind. I knew South Side Sam when he first joined the force. I watched him turn graft and corruption into an art form. Anyone that spoke out against him was suddenly transferred. His filthy money filtered through the department like termites. Well, you know what, Officer? I won't have it happen again."

"It won't happen with me, sir."

"I wish I could believe that, Carson. But Brody raised you. You're full of his influence. It seems you've tried to straighten yourself out, but you can't leave your past behind."

I flinched. "C'mon, Captain. Maybe I shouldn't have gone to Mona's, but I plugged the guy, didn't I? He'd killed two people, and I got him right away. I know people at the *Daily*. I'll have 'em say I was passing by."

"There it is. 'Maybe' you shouldn't have gone there? You still don't see that it's wrong. And what do you see as the problem? The department's image? Well, thank you for being so thoughtful, Officer. The department thanks you."

He stood up, walked around the desk, stood over me. "I am responsible for the department's image, Officer, and I will handle it with the press. But the real problem escapes you. The problem isn't what the press reports; the problem is how you behaved. You simply do not know right from wrong, and that cannot be tolerated. You are hereby suspended until further notice. Until this matter has been thoroughly investigated, I don't even want to see you around here. If I decide to reinstate you, and that's a big if, you will have a strict code of conduct with which to comply. And I might say that it will be much stiffer than that of your fellow officers. Good day, Officer."

I gripped the arm of the chair hard like a nightstick, fought the urge. "How long did it take the mayor to call you?"

"Excuse me?"

"You heard me. This beef's coming from the top. You and I haven't had any problems, and you can forget about lumping me with Sam. Mayor Kelly called you, and you didn't even stick up for one of your own men. I know *your* kind. You threw me to the fire like a dirty champagne glass."

"Get out!!" he screamed. I slammed the door behind me, grabbed my coat and walked out of his office. He was still standing, red-faced, glaring, when I left the squad room. I blew outside, stormed through the lot, found my car when it dawned on me: He hadn't asked for my badge... or my gun.

I DROVE INTO THE LOOP, parked and walked. I looked for something to kick, shook my head at the thought of the suspension. There was a line in front of a small diner. I took it as a recommendation, grabbed a newspaper and stepped into line.

The newspaper said that the coal miners' strike wasn't over—a two-week truce had been called. John L. Lewis wanted a seven-percent payroll assessment for a miners' welfare fund. I skimmed until I found what I wanted—no further restrictions were expected.

I tracked the headlines: ALLIES TO DIVIDE JAP WAR PLANTS; BOWLES WANTS TO RESTORE FOOD RATIONING; 61 NAZIS MEMBERS OF MURDER MILL CONVICTED BY U.S.; RACKET CHARGED IN VET PRIORITY SALES. They didn't get any better. I flipped the pages: no mention of the shootings. I hit the comics, read *The Gumps, Harold Teen* and *Smitty*. Hedda Hopper welcomed back Jimmy Stewart—*that* got me thinking. The dimout was over; the theaters would be open.

I flipped through the newspaper, found the movie ads. Two hours without thinking sounded like aspirin for a headache. *Lost Weekend* was showing at the Uptown—I'd seen the preview; Ray Milland stumbling around drunk would seem like just another night at Harry's. Ingrid Bergman and Gregory Peck in Hitchcock's *Spellbound*—up north on Milwaukee, too far to walk. Randolph Scott and Gabby Hayes in *Badman's Territory* at the Palace; a Sherlock Holmes flick was the second feature. I looked at the Balaban & Katz listings. I wanted escape—I found it. *The Ziegfield Follies of 1946* was showing at Randolph and Dearborn. I decided to skip the lunch.

I walked to the theater, forked over my twenty-five cents and sat through the show twice. Red Skelton owed me a popcorn—a gut-busting laugh had launched mine to the floor. The afternoon was nearly over by the time I ate a Wimpy burger and drove home.

EARLY EVENING: the ringing telephone slapped me out of my nap. I figured Tony Carvone. "Carson," I said.

"Officer Carson, this is Chief Hogan."

"And this is Walter Winchell."

"Very funny, Officer. This *is* Chief Hogan. I need you to meet me at Fourteen East Alibaster. Park in front of the house and meet me inside."

"What's this about, Chief?"

"I'll get into it when you arrive. We're meeting with Arvis Hypoole."

That got my attention; the name Hypoole rang like a church bell. "Related to Eustace Hypoole?"

"The son. Now meet me there, lickety-split."

I splashed cold water on my face, rubbed some Brylcreem in my hair, ran a comb through it and threw on some cologne. I called Tony Carvone and told him I'd meet him at the High Roller but couldn't promise a time.

I DROVE NORTH ON STATE STREET, found 14 East Alibaster, parked my Olds in front. I walked toward the gate, paused to look at the house. It was the kind of house that adults drove by just to see but scared children. It was Victorian: gray stone and dark windows. Fancy designs were etched in the stone above the windows, and it wore a cross above the alcove at its forehead. It was big and dark and cold.

The gate was open. I walked up the steps, grabbed the brass door-knocker and knocked. It must've been the butler's night off; Chief Hogan answered the door.

"Come on in, Carson," he said as he shook my hand. He was broad and thick and red. His white hair peeked out from under his hat, and he still wore his trench coat, so I followed suit.

He led me through the foyer and living room and into the library. Behind a large walnut desk stood a man. His hands were drawn behind his back and he faced the window, but his head was reared back and his gaze was cast at the corner of the ceiling. I followed his gaze and saw a spiderweb. A tiny spider crawled into the corner.

"What do you see there, gentlemen?" he asked, his gaze not leaving the corner.

"A spiderweb," said Chief Hogan.

"A maid who's about to be fired," I said as I slipped off my trench coat, draped it over my arm.

Arvis Hypoole turned and looked at me. "Excellent."

He strode out from behind the desk and reached for my hand. "You must be Officer Carson."

"I must be," I said, taking his hand—it was as cold as a divorcée's kiss.

Chief Hogan didn't like having his thunder stolen. "Carson, please. Mr. Hypoole is a friend of the department, and you'll treat him with respect."

"Nonsense," said Hypoole. His voice was shrill and sounded like he had phlegm caught in his throat, but he went on, didn't clear it. I realized a moment later that it was his natural voice—as annoying as a loud clock in a silent bedroom. "I want Officer Carson to feel at ease with me. If he accepts our offer, we're going to be dealing in trust, and the only way for us to develop it is to drop our guards and get to know one another."

"Sure, Mr. Hypoole, but..."

Hypoole held up a hand. "Chief, I'll beg your pardon, but the only reason that I wanted you here tonight was to convince Officer Carson of the validity of my offer and to show him that I do have some clout within the department. Having done that, I don't see any further reason for you to stay."

Hogan's red face went crimson. "Well, sure, Mr. Hypoole. If you say so. Officer, give this man full consideration. He is well respected within the department." He nodded at both of us, walked out.

Hypoole motioned toward two overstuffed chairs on either side of a coffee table. We each sat in one.

We sat quietly for a moment, each getting his first good look at the other. I noted his features like I was writing a report: sixtyish, slight, medium height, bald—with short silver and black hair on the sides, high, sharp cheekbones, thick gray eyebrows and large ears. He wore his money in his clothes—a hundred-dollar suit with a gold pocket watch that dangled from the pocket of the black vest. The kind of man that adults walked by just to see but scared children. Not so big, but dark and cold.

"I suppose you know of me, at least my family name," he said. He pretended to flick some dirt from underneath a fingernail, dropped his eyes to avoid meeting mine.

"Everyone knows the name Hypoole," I said. "People still talk about your father. He was the Republican version of Pat Nash."

He winced, lifted his head, smirked. "The only thing better for the Democrats than the Depression was my father's death. There hasn't been a Republican mayor since he helped put William Hale Thompson into office."

"When did he die?" I asked.

"Thirty-one. He was sixty-three years old, only three years older than I am now." He noted my surprise, didn't mistake it for a compliment. "He was eighteen when I was born. Toward the end of his life we were more like contemporaries than father and son."

"I know that feeling," I said.

Hypoole ignored my comment. "I suppose you're wondering why I asked you to come here," he said.

"You didn't ask me, the chief did, but yes, I'm wondering."

"What do you think of policy, Officer Carson, and may I call you Gus?"

"I don't play the numbers and yes, you can call me Gus."

"Well, Gus, I abhor policy. You see, I'm an investor, and I consider Chicago my biggest investment. And when I invest in something, I watch out for problems. The way I see it, the blight in our city is policy. It is the single greatest element that is stopping the Negroes from becoming productive members of our society. Do you agree with that assessment?"

"I know a lot of colored men who would probably sock you in the teeth for that statement, but I do agree that it's a problem."

"Don't misunderstand me, Gus. I'm a friend of the Negro. My wife and I were committed to helping them. In fact, I think they have tremendous potential. They're not unlike any other group that came to this country and had to work its way out of poverty."

"They didn't come by choice," I said. "But I'm not here to talk about your views of society, am I?"

"To the point, eh? Well, all right, I'll get down to it." He folded his hands in his lap, looked directly into my eyes as he spoke. His voice softened, cadence slowed. He blew me a politician's speech—rehearsed and condescending. "The only way for us to have a city that is working on all cylinders is to have all of us working productively. And the Negro will never pull his share of the load while he's destitute. Why is he destitute? Because he spends all of his money playing the numbers. The policy rackets may seem like a harmless diversion, but they are taking staggering amounts of money out of the Negroes' pockets and banks and putting it into the pockets of common criminals. The largest policy operators, Gus, are Ed Jones and his brother George. Ed Jones has been kidnapped. I want you to find him."

"I've been suspended."

"I'm aware of that. If you are able to find Jones and deliver him to me, I will make sure that you are reinstated. You will also be moved to the top of the list for the sergeant's exam, and I'm sure you will pass. Shortly after that, I'm confident that you'll have the opportunity to become a detective. Finally, I will personally write you a check for five hundred dollars."

Six months salary. "That's a lot of cash. Why not save yourself some money and let the department handle it?"

"We won't interfere with their investigation, but I'm sure it will be halfhearted, at best."

"Why me?"

His lips formed a narrow smile. "You're available. Your file is excellent."

"You must be reading the wrong file."

"No," he said, "I just read it the right way. Your experience in the seamier sides of life should prove useful. You can navigate the colored community better than most, and you'll know where to look for Mr. Jones. I also believe that certain methods might be necessary. Methods such as those that you have employed throughout your career."

I didn't tell him that I didn't use those methods anymore. "When was he kidnapped?"

"Earlier this evening."

"And you just called up Chief Hogan and he thought of me immediately? He grabbed my file and rushed right over? I'm not buying it."

He shook his head. "Your skepticism is warranted. I sit on the crime commission. Yesterday a man informed me that Mr. Jones would be kidnapped. I contacted the chief of the uniformed force, Chief Hogan, and told him. Both of our attempts at contacting Mr. Jones were unsuccessful."

"How hard did you try? I'm sure somebody would've told him."

"We left messages at the Ben Franklin store he owns, and Chief Hogan had his men put the word out on the street. We tried to contact his brother, but he was out of town. We also sent men to his home, but there was no answer."

"Policy operator sees a cop at the door, he's not hot to answer. You fellows may not have found him, but someone did. Why don't you ask your stoolie where he is?"

His face went blank. "Not possible."

"What does that mean?"

"It means that he is unable to offer any more information. It's going to be up to you, Gus, if you'll take the assignment."

My turn to smile. "What's in it for Chief Hogan?"

"He's ambitious. He wants to be chief of police someday."

"And you?"

"I want to stamp out policy. When you turn Mr. Jones over to me, I'm going to take him to the newspapers and then directly to the grand jury. We will give him full immunity. He will tell us everything we need to know in order to stamp out the policy rackets and then he will cease his operations."

"Or what?"

"Or he will go to jail. For a long, long time."

"Who's handling the case?"

"Wabash Avenue station."

It was my turn to shake my head. "I won't be welcome."

"I'll have Chief Hogan get you copies of the reports. You shouldn't have to talk to the officers on the case."

"Then what do I do?"

"Consider other alternatives. The department is talking to his brother and family and interviewing his employees. You can talk to his gambling associates and other policy racketeers. Use your imagination—you know much more about this sort of thing than me. Oh, yes, and you'll also need to watch his girlfriend's home."

I raised an eyebrow. "What girlfriend?"

"Her name is Martha Lewis. I'll get you the address. I've got Detective McGuire watching her home during the day; you watch it from six p.m. until six a.m."

"If I'm watching her place all night and working the case during the day, when am I supposed to sleep?"

"Five hundred dollars will buy you a lot of rest after you find Ed Jones."

"Is McGuire talking to the girlfriend?"

"No," he said. He shook his head. "And neither should you. We do not want her to alert him that she's being watched, should he call her."

"Maybe she knows something."

"The department will contact her. Let's leave it at that. I've got another man over there tonight and tomorrow night, so if you decide to accept my offer, you'll need to start there Monday night."

"What's the catch?" I asked.

"There isn't a catch, but there is a rather quick deadline. Per federal regulations, you have seven days until the FBI is brought in. If you can't find him before they take over the case, you're no good to me."

"Seven days isn't much time."

His voice hardened. "I didn't set the deadline. Five hundred dollars is a nice week's pay."

"Sure is."

"Well," he said as he rocked forward. "Drink?"

The sudden shift in conversation surprised me, but not my whistle— it preferred wet. "White," I said, "straight up."

He left, came back with two tumblers full of gin. "Before I hear your answer, why don't we get to know each other a bit better. I've read your file, but tell me, Gus," he said as he handed me my drink, "what did you do during the war?"

I focused on his teeth; he leered. His look said it all—he thought he knew me. I gripped the tumbler tight, mumbled a response. I didn't tell him that I enlisted at Chief Hansen's suggestion: I had pushed Mayor Kelly's right-hand man through a plateglass window after I'd busted up an opium party at his house—replete with Joliet Josies and teenage boys. It was the cooler or the Marines, Military Police. I enlisted the next day, stayed stateside.

I didn't tell him that my cush duty ended when a greaser named Francisco Juarez raped and killed a general's wife while on leave. Somehow he made his ship. *I* got to drag him back for trial. The general gave it to me straight: Any problem getting him back and I should kill him on the spot—he gave me his own pearl-handled revolver to use.

I didn't tell him that I found Francisco Juarez in Guam, used the revolver to beat him unconscious. I dragged Juarez to a ship; we'd catch a lift back to Pearl Harbor on a cruiser. I threw him in the brig—hated him more for making me stay in the heat in the belly of the ship. The sailors brought him food; I didn't tell them he was a murdering rapist.

Two days from Pearl Harbor, an explosion knocked me out of my bunk. Another one sent me back to the floor. Men took the ladder in two strides. Word filtered down: We'd caught two torpedoes from a Jap sub. Juarez screamed for me to let him out. I raised the revolver. Judge, jury, executioner: I tucked it back into my pants, bolted up the stairs. "I'll kill you, Carson," he screamed as I sealed off the compartment, locked the hatch tight.

I didn't tell him that fire had turned the deck into a grill; my hands were burned when I fell. I fought through the smoke, grabbed a kapok life jacket with my wrist, started to go over the side. I saw two men try the high side, get caught in the propellers: The ship's engines hadn't been cut. We steamed forward; I followed the last group of men over the side. We hit the water a few hundred yards from the bulk of the group— oil covered us. Someone grabbed a floater net and we held on for our lives. The swells were high; we couldn't see the other groups. The swells fell for a moment—long enough for us to see the Jap sub rise out of the water and soldiers pile out, machine guns aimed. I cupped my burned hands over the mouth of the man next to me as he screamed while the Japs shot his buddies.

I didn't tell him that there were fifteen of us on that floater net. Our only luck was that the sub didn't see us, took off. I didn't tell him what it was like to watch men go crazy, dive for clean water, drink the salt water and die. I didn't tell him about the sharks—the group slaughter brought hundreds. They would circle beneath us; the clear water gave us a sight line. We watched as they picked us off, one by one. Fifteen became fourteen, became thirteen, became twelve. The sun beat us during the day; the cold and the sharks got us at night.

I didn't tell him that it finally became two: me and Sollie the Jew. Sollie held my head out of the water, kept me sane with his talk. He named everyone he could remember from the ship, made me remember them, too. He let me rest on his shoulder. He made me a promise: We'd both live.

I didn't tell him about the morning when Sollie the Jew started screaming—we'd been spotted by a plane. It dropped out of the sky and landed on the water. A man peered out of the plane, asked us where the Cubs played. I didn't tell him that Sollie didn't answer but I let out a scream that made my insides hurt. "Chicago!" I'd yelled, and they dragged me on board. Five days of hell were over.

I didn't tell him that when I awoke, the next day, on another ship, the first thing I asked was, "Where's Sollie?" I didn't tell him about the blank stares, the "Who's Sollie?"

I told him I had it easy: Worst thing that had happened to me was that a guy lied to me once. I told him that I'd take the job. I thanked him for the gin and left.

I PULLED UP IN FRONT OF THE HIGH ROLLER, parked my car in front. A valet yelled at me; I flashed him my badge and went inside. I checked my coat and pushed through the crowd. Three levels, a dance floor, a stage with instruments and no band. People sat in black high-back chairs at white-tableclothed tables. It reeked nightclub: that funny mixture of food, booze, cigarettes and perfume.

Crowd noise drowned out my thoughts. I felt a tug at my sleeve. A fat guy in a cheap tux threw together an improv magic act: He pulled a coin out of my ear. I pushed him away: "Disappear."

I looked above the crowd, spotted Tony Carvone near the staircase. He wore a dark suit, maroon patterned tie. His black hair was slicked back and his shoes were shined. He was talking to a tall drink. I interrupted. She decided to powder her nose.

He grinned. "Thanks, Gussie, you show up just in time to run off the dames. Where you been?"

I didn't tell him about Arvis Hypoole. I told him I'd fallen back to sleep. I told him I'd been suspended.

"Those rotten mugs upstairs," he said. "They wouldn't recognize a real cop if one arrested 'em. Whatcha gonna do?"

"I'm not sure," I said. "But I've got plenty of time to think about it."

The band came back out, broke into swing. The crowd spilled onto the dance floor, a handsome singer juked 'em like a jockey whipping his horse. I waded toward the bar; Tony held his drink high, mouthed, "Bourbon, soda back." I grabbed the drinks and walked back toward the staircase.

I reached out to hand Tony his drink. He ignored me, gazed up the stairs. "Will you look at the gamsel in dis dress," he said.

I looked up the stairs. A girl in a dark green dress cascaded down the steps. Her long, black hair was pulled back from her face, which glowed. Attention spilled in front of her like a red carpet. She rode it down the stairs, stopped in front of Tony and turned to me. She smiled and raised a dark brow. Her eyes were so green they brought out the color in her dress, and she batted long lashes as her cheeks rose over high cheekbones, tried to lift a smile.

"A big, hulking brute. I like," she said.

"I like back," I said.

"How 'bout the front?"

"Never been there. Heard it's dangerous."

"Would a big, hulking brute like you be afraid of a little danger?"

I took her hands, pulled her close. "When danger's wrapped in that green dress and that hair and those eyes, this big, hulking brute is afraid. I'm afraid we've skipped introductions." I spun her around. "Sheila, this is Tony Carvone."

Tony whistled. "And Gussie is full of surprises. How are you, Sheila?"

Sheila flashed teeth as white as fine linen. "I'm fine, Mr. Carvone, and as you can see, I'm now wearing the latest coat. It's called a Carson. It's big and warm and protective, and I haven't tried it on for quite some time. May I be so bold as to ask you if I can steal your friend?"

Tony was a sport. "You may and you can. I'll catch up with ya, Gussie." He whistled again and walked off.

Sheila dragged me away like a carny prize. She stopped at a table, dropped her purse on it, opened a deck and pulled out a cigarette. I sat down across from her, lit her stick.

"How have you been, Sheila?" I asked.

She blew smoke. "Fine. I've just got back from school. Oh, Gus, I'm so sorry I haven't talked to you in such a long time. It's just that I didn't come home last summer, and, oh, you know how it is between Mother and me."

"And how is Virginia?"

She stubbed out her cigarette, early, ignored the question. "Daddy told me he'd seen you, so I thought I might find you here. He said he'd heard that you had it just awful during the war. Oh, I'm sorry, Gus. Did you have it that awful?"

"Not me, doll. I made it home." I motioned to the waiter, ordered two Spotted Owls and a Guinness. "And now you're home."

"And now I'm home," she repeated. "So do we take up where we left off?"

"Where we left off was me heading to war, you heading to college. At least one of us learned something. As for me, I'm different now, not so exciting anymore. And if I remember right, you like excitement."

"If you remember right, I like you."

"I'm suspended, out of work."

"Then you'll have more time for me."

"No, I picked up a side job. It's gonna take up all of my time."

The waiter arrived, set the Spotted Owls in front of us. I took the Guinness from him and handed him a single. "Keep it."

Sheila moved to my side of the table, grabbed her shot. We clinked glasses and drank. "What did you do to get suspended?" she asked.

"Too many misspellings in my reports."

"A suspension sounds a bit harsh," she said.

"Not when most of them were my own name. Say, I could probably misspell yours, if you like."

"Let me help you spell it," she said. She leaned into me, moved her lips next to mine. She wrapped a cool hand around the back of my neck. "S," she said as she moved her cheek against mine. "H." Her breath came in a sweet puff. "E." Her eyes rolled back. "I." Our eyes locked. "L." Our lips met. "Aaaaaa."

The music stopped. We continued. People walked by our table, whistled, clapped. I pulled back. "I'm ready for the spelling bee, now, ma'am."

"If you need help boning up, I'm available."

"What are you doing tonight?"

"We're having a party tomorrow, Gus. I'd like you to come."

"Sister," I said, "I'd forgotten, but you change subjects faster than outfits."

"We'll see about that. Tonight, I'm staying with you. Tomorrow, I'd like you to come to our party."

"It's Sunday. Who has a party on Sunday?"

"It's Mother's Day, silly," she said. She brought her hand to her mouth. "Gus, I'm sorry. I didn't think."

I let it slide, smiled. It had been too long. "You won't need to."

We left the club, went to my place, made up for lost time.

## SUNDAY, MAY 12

WE WOKE UP EARLY. I drove Sheila to her car, went back home and found a file waiting for me, courtesy of Chief Hogan. I sat down with a cup of coffee, lit up a smoke. Summary: Two swarthy "Italians" curbed Ed Jones's auto at 4328 South Parkway, pulled him out of the car in front of his wife, an unidentified second woman and chauffeur, hit him over the head with a revolver and drove north on South Parkway. Jones's wife flagged down two cops. They chased the vehicle, got the license plate, Illinois 533-548, and a windshield full of lead. One officer was cut above the eye; his partner stopped to tend to him. Police and park district squad cars gave chase. The kidnappers got away.

Enclosures: a picture of Jones, another of his brother, a third of another brother—deceased. I committed the first two to memory, scanned the third. Report: Jones's holdings: a Ben Franklin store on 47th Street, bathhouse, several apartment buildings, hotel, two villas— one in France, the other in Mexico, a summer home in Joliet. Report: an arrest file; convicted: Jones did over two years in Terre Haute for income tax evasion, paid an IRS tab of over four hundred and eighty thousand dollars. The man had money. Money meant motive.

The cops on the case would run the tags, cover the wife, chauffeur, unidentified woman. They'd canvas the kidnapping area, check out the Ben Franklin. They'd sit tight, wait for the phone to ring.

I'd play a source, cover the girlfriend, policy wheels, enemies. I'd check out the Italians, sift through his two years at Terre Haute. Five C notes just begging to be picked up.

I fired up my machine and drove to the South Side.

I PARKED IN FRONT OF A STOP AND TRADE FOOD SHOP, flashed the owner my badge, cut down an alley as he cursed me. Three-story tenement houses grew on both sides of the alley, trash strewn everywhere. A colored woman stepped onto her back porch, dressed in a tattered housecoat with a red and black checked scarf wrapped around her head. She saw me, grunted and dumped her trash over the rail.

I came out of the alley, hit the street, walked near the buildings to skip attention. I watched the windows, scanned the reflections, feigned interest in the specials: small, fat chickens—thirty-nine cents; pigs' feet—ten cents; pork roast—thirty-nine cents.

I passed a barbershop, bank, a blind man playing a street piano.

"Whatta ya say, friend?" asked the blind man as I passed. "Wanna hear some Armstrong?"

"Pass," I said.

He lifted the front of the piano box, let it hit the ground. The keys jumped, sounded off as it landed. "See," he said, "ain't my arms strong?"

I passed a tavern, saw the rabbits on the other side of the street, decided to cross. I moved forward, stepped over the streetcar tracks, and crept up the sidewalk. A dozen dead rabbits hung, upside down, from a rope stretched between a second-story window and a telephone pole. Each of the rabbits' feet were bundled together; paws fell forward, their ears fell back.

Two colored men stood underneath the rabbits, laughing. The younger of the two leaned against the telephone pole. He wore a wide-brim, light brown felt hat, white dress shirt with no tie, dark slacks and shoes and an oversize tan overcoat. The overcoat nearly fell off his slight shoulders. Cars drove by, and occasionally he lifted a hand, waved.

I walked up behind him: "Big ones today. Good stew rabbits for sale, eh, Bunny?"

The skinny man's eyes bugged, he turned slightly, caught me over his shoulder. "Shiiiit." He spun, ran.

"What the hell?" yelled the other man.

I ran after Bunny. He cut back across the street, ran past the pool hall, jumped the blind piano player's piano. He turned into the alley, looked back and slid through the trash like a puppy on ice.

I picked him up, led him under a porch, slammed him up against a brick wall. "Some greeting I get. I haven't seen you in years, and do you even ask how I've been?"

I brushed his coat, straightened his hat. "You know what you miss when you leave a place, Bunny? The little things. I miss my morning coffee at Myrna's. I miss watching the jabbers dance when they wake up in the alley and I miss having our little chats. What about you? Do you miss me, Bunny?"

Bunny covered his face with his hands. "You ain't got no business with me, Officer Carson. I ain't done nothing."

"You got me all wrong, Bunny," I said. "I come in peace—I really do. I need your help."

He looked at me like I'd told him I was in love with him. "You need what?"

"I need your help," I said. "I'm looking for Ed Jones."

He brushed himself off. "You and everybody else."

"What's the street say?"

"Street says the Eye-talians."

"That's what this morning's paper said. I asked you what the street said."

"Ain't much else to say."

"Why?"

"'Cause there just ain't."

"No, why did they grab him? What's new in his world?"

"You talkin' to the wrong guy. All I know is he runs the numbers. All the guys report to him. But that sure ain't new."

I threw him a half. He caught it, inspected it, put it in his pocket. "What's with this Santa Claus shit? Somebody watching us? What you want me to do?"

"No act. So you're telling me he isn't into anything new, like drugs, women?"

"Shit no. Even the newspapers call him the 'Negro Robin Hood.' Man ain't runnin' no women or drugs."

"Enemies?"

"Man with that kind of money's got enemies. Lotsa guys wouldn't mind having his racket."

"Such as?"

"Such as me," he said. "Such as you. Such as Lincoln Johnson."

"Lincoln Johnson?"

"Fat mother wants to run Bronzeville. Wants to be another Big Jim. Another Dawson."

"I know who he is. Didn't know he was into the numbers. Where do I find him?"

"You don't. Catch one of his runners, you might get lucky. Other than that, line up at a parade. Fat mother likes to kiss babies, kiss asses."

"Where can I grab one of his runners?"

"What is it, eleven? You know the pool hall 'round the corner from Jones Brothers Funeral Home?"

I nodded.

"Watch there 'bout half an hour. One of the last stops a kid makes before their noon game. That's one of Busy Jackson's wheels. Busy works for Lincoln Johnson. You show him how you got me these gold teeth, he'll take you to Johnson on his back."

"What else?"

"Nothin' I know. But something's gotta happen. Paper said eighty thousand Negroes was out of work on accounta the dimout. People's broke. People's hungry, and now people ain't gonna get to play their numbers. Paper said cops gonna come down here and bust up the numbers game. That ain't right. First they take everybody's money, now they gonna take policy. I tell you what...people ain't gonna stand for it."

"Papers this, papers that. You been doing a lot of reading?"

He shrugged. "Nah. Just use 'em for customers. People don't like to touch the rabbits."

THE POOL HALL WAS A FEW MILES AWAY, so I grabbed my car, drove, found it easily. I got lucky—a spot opened up across the street from the pool hall. I stayed in the car, put on a brown fedora, pulled it low over my eyes and slumped down in the seat.

The pool hall was on the first level of a four-story brick building. A big sign on the door said, MILLER'S POOL HALL, 5 CENTS PER CUE, 90 CENTS PER HOUR, NO PROFANITY, NO GAMBLING, ALL HOURS. I figured Miller had wasted his time with the rules—no one read 'em. No one cared.

A couple dozen colored men filled the room. I watched the men shoot pool—cool and deliberate when they shot, excited and animated when it was an opponent's turn. They all wore overcoats and hats, held pool cues regardless of whether they were actually playing a game. Cigarettes burned to the nub, smoke pooled under the overhead lights; the older men in the group held their cues like soldiers relaxing with their rifles. A boy suddenly appeared, and the men began handing him slips of paper and cash—coins and bills. He weaved in and out of the group; players stopped in mid-stroke to play their numbers. He filled a bushel basket with the money and slips.

The front door came open and the boy sauntered out, set down the basket and counted the money. He looked like he was in his early teens, but he wore a flight jacket with ribbons pinned across the left breast, slacks and leather work boots. Satisfied with the count, he wandered off, didn't look for a tail, so I gave him a half-block lead and trailed him.

His next stop was across the street. He checked traffic—two cars rolled to a stop to let him pass. One driver rolled down his window, beckoned the boy over, handed him a slip of paper and some coins. The boy dumped the coins in the basket, marked the bet on a tally sheet, finished crossing the street and stepped inside another storefront.

If I hadn't known better, I'd have sworn it was Duke Ellington who walked into the beauty parlor—the women fawned over him, tousled his hair, dropped their coins into the basket after they'd handed him their slips, played their numbers. By the time he left the beauty parlor his shoulders had begun to sag under the weight of the basket.

Two blocks later, he'd collected from a bootblack, a newsstand operator, an ice truck driver and a group of rummies who stood in an alley, slugging from brown paper bags. He still hadn't noticed me when I saw a tall, lanky Negro cop step out of a tavern and flag him down. The cop had sergeant's stripes on his shoulder, a jailer's biceps.

I was close enough to hear the shouts, cursed my luck as I faded into a doorway. If the kid got busted, I'd lose a shot at Busy Jackson.

"What you thinking there, boy?" yelled the cop. I peered out of the doorway, watched as the boy set the basket on the sidewalk, flipped his hands up in front of his chest as he protested his innocence.

"I don't know what you're talking about, Sergeant! I'm jist doing mah job." His voice was shrill, and it cracked so often that it broke the word 'job' into three syllables.

"Your job? You keep acting like this, you ain't gonna have no job." The cop sounded angry enough that I thought he might hit the kid.

"Whatchou mean the way I'm actin'?" yelled the boy.

"Boy, you know the morning drawing's in less than half an hour!"

"So?"

"So? I damn near missed you! From now on, make sure you see me first thing in the mornin'." The cop pulled a slip of paper out of his pocket, handed the boy some coins. "Them's my lucky numbers today. Four, thirty-two, fifty. Four, thirty-two, fifty."

The boy dropped the coins in the basket, lifted it and took off as the cop slapped him on the back. "Four, thirty-two, fifty. I'll be seeing you tomorrow, so I can collect!"

The boy covered three more blocks, stopped in stores, a barbershop and a liquor store—the basket was filled to the brim. He stopped in front of a large, brick warehouse, knocked on an overhead door. It slowly rose, stopped halfway up, and he slipped underneath.

I rolled the car to the curb, surveyed the building. Two stories with tall, dirty windows. Two overhead doors in front, an entrance on the side marked DISPATCH. Above the overhead doors, in big, black painted letters, JACKSON CARTAGE. I stepped out of the car and walked to the side entrance.

I opened the door, stepped into the dispatch office. It was a small room, with a narrow table and two chairs. A time clock sat on the table, near the door, and a small metal rack that held half a dozen time cards had been nailed to the wall. Coffee stained a pile of work orders that had been pushed toward a corner, and a short, squat colored man used a second pile to cushion his feet, which were propped on the table. A newspaper was open in his lap, and he ignored me as he peered at the comics section. His fat fingers traced the captions for *Speed Jaxon*. When his finger traced the last pane of the comic strip, he looked up at me, no emotion: "We paid up."

"What?"

"We paid up. They came by this morning."

"I don't know what you're talking about."

"Sure you do. You a cop. Yo boss came by this morning. We's paid up."

I leaned over the dispatch counter, "You might be paid up, but not with me. I need to see Busy Jackson."

"Sunday, he's not here," he muttered.

"You're just getting ready for your noon drawing, so he's here."

"I don't know what you're talking about. He ain't here."

"Then why did that kid just hightail it in here with a basketful of coins and a fistful of betting slips?"

He folded the comics section, eyed me. Dark half-moons grew underneath his eyes; his fleshy face looked tired. "Mister, you way off. Any kid came in here, he better be ready to work. Even though it's Sunday, we got four shipments coming in this afternoon. Matter of fact, I'm busy. Come back on Monday, maybe Mr. Jackson'll be here."

"Not the way it's gonna work. I'm gonna step around this counter in about three seconds, and I hear any lip from you, you get a first-class room in the hoosegow."

"Hoosegow" got his attention like a rap on a chalkboard. "Just doin' my job," he mumbled.

"If I'm you, I'd step into that shitter around the corner. That way, after I leave, you can tell 'em you were in the washroom and never saw me come in."

"Please, mister," he said. "They's already a lady back there raising hell. I'm already in trouble. Can't you come back Monday?"

I pointed to the can. He followed my finger like a kid going to his room. I pushed through the swinging door at the counter, stepped behind it and opened the door to the warehouse. It was a cavernous gray room with a huge freight elevator off to one side. Boxes were stacked eight feet high in rows marked by letters and numbers written on pieces of tape stuck to the floor. Near the rear of the warehouse, two large sliding doors opened up into another room and I could hear the roar of forklifts, but they were nearly drowned out by the shouts from a woman.

"Them's always my numbers!"

I slipped down an aisle, stopped two feet short of a gap between the rows. Two enormous colored men in dark suits leaned on a pile of wooden pallets—the revolvers that bulged under their jackets weren't company-issued. Four other colored men sat on folding chairs surrounding two folding tables, tallying bets, dumping coins into a couple of change-counting machines. A small steel-mesh barrel filled with numbered marbles sat on a table in the middle of the group. The young boy sat behind the barrel, reading slips.

One of them stood up, pushed his face inches from that of the screaming woman. He was tall and slender, dressed in a dark suit with a dark shirt and a diamond pin in place of a necktie. He wore his wide-brim hat sideways. "I know you say them was your numbers," he said. "But this here's your slip and it don't show that."

The woman grabbed at the slip. She was huge—dressed in a skirt that looked like it had been made from a bed sheet and a blouse that had come from a quilt. She had a dirty white scarf tied around her head. "Lies, all lies!" she yelled. "I play the same numbers every day and you know that! I play my son's birthday: twelve, twenty-one, forty-one, and them was winning numbers yesterday."

"I know that, Roleen, but yesterday you had twelve, twenty-one, seventy-one. I remember remarking how odd that was, you changing your numbers all of a sudden. Look here, here's your slip."

The man held out a slip and the woman grabbed it, studied it. "They changed it!" she yelled. "Look here how the top of the four's been rubbed in to make it look like the top of a seven. I didn't do that, they did!"

The woman stomped her feet, threw the paper down on the floor. She tried to kick at the table, but the man grabbed her. "Now, Roleen, you calm down. I shouldn't do this, but I'm gonna give you your money back from yesterday. Only, if I give you your money back, you ain't gonna play here no more."

"Why play if I can't win?"

"That's your call. Yesterday you made an honest mistake. Who knows, if God is just, you just might win today!"

"Hey!" A man yelled behind me. I stepped into the crowd, held my badge high.

"Who the hell are you?" asked the tall man.

"I'm the guy that's not busting your wheel, that's who."

The two men stepped down off of the fork trucks, scurried over. The man behind me stepped forward. "I'm looking for Busy Jackson," I said to the tall man, "and I'm betting that's you."

"You a police officer?" asked the woman.

I nodded.

"Then you the one I need. These men trying to rob me. I won yesterday evening and now they trying to cheat me."

"Roleen!" yelled one of the men.

I slipped my badge back into my pocket. "Policy is illegal, ma'am," I said. "I'm not going to be able to help you."

"You don't understand," she said. She was so excited that she spit as she talked. "I . . . I always plays the same numbers. My son was born on December twenty-first, nineteen forty-one, so I always plays twelve, twenty-one, forty-one. I got all three numbers in one row, so I got a gig! A gig pays a hundred to one. I bet fifty cents, so they owe me fifty dollars!"

The tall man stepped toward me, looked over his shoulder. "Alex, you go find out where the hell Jessie is. Ask him how the hell two people got back here!" He turned back to me. "You in the wrong place, my friend." He stretched the word "friend" so far that it didn't even make me a neighbor.

"Not if you're Busy Jackson, I'm not."

"Gravy," he said to one of the big men, "take Roleen out of here. Give her fifty cents and tell her she's not playing no more."

The big woman shrieked. "No, no, no. You owe me!"

"Can't have it both ways."

She panicked. "All right then. Keep my fifty cents. Here's my fifty cents for today. But someone's gonna hear about this." She pitched the coins onto one of the tables.

The big man took her by the arm, led her toward the overhead doors. The tall man looked back at me. "What the hell do you think you're doing, coming in here like this? We pay damn good money and your people got theirs today."

"I'm not here to bust your wheel," I said. "I'm looking for Lincoln Johnson. I was told that Busy Jackson could help me find him."

"Why you looking for Lincoln Johnson?"

"I'm looking for Ed Jones."

"I thought you just said you was looking for Lincoln Johnson?"

"I did. I think Lincoln Johnson might be able to help me find Ed Jones."

The man laughed. "Listen, I am Busy Jackson. I run an honest moving and storage company and on the weekends, my friends and I here play some numbers, just for fun. Only thing I know about Lincoln Johnson is what I read in *The Avenger*. Why don't you just take out a ad?"

The rest of the men laughed; I didn't. "Your protection money isn't gonna go too far. Read today's paper. Commissioner Prendergast is going to feel a lot of pressure to close the wheels. I have no problem pointing to yours. I find Lincoln Johnson without your help, I'll have him busted, tell him you sent me. I find out he kidnapped Ed Jones, I'll tie you in as an accessory."

Busy looked at me, sized me up. "You think you can come into my place and make those kinda threats and just walk outta here? You might be a cop, but cops been known to disappear, too."

I let it pass. "All I want is to talk to Lincoln Johnson. Chances are, he had nothing to do with Jones's kidnapping, but he might know something that can help me."

"You never answered my question. What makes you think you can come in here and talk to me like this?"

"Remember when Clubber Jones spilled on Theo Black?"

"Uh-huh."

"Ever hear how it happened?"

One of the other men yelled, "Yeah. Clubber lived in that basement apartment off Forty-seventh. South Side Sam and three cops broke in, took his own club to him."

I shook my head. "Just me and Sam."

Busy bit his lower lip, rubbed his nose with a thumb and forefinger, turned to the men. "Time for the drawing. Let Reg draw today."

The young man clapped his hands, set the slips on the table and started to spin the barrel. The others gathered around the table. Busy walked down the aisle, motioned for me to follow. He walked about ten yards, stopped. "Big man, South Side Sam's away, can't help you now."

"I don't need his help," I said. "I need yours. I'll tell you what, you tell me where I can find Lincoln Johnson, call him and tell him I'm coming. You tell him it's Gus Carson, he won't even ask you why you told me."

"You sure 'bout that?"

"Sure as shit."

He took a box down, sat on it. "You know," he said, "he may just want to talk to you."

"Why's that?"

"'Cause none of us had nothing to do with Ed, but he might wanna know who did. You find Ed Jones, Lincoln might have something else to talk to you about."

He tore a corner off one of the boxes, pulled a pencil out of his shirt pocket and started to write. I looked over his shoulder, watched the young man pull colored marbles from the barrel. He set the marbles on the table, and another man wrote down the number printed on the marble. The young man gave a yell, reached in and pulled out one last marble. "Fourteen," he yelled. The other man wrote the number down in the second of two rows. Two rows, twelve numbers in each row. A bettor got all three of his numbers in one row, it paid a hundred to one; two in one row and one in another paid ten to one.

"Here," said Busy. He handed me the cardboard. An address was written on it and the name "Ruffin." "That's the address for the Baptist Church where they's having Albert Ruffin's funeral. Lincoln'll be there. You can even tell him I told ya to come."

"Thanks," I said. I pocketed the cardboard.

"Now, the heat comes down, you're not gonna say anything about this wheel, are you? It's the California Gold Rush Wheel, my best, and I'd be grateful if you didn't say anything."

He pulled two sawbucks from his pocket, folded them and reached for my hand. "No thanks," I said. "I'm not on duty right now, so I don't see any need to report you, but I also don't see any need to take your money."

"Legit?"

"Legit."

I looked over his shoulder, watched as the young man shook his head, looked back at a slip of paper.

"Tell me one thing," said Busy. "What really happened with Clubber Jones? He's the meanest cat I ever met. What you got to say about that?"

"You just met me," I said. I turned and walked toward the overhead door. Busy whistled after me, walked back to the group. Over my shoulder I heard the young man yelling at Busy.

"What you yellin' 'bout, boy?"

"She hit it again. Look, Roleen's numbers are all in the first row."

I lifted the overhead door, slipped underneath. My eyes adjusted to the sunlight as the door fell back down. I heard Busy shouting from inside the warehouse. "I wasn't here, so it don't count," he said. "Draw again."

PALLBEARERS WERE CARRYING THE CASKET out of the Baptist Church as I pulled up. I parked and watched the mourners pour out of the church. Albert Ruffin would've enjoyed his funeral—women wilted like damp hair, men eyed the sidewalk.

Lincoln Johnson walked out, the widow on his arm, his wife two steps behind. He wore a dark three-piece suit with a spotted bow tie and a white hat with a brown band. I figured he paid double for his suits—he was so big around that they'd have to load him in a piano case at *his* funeral. He stopped in front of the hearse, hugged the widow, ran a hand across the small of her back. He opened the door to a black limousine, gave the widow a final hug and she slipped inside. His wife climbed in after her. Johnson looked around, saw me, closed the door and came over.

He opened the passenger door and climbed in next to me. The seat screamed as he sat down; his weight nearly broke its back. He was winded from the short walk to the car, and he sat still for a moment, caught his breath. When he spoke, his voice was surprisingly high: "Officer Carson, I can honestly say that your timing is impeccable. As much as I love and respected brother Ruffin, I'm not really up to driving out to the cemetery today. Since you desire to chat and I need a ride, why don't we depart before the procession begins."

"Sounds good to me," I said as I pulled away from the curb. "Who was the deceased?"

"Albert Ruffin was the finest barber in Bronzeville. He took over his father's practice and . . . take a left here. And he turned it into a fine business. His father cut my hair for the first twenty-five years of my life, and Albert cut it for the past ten. So I am now without a barber for the first time in my life."

"Must feel like quite a loss for you."

"You are being cynical, Officer Carson. Of course, I am aware that others have lost a great deal more than me. I plan on consoling the widow once she is through with her familial obligations."

"I'll bet you will," I said. "Where are we heading?"

"If you could drop me at the Delilah Café, I'd greatly appreciate it."

"Maybe Delilah can cut your hair."

"Very amusing," he said. "I loaned them two portable gas generators so they could stay open during the dimout, and I need to see that they're returned."

"Coincidence; I want to make sure Ed Jones is returned."

"I received a call from Busy Jackson, telling me so. He also informed me that you left him his teeth and his money. You have obviously changed since we last met."

"And so have you. Last time I saw you, I was working security at one of Congressman Dawson's rallies. You were smoking reefer and hitting up young girls. Now you're some kind of policy baron."

He frowned at me, dropped the air of politeness. "You're still a bit direct for me, but so be it. Since we both know that you didn't end up with the case, can you tell me why you're so interested in finding Ed Jones?"

I checked traffic in the rearview mirror, gave him a tight grin. "I'm a good citizen."

"That kind of attitude isn't going to get anything out of me."

"I'm being paid. A private citizen wants him found. He just wants the credit for finding him."

"Who is your client?" he asked.

"Doesn't matter."

"Negro or white?"

"White guy. Doesn't matter."

"The 'who' may not matter, but the 'why' does," he said. He pushed the legs of his slacks down, frowned at the wrinkles that grew around his thighs. "I don't want to help someone who has intentions of undermining our games. The numbers games generate a lot of revenue for us, the police and the politicians, and nobody wants to see that harmed."

"Who snatched Jones?"

"The papers said it was the Italians. The 'why' will lead you to the 'who.' Whoever kidnapped Ed did so for a reason. If they just wanted him out of the way, they could've killed him."

"Then why do you think they grabbed him?"

He glanced out the window, rubbed his chin. "Lot of reasons. Ed makes friends too quickly. He has made a lot of money because people like and trust him, but he offers the same without discretion. His financial holdings are all tended by white people, as are his real-estate holdings. Pardon the pun, but that's not good policy. You know, I understand he placed a large order for jukeboxes recently. You might start with them."

"Who's them?"

"The Kingdom Come Novelty Company. They're in Terre Haute."

"What could they tell me?"

"With your persuasive methods, I'm sure they could tell you who their other major customers are. I don't imagine that they would have been too pleased to find out that Ed intended to offer competition."

"Not bad," I said as I pulled in front of the Delilah Café.

"One other thing," said Johnson. "If you find Ed Jones, I'd like to see him first."

"Why?"

"We have business opportunities to discuss. I'd make it worth your while."

"What's my while worth?"

He looked me straight in the eye. "Say five hundred dollars."

"Must be the going rate."

"Make it a thousand."

"You're competing with fringe benefits that you can't supply," I said. "But I'd be happy to pass on a message for you."

"Good. Tell him if he's done something that screws up my games, I'm going to kill him."

I frowned. "That's the kind of message that had better be delivered in person."

He nodded. "My sentiments exactly. If you find him, bring him to me."

"Don't count on it."

"In fact, I'd be interested in anything you find out."

"Not likely, but you never know. How can I reach you?"

He looked out the window, watched a couple leave the café. "My sister is a spiritualist. She's at Two-thirty West Forty-seventh, a half of a block west of Wentworth Avenue. You can leave a message for me with her. I contact her several times a day. Madame Gail."

"What does she do?"

"Who knows? Convenes with God. Talks to the dead. Sees the future."

"Maybe I should stop and see her."

"To help you find Ed? No, I don't think so," he said as he opened the car door.

"Maybe she can look into her crystal ball and tell me how things are gonna turn out."

Johnson struggled out of the car, hesitated before he shut the door. "You know, Officer, she might tell you that if you find Ed Jones and turn him over to the wrong people, she couldn't read your future. Know why? Because you won't have one."

PLAYBACK: Bunny to Busy Jackson to Lincoln Johnson. Johnson says the Italians. Johnson says jukeboxes. Johnson threatens Jones, threatens me. Johnson doesn't have Jones.

Bix Bennett: "Harry says to give it six plays every hour." Find out where Harry bought his jukebox, who picks the tunes. A quick trip to Terre Haute and the Kingdom Come Novelty Company, stop and see Sam. Bad memories dredged up for a no-win case. My pre-war luck holding true. Fuck that. Water thoughts: Everything post-war is gravy.

I glanced at my watch: two o'clock, Sunday afternoon. I pulled into a gas station, grabbed a pay phone, dialed the station. I got Sally Rand on the line, blew compliments, begged: "What's the word on my shooting?"

"Word is, you got suspended."

"C'mon, Sal. I've always done you straight."

"You sure did, four years ago after the Christmas party."

"You were too good for me then and you're too good for me now. Come on, what gives?"

"Jameson and McGuire've got it. They aren't playing it like a straight shooting."

"Assholes. Who was the colored guy?"

"Don't have the file in front of me."

"What will it take for you to get it?"

"Flowers. Dinner at Pat Kelly's."

"Dozen roses, dinner next week."

"Let me call you back. What's the number, handsome?"

"Kenwood nine zero two zero."

I hung up, lit a cigarette, burned through it and lit another. The phone rang as I smoked the nub. "Yeah."

"Here it is in a nutshell, and get ready for this: The white man was an attorney named Don Cordell. The woman was Jane Vance, prostitute, multiple arrests. The Negro was Vaughn White, juvy arrest record, Forty-seven Thirty South Switzer."

"I knew the name Cordell; the rest is new. How old was White?"

"Thirty-seven."

At least nineteen years since his last arrest. "What's the motive?"

"Robbery."

"Robbery? Next thing you know they'll be busting Cordell for rape."

Sal sighed: "Hey, I don't know anything. I'm just reporting the news. You got a problem, talk to Jameson."

"What else?"

"I haven't seen their full report. I think they're going to file it three dead under 'who gives a fuck' and move on."

"Keep me posted. I owe you."

"No kidding you do. Griffin reinstates you, you got flowers and dinner for me."

I hung up, dialed the operator, got a listing for Don Cordell, Attorney at Law. I wrote down the phone number and address—North Wabash in the heart of the Loop. Didn't make sense—why would a Negro bust into a brothel to kill Cordell? Robbery was bullshit. Robbery meant "File it away." Robbery meant "Who cares?" Sal had that right. I looked at my watch again: two thirty. Plenty of time. I jumped back in my car and drove to 4730 South Switzer.

THE TENEMENT WAS MADE OF BRICK AND ROTTEN WOOD and looked like a strong wind would topple it. Two colored women, dressed in tattered white dresses and sweaters, stood on the back porch, smoking cigarettes. They looked down at me as I walked toward the building. In the background, a small child looked out from behind a barred window. The back door of the apartment was partially open, and its screen was torn out. The women looked at me with vacant eyes, didn't say a word.

"Excuse me, ladies," I said. "What unit did Vaughn White live in?"

They looked at each other, back at me. "Did?" said one.

I wasn't a reporter, not my job to spread the news: "I'm sorry, what unit?"

They shrugged. "First floor, second one on your left. Wife's there."

I stepped inside. Paint peeled off the walls; the floors were so filthy I could've written my name in the dirt. I found the unit and knocked. A moment later, a small woman came to the door. "Huh," she said. She held the door open; it was still chain-locked.

"My name is Carson," I said. "I'm with the Chicago Police Department. I'd like to talk to you about Vaughn."

"What? Oh no," she said. She unhooked the chain, opened the door wide, let me inside.

One room: a sink and stove off to one side; a shelf hanging from the wall held oatmeal, a can of coffee and rat poison. Two single beds and a dresser filled the rest of the room; a young boy lay in one of them, reading a comic book.

I looked at the woman, a dishtowel wrapped around her head, a dirty, ragged dress and saddle shoes. She was as frail as the tenement house, and she was scared. "What 'bout 'im?"

"Haven't you heard?"

"Heard what?"

I hesitated. "Anything. I mean, haven't you heard from him?"

The boy put down the comic book, eyed me. The woman glanced at him, grabbed the comic. "Donnie, you run on down the hall and see if Cecil can play. Mommy's got to talk for a while."

"Awright," he said. He jumped up off the bed and ran to the door.

The woman held out her small hand. It trembled. "Lydia White."

"Mrs. White," I said, shaking her hand, "I'm sorry to barge in on you like this."

"What is it?"

My stomach knotted. The bastards hadn't even told her yet. She read my thoughts: "Somethin' happen to mah husban'?"

I tried to rationalize a good lie—for the case, for her sake, for the kid. None of them worked—I knew I'd elected myself bearer of the worst news. "Mrs. White," I said, "your husband is dead."

She didn't scream, didn't cry, at least not immediately. She calmly stepped back to one of the beds and sat down. She crossed her legs at the ankles, folded her hands in her lap and quietly spoke. "Ain't no way. Why you think it was Vaughn?"

I didn't tell her he'd broken into a brothel and killed two people. I didn't tell her the names of the dead. I didn't tell her the department was filing it away and I didn't tell her I'd killed her husband. I told her that he'd entered a residence, robbed a man, shot him and was killed before he could escape.

She laughed, quietly. "Oh no, not Vaughn. Not in a million years, somethin' like that. He's quiet, makes me look like a fighter. He's a gardener. Why they think it was him?"

"I'm not sure," I said. "That was just the information I was given. Maybe he had identification on him, or he might've been fingerprinted at some point. Was he ever arrested, in the service?"

"Huh-uh. Like I said, he was just a gardener."

"Mrs. White, I'm awfully sorry for the confusion. I promise you I'll go back to the station and get to the bottom of this immediately. But have you seen your husband since Friday night?"

She paused, began to tap her knees with the palms of her hands. "No, can't say I have, but sometimes he gets jobs way up north and he stays 'til he's done. He was workin' this weeken', so I just figured he stayed."

"Do you know where he was working?"

"No. But he was all excited about it. Lotsa flowers and the like. He was working with some crew, one of the ones he worked with now and again."

"Do you know their name?"

"No. There was a lot of 'em. Well," she said, looking around the room. "I guess there wasn't that many. Vaughn just couldn't work with nothin' but flowers."

I kneeled down next to her. "Mrs. White, I'm hoping like hell that the man I saw isn't your husband, but if it was, I've got to know anything that you might be able to tell me about him that might help me figure out what happened. The man that I was told was your husband slipped into a, uh, house and killed a lawyer. I was told it was robbery, but I don't believe that. Your husband had a juvenile arrest record, but that was a long time ago. It just doesn't make sense."

"You just say you saw him?"

"I did and anything that you might..."

She cut me off. "Oh!" she cried. She jumped up off the bed, ran over to the dresser and picked up a framed picture. The glass was cracked; it had fallen over and I'd missed it when I came into the room. "Here, this here's mah husban'. This the man you saw?"

"Anything you might be able to tell me," I said, as I gazed at the picture, continued to kneel, "might be of some significance. See I just can't figure out what..."

"Is it him?" she yelled.

"...why he would just..."

"Is it him?"

"...break into the room and kill this lawyer...and this woman..."

"Is it him?"

"...for no apparent reason."

"Is it him?"

I raised my eyes and she screamed.

I DROVE NORTH ALONG THE LAKE for what seemed like an eternity, watched trees fill the landscape as I entered Lake Forest. Giant oaks seemed to guard the area, while pines, maples, elms and all sorts of other trees fought for room. The plant life and vegetation was a stark contrast to downtown, and I could understand why the rich had bought summer homes in the area and eventually built the huge mansions that housed the "Who's Who" of Chicago society.

Finally I wound around a bend and saw the driveway that led to the Prescott estate. Most of the homes in Lake Forest were only a hundred feet or so from the street. But the Prescott estate sat back at least a couple of hundred yards, and while the estate wasn't fenced off from the other properties, a waist-high stone wall ran along its edge, near the street. I figured they didn't need a fence anyway; the estate sat on more than one hundred acres, and their nearest neighbors lived in the servants' quarters and, occasionally, the guest house. I slowed down and coasted toward the stone arch over the gate to the estate.

When I looked through the gate, up the driveway, and saw the Rolls-Royces lined up, I finally started to forget about Lydia White. I'd called the station, raised hell with Captain Griffin, told him he'd suspended the wrong mug. He fired back about my suspension, got quiet when I bullshitted him—the good Christian in me had to pay respects to the widow. He promised to visit her himself, offer condolences. He told me to stay the heck out of the department's business. He sounded like a man just following orders—as involved as a jailer near a vacant cell.

I pulled forward, rolled down the window and told the guard my name. He checked my name off a list and let me in—I noted the snub-nosed revolver under his jacket and remembered that I was about to meet up with Chicago society.

A valet greeted me at the top of the circle driveway and took the keys to my car. "Mix 'em up with the keys to the big silver one," I said, pointing to a Rolls.

"Excuse me, sir?"

"Never mind; even my jokes aren't worthy."

He glanced at my car, then me and sneered. I watched him take off down the driveway, turn down the street and park my car as far from the house as possible. I wondered if he'd expect a tip.

"I hope he makes it back before you return for your keys, Gus."

I turned around and shook hands with Nathaniel Prescott. His hand felt small inside mine, and I remembered that I usually got his fingers—he shrank back when someone offered a handshake. He wasn't short, but he sure wasn't tall, and his slender frame couldn't hide the slight gut that dipped over his belt. He had that pampered paunch of the very rich. "I'm not so worried about the keys, Mr. Prescott. I'm just hoping he doesn't drink my bottle of hooch on his way back."

Prescott laughed. "You haven't changed a bit, Gus. But remember, it's Nat. We're chums! I don't know who was most excited when Sheila said she'd run into you and invited you to our little party. Let's step inside our happy home and get you a drink."

The drink sounded good, but the happy home was an understatement. Well, the 'happy' I wasn't sure about, but 'home' didn't do the manor justice. Everyone referred to it as the Prescott estate, and while I knew they were referring to the guest house, dog run, stables, pool, cabanas, lawn, gardens, driveway, trees, nuts and berries, I figured just the house could be called an estate. Or an ecountry or an econtinent. It was just plain huge.

Sheila raced up to me as we entered the house. She wore a light green evening gown. Its cut showed off her slender waist and hips, while her delicate arms peeked out of short sleeves. She wore long white gloves, and she gently pressed them against her hair, which was set in a pompadour.

"You didn't have to doll up just for me," I said. "But I'm glad you did. You'd make Hedy Lamarr jealous."

"You're so sweet. You look great, too," she said as she grabbed me by the arm and dragged me through the foyer and into the great room, where two bars had been set up and a crowd had gathered. I'd never felt under-dressed in my double-breasted charcoal pinstripe suit before, but the men in their tuxedos and women in their gowns had me feeling like a monkey in the gorilla cage.

"I forgot what I was stepping into," I said.

Sheila ran her hands across her light green gown. "What do you mean, Gus?"

"A woman of your persuasion would call it doo-doo."

"Very funny."

"Christ, I'm so under-dressed, I wouldn't be surprised if someone gave me a drink order."

I felt a tap on my shoulder. A tall, tanned man with slick hair and a face that didn't age said, "Excuse me, but I'd really like a martini. Extra olives."

I looked at Sheila. "See what I mean?"

She laughed. Her eyes sparkled. "Oh, Gus, you've been had. Don't you remember Uncle Zack?"

I turned, smiled. "Of course I do. Nice to see you, Uncle."

Zachary Bloodworth laughed, took my hand. He was no real uncle, just a friend of the family that took the title, but I'd met him several times. Yet I was surprised to feel his grip—I figured him for a pair of white gloves. "Just pulling your leg, Gus," he said. "I haven't seen you in a few years. What've you been doing with yourself?"

"Gus was a Marine," said Sheila.

I was saved by Nat Prescott, two drinks in his hand. "Bourbon, straight up, eh Gus?"

"Fine," I said, accepting the drink. Prescott stood next to me, his back to Bloodworth. He was probably the same age as Bloodworth, early fifties, but he looked it. The years hadn't been kind to him, nor, I figured, had his wife. He was still handsome, but his face was deeply lined and hung loose, like a mask slipping off. His eyes, though, were full of laughter.

"Have you been following the Cubs at all, Gus?" he asked.

"Not much. How're they doing?"

"Slow start. After the World Series last year, I'd hoped they'd get back there and win it this year, but it's not looking good."

"I'm afraid baseball is much too slow for me," said Bloodworth. "I prefer the horses. In fact, I'm thinking of joining the Lavins next week at the Preakness."

"Are you, now?" asked Prescott. "I'm sure that would be a bit of news to the Lavins."

Bloodworth ignored the comment. Sheila took my drink from my hand and took a sip. "So what horse do you like?" she asked.

Bloodworth beamed. "I really like Assault. Great horse. Won the Kentucky Derby, you know. Truly great beast."

All I knew about horses I'd learned from Randolph Scott, so I changed the subject quicker than a wet diaper. "Some party, Mr. P...Nat."

Prescott smiled. "Well, with Mother's Day and the fact that the Lavins are leaving tomorrow and we won't see them for two weeks, we decided to have a few people over. You know how these things happen; you start inviting people and when you invite one, you've got to invite the next and the next. Feelings and all."

"Kinda like when it's my round at the bar," I said.

Prescott laughed. "Exactly. People just start showing up!" He looked out of the corner of his eye at Bloodworth, who averted his gaze.

A lull in the conversation. I dug my feet into the thick beige carpet like a hitter in the batter's box, looked around the room, cased the joint: A large crystal chandelier hung from the ceiling, candles everywhere. A black grand piano sat in the corner—a man, thirtyish, dressed in a tux, played, oblivious to the crowd. Occasionally he would look up, acknowledge a request with a slight smile and go back to playing whatever it was he was playing. I fought the burning desire to join him in chopsticks.

"What are you thinking about, Gus?" asked Sheila as she took my hand.

I shook my head. "Not much at all. Just looking around the room."

"I have the most marvelous news, Gus," she said. "Daddy just ordered me a Cadillac!"

"Gee," I said, "that's swell."

"She's a bit of an optimist, Gus," said Prescott. "They told me I probably wouldn't get it until forty-nine."

"Hooey," said Sheila. "They haven't made new cars in years; it can't take that long."

Bloodworth chimed in: "Well, with the rationing and since you do want all new materials..."

"Rationing, my..." said Sheila. "When everyone else got A or B ration coupons for gasoline, they treated Daddy like a politician. He got all the gasoline he needed. I'm sure we'll get the car soon."

Prescott frowned, bit his lip. "Sheila is exaggerating, as usual. I got by with three gallons of gas, just like everyone else. She was away so often that she didn't notice. She's just lucky they didn't ration the fuel it takes for her to concoct that story."

I laughed to cut short Sheila's embarrassment. "Well, if there's a lot of bull being thrown around, let's talk politics."

Bloodworth smiled. "Big fan of Mayor Kelly, are you?"

"I've got about as much use for him as a boxer does a glass cup," I said.

"Ouch," said Bloodworth, "are you a Republican?"

"I didn't say that," I said. "I'm just not a big fan."

"You're certainly in the majority, right now," said Prescott. "He's under a lot of fire. I'd say the Republicans have as great a chance in next year's election as they've had in a long time."

"Now it's you who are being a bit optimistic," said Bloodworth. Sheila smiled slightly. "The Democrats are simply going to find someone to run in Kelly's place. They're not blind. They read the papers, too. It's not the Democrats that are under fire, it's Kelly."

"Too much graft and corruption. Did you read the article on that Negro policy racketeer that got kidnapped?" asked Prescott. "The paper said that it's a ten-million-dollar-a-year industry in Chicago. Can you believe that? That's a fantastic year for entire companies, let alone some colored gamblers. And you wonder how much of that goes into the Democrats' pockets?"

"Jealous?" asked Bloodworth, as he lit a pipe.

"You're intolerable," said Prescott. "Here I am, seriously debating the shortcomings of our mayor and you're baiting me. Well, it'll serve you good when the construction boom hits all over the country, and we miss out here because we've got a corrupt, incompetent mayor."

Bloodworth drew on his pipe. "Aren't you forgetting that you're in the construction business and I am not?"

Prescott threw back his drink. "Jesus, Bloodworth, I'm just trying to make a point. Our city can't run on all cylinders if our government is corrupt."

"Kinda like asking the sheep to keep an eye on the shepherds," I said.

Bomb defused. They all laughed. We turned to small talk; I watched the crowd, tried to figure them out. I never understood people born into money—they always looked like their parents had dressed them and they didn't really have anything to say. The corner of my eye: Prescott helped Sheila with her zipper; she asked him, again, about the Caddy.

I filled my drink, walked through the crowd. No one felt obligated to trade quips with me, so I made friends with the bartender. Sheila and Bloodworth exchanged gossip in a corner, Prescott made the rounds. I fished another penny from my right pocket, went to slip it into my left when it dawned on me that I wasn't paying for the drinks and didn't feel like keeping track just to fight off the hangover. I'd decided to drive to Terre Haute the next day, anyway, and that didn't require much energy. I polished off the drink and signaled for another.

"And who might you be?"

I turned away from the bartender and saw a gray-haired matron smiling at me. Her navy blue gown was tasteful, and she cocked her head back with poise and confidence. "I might be Gus Carson," I said. "But I've had enough of these to make me wonder."

"Well, since you're wondering, I'm Gloria Blanchard, and that tall, boring fellow behind me with the hideous polka-dot bow tie is my husband, Gerald. He's actually a decent fellow, but parties aren't for spending time with your spouse."

"Well, don't worry," I said. "I don't have a spouse, so I won't ask you to spend time with her." I reached over and grabbed my drink from the bar.

She laughed. "And there you have it, young man. Within a few seconds you've shown more wit than Gerald has in the last thirty years of our marriage." She ran a forefinger around the rim of her wineglass. "Now, didn't I see you with Sheila Prescott?"

"You might have."

"And what is your relationship with her?"

"Are you Hedda Hopper?"

She put her fingers to her lips and made a twisting motion. "Your secret is safe with me."

I leaned into her. "I'm madly in love with her, but I want her to give all of this up and come live with me in my one-bedroom apartment."

"Maybe it's the rest of the apartment that scares her. The one bedroom sounds ideal." She cackled, threw back her head. I grinned, heard the crowd murmur. I watched heads turn like willows in a breeze, knew what drew the attention. Unconsciously, I followed their gaze—Virginia Prescott made her entrance.

She moved gracefully down the staircase, not quite in full view, turned and came toward the great room. All eyes were on her as she sifted through the crowd, said pleasant hellos, shook hands and gave quick embraces. When she finally entered the room, the crowd parted slowly, and I got the full view. A gorgeous black gown wore Virginia Prescott. It was a piece of cloth without her, but a work of erotic art when she slipped inside. The hemline barely beat my tongue to the floor. It had company. Guests flocked to her like it was closing time and she held all of the car keys. I turned back to Gloria Blanchard, and we exchanged knowing grins.

"Believe it or not, in my day, I got a few of those looks, too," she said.

"I believe it. You'd better be glad this isn't your day because there aren't a pair of eyeballs to spare."

She howled. "Gus, I've enjoyed talking to you, but you'd better go say hello to Sheila. I don't think her mother's entrance has done a whole lot for her confidence."

I shook her hand. "I guess it's not called Daughter's Day for a reason."

She smiled, sighed. "Well, that would be another excuse for a good party."

"Who's ever needed an excuse?" I asked as I tipped my glass toward her.

She chuckled. "No excuses necessary, but a change in neighbors means a change in the social venue."

"What do you mean?" I asked.

"These parties," she said, sweeping her hand across the room. "I mean, there will always be wonderful social occasions, but the day of these grand estates has almost passed."

She saw the confusion on my face, continued. "Huge estates like this are being redeveloped into subdivisions, with middle-class houses being built on an acre or less." She crinkled her nose like someone had said the word "poop." "In fact, I dare say the Prescott estate is the last of the great estates. And even people as rich as the Prescotts can't turn down the developers' money forever."

"I don't follow you," I said. "What is there to miss? A little booze and some good gossip and you can have a party."

"Money and excess bring out people's eccentricities," she said. "Look at this wonderful, horrible, eccentric family." She glanced briefly at Nat Prescott, Sheila and Virginia. "Watching them is grand entertainment. No, when the middle class moves in here, I think these crazy, rich people will simply slink into the shadows, and God how I'll miss them."

"I thought you shared soup spoons with them," I said. "You weren't invited here because you date the daughter."

She chuckled again, finished her wine and searched the crowd. "My husband and I might be in their class," she said, "but we're older and boring. Gerald is too homely to find a stunning young wife, and I'm too lazy to compete with a daughter." She finally saw her husband, said good-bye again and walked off to join him. As she sidled up next to him, she looked back at me and rolled her eyes. I smiled at her and winked.

I saw that a crowd of guests was still gathered around Virginia and I remembered Gloria Blanchard's suggestion about Sheila, so I turned around and looked for her. I spotted her, then again caught Nat Prescott out of the corner of my eye. As his wife sifted through the crowd, he moved to the other side of the room like she carried a subpoena with his name on it. He settled in at the bar and gently hoisted the bottom of the bottle as the bartender filled his glass with scotch.

I stifled a laugh and walked over to Sheila, who stood, alone, sipping a glass of wine. She stared at her mother, barely noticed me stand beside her. "Isn't that gaudy," she said. "She always has to call attention to herself. I don't understand it."

"Maybe it's because she has a beautiful daughter and she knows her days are numbered," I said.

Sheila smiled. "Do you think so? Well, yes, you're probably right." She took the rest of her wine in one gulp. "Oh, look at me, jealous of my own mother. I'm so embarrassed. It's just that I see all of these men looking at her, and I know what it must do to Daddy."

"I'll tell you exactly what it does. It makes him damn proud. She's his girl, no one else's."

"But he's older than her, Gus, and when she dresses like that, it just makes it more obvious."

"Sister," I said, "we could fill a planet with all of the older men who would trade places with your old man and a solar system with the younger women who would trade places with your mother."

"You're right." She grabbed my hand, locked her fingers inside mine. "Let's go out by the pool."

"Little cold, don't you think?"

"No," she said as she guided me down the hall and out the back door. We stepped outside into the cool night air. I couldn't see my breath, but it was chilly. She guided me down three flights of concrete steps toward the pool. It was light outside; I could see the bushes and flowers that lined the steps and the tight manicure of the lawn. As we got closer to the pool, I saw the tall torches burning and could hear the hum of the portable generators. Nat Prescott had made sure that it would be light and warm for his party.

We walked between the cabanas and onto the deck surrounding the water. Several others had had the same idea and a waiter weaved through the group, taking drink orders. Another waiter, dressed in black slacks and a white dinner jacket, served hors d'oeuvres off a tray. The flames from the torches reflected in the pool, which seemed as wide as Sheila's smile.

"Thanks for coming, Gus, and thanks for babying me." She leaned forward and gave me a quick kiss. I started to respond, but she pushed me back, looked around at the crowd.

"Later, later. You don't have to rush off, do you?"

"I'm heading out of town tomorrow, ten hours round-trip and a few hours in the city, so I can't stay too late."

"Where are you going?"

"Doesn't matter. Remember the side job I told you about? I've got to be back in Chicago by six, too, so I'm gonna have to leave about five in the morning."

The waiter stopped by, took our drink orders. Sheila pulled me away from the crowd. "Why don't you just stay here, in the guest house? That way, you can just get up and go. If you drive home tonight, you'll have to go back into the city, and then back out again tomorrow morning."

"Why would I want to stay out here tonight?"

She moved forward, brushed a hand against me. "Remember last night?"

Falsetto: "As if it was almost yesterday."

"Then I'm not even going to ask again. It's settled. If you dare reconsider, you'd better kiss me good-bye."

"Kiss you, yes, good-bye, no. I guess I'm staying. I don't really need a change of clothes for the people I'm seeing, anyway."

The waiter strode up with my drink, told Sheila he'd be right back with her wine. I could see Virginia making her way toward us. She stopped, chatted briefly with a couple seated near the water's edge and then walked over to us. Sheila grabbed my glass and took a swift drink as Virginia joined us.

"Hello, Gus," said Virginia. She leaned forward, kissed me on the cheek. I patted her shoulders. "Sheila," she said, turning to her daughter, "I don't think Gus needs help with his drink. You don't need to start mixing liquor and wine."

"I was just tasting it, Mother," said Sheila. She rolled her eyes. "You don't have to worry about my every move."

"Well, God knows your father doesn't set any kind of example," said Virginia. "I'm sure he's already half in the bag."

"Daddy's fine!" said Sheila, venom in her voice. "Somebody gives him that edge he likes to take off."

That somebody looked back at me, ignored her daughter. "I'm glad you made it home safe, Gus. Nat said he'd seen you, but I wish you'd have come by the house. We were all worried about you."

"Thanks. I'm fine. How have you been?"

"I understand you're not fine. I heard you had a terrible time in the war, and now I hear you've been suspended."

"Really, Mother!" said Sheila. "She didn't hear that from me."

"I'm not prying, dear, I'm just concerned for Gus. Gus, is there anything we can do?"

"No," I said. "Nothing important. It'll blow over. I've got plenty of other stuff to do."

"Such as?"

"Such as what?"

"What are you going to do with yourself?"

"I've got some work."

"Listen," said Virginia. "I can help you. There are several people here tonight that you should meet. A lot of them hire private security."

"You mean security like the man at your gate?"

"Yes, like the man at the gate. We've had threats, burglary attempts. And I'm sure they make a lot more than you make now," said Virginia.

"Oh, God," said Sheila. "I don't believe this. Gus, I'm sorry…"

I waved her off. "Money's not everything," I said.

Virginia slowly shook her head. "Oh, Gus, once you have money, you see things differently. You stop worrying about missing the boat and start thinking about buying one. And there's plenty of money for a smart man to make. You just have to put your mind to it."

The waiter returned with a glass of wine. Sheila insisted it wasn't what she'd ordered, also insisted she'd select it herself. She trotted off with the waiter, escaped.

Virginia grabbed my hand and led me to the other side of the pool. As I followed her, I noted her long, blonde hair was piled on top of her head—the nape of her neck still looked young and fresh. She stopped, looked up to make sure that no one was looking and lashed into me. "I know exactly why you've been suspended, and I think it's horrible. A prostitute, Gus; you visited a prostitute and now you're seeing my daughter? I'd have told her, but the silly girl really likes you. The whole thing disgusts me. Did you at least wear protection?"

"Of course."

"Don't 'of course' me. Sex can kill. Look at Al Capone. I hear the syphilis is eating him alive."

"You don't have anything to worry about."

She pulled back, threw an open hand across her breasts. "Of course I have nothing to worry about; it's my daughter I'm thinking about. What's gotten into you, Gus?"

I shook my head, not buying the act. "Virginia…"

"It's Mrs. Prescott."

"Mrs. Prescott, that's not what I meant."

"Frankly, I don't care what you meant. If my daughter gets in any trouble over you, I'll ruin you. You think a suspension is rough; just wait and see what our friends can do."

"I don't like threats, Mrs. Prescott, so you'd better watch 'em. And I don't need the 'leave my daughter alone' lecture from you either. You and I both know you don't care if she sees me. It's not gonna last. I'm from the wrong side of town, and it's just fun for her now."

"Have you got a cigarette?"

I pulled out a Lucky Strike, handed it to her. She placed it between her lips, leaned toward me and cupped her hands around mine when I lit it. She inhaled, deeply, and sighed. "I'm sorry. With this party and everything, I've been on edge. I heard about your suspension and I felt horrible for you. Rather than offer you my sympathy, I lost my temper. I'm sorry."

"No problem."

"Who was the man you killed?"

Her abruptness struck me like a lead jab. "Why?"

"Guess I'm just curious. It sounded so odd. I just wondered if there was anything more to it. After all, my daughter may be spending time with you; I think I've got a right to ask."

I didn't tell her his name. I didn't tell her about my trip to the tenement, my conversation with the dead man's wife. I didn't tell her that I didn't want to talk about killing and poverty and despair while I was surrounded by wealth and insincerity and deceit. I told her I didn't know his name, he was just a stupid burglar. The department didn't care and neither did I. I told her he was just some shine.

She studied me, swallowed it. Sheila came back, wine in hand, and the cloak went back on. "Why don't you introduce Gus around, dear," said Virginia. "You never know when a splendid opportunity might present itself."

"That's exactly what I was about to do, Mother," said Sheila. She turned to me. "Daddy just sent me to fetch you. He wants you to meet someone, so come along."

We started to move away. "Have you got one more cigarette, before you go, Gus?" asked Virginia. I saw the twinkle in her eye, said yes. She repeated the performance for Sheila, cupped my hand as I lit the cigarette. I caught Sheila's glare. She gulped her wine like it was punch.

"How old are you, Gus?" asked Virginia.

"Twenty-nine."

She blew smoke. "I thought you were a bit older than that. I guess it's your size. When is your birthday?"

"Why?"

"Because you're right in between Sheila and me."

"Mother's nearly forty," said Sheila, gleefully.

Virginia threw Sheila a look of annoyance, turned back to me and smiled as she pulled the cigarette from her lips. "C'mon, Gus. Humor us."

The raven-haired daughter, golden-haired mother: Sheila stared at me like a patient waiting for a diagnosis; Virginia waited, eyes gleaming. "June twenty-fourth," I said.

A smile crept across Virginia's face. Sheila looked ashen. "How funny," said Virginia. "You're closer to me."

Sheila grabbed my arm and led me back to the house.

"SHE'S JUST VULGAR WHEN SHE'S LIKE THIS," said Sheila as we entered the house. "But I won't have to put up with it much longer. Once my car arrives, I'm going to convince Daddy to set me up on my own. I can handle it, you know." She looked at me for approval.

"Of course you can, kid," I said. "Wouldn't worry about it for a second."

We walked down the hall and into the den. More Persian rugs covered the floor; a couple of bookshelves, a German shrunk and a glass gun case had the perimeter. Four wood chairs surrounded a small table in the center of the room—a chessboard sat on top, its pieces set up for battle. A cowboy hat sat in one chair. In the corner of the room, staring into the gun rack, stood a short, white-haired man.

"Mr. Tanner," said Sheila. "This is Gus Carson."

The short man stepped forward, shook my hand. His grip was strong and firm, and he pumped my hand enthusiastically. "Pleased to make your acquaintance, Mister Carson. I'm Lucas Tanner. Luke, to my friends." His voice carried a soft Southern twang.

"Gus," I said.

Sheila excused herself. She swayed a bit as she walked. Her mother and the wine had started to affect her.

I looked at Tanner while he sized me up. He was short and slender, but there was a lean, hard look to his body. He was probably in his late fifties—the white hair and thick, white moustache were a giveaway; he looked like a man who had worked hard for most of his life. I'd felt the calluses on his hands, noticed his weather-beaten skin.

"How're you liking the party?" he said. It took effort for him to make small talk; he smiled uncomfortably as he asked.

"A little much for me," I said. "I'm not used to drinking in a place with clean floors."

He slapped a knee. "I'm right there with you. This is just a little high-fallutin' for me."

"Maybe we'll have to do something about the floors," I said.

He laughed. "Well, did you at least call your mother today and wish her a happy Mother's Day?"

"If she was alive, I'd have called."

"Oh Christ, I'm sorry," he said. "There I go, not knowing you for three minutes and I've already shoved my boot in my mouth."

"Don't worry about it," I said, finishing my drink. "Long time ago. I'm over it."

"Man never gets over something like that," he said. "Sometimes life just goes and kicks the teeth out of you." He noticed my empty glass, drained his. "Gus," he said as he pulled a bottle from behind a vase full of flowers, "care to join me in a glass of Kentucky bourbon?"

I held out my glass; he filled it to the brim. "You grow up around here?" he asked.

"City."

"Me, I'm from Kansas, just outside Kansas City. Cattle business, some oil. Spent most of my life on a horse or doing chores. Kinda miss it. Then again, my back don't."

"How'd you end up here?"

"Took a Pullman car from KC to Chicago to visit friends and ended up in a poker game with a couple of rascals. One of 'em was a Jew doctor named Green. Took one of his houses, a small plane and a load of cash. Funny thing was, we wouldn't have hit the train station, he'd have wanted to keep on playing. Man just didn't know when to quit."

"He offer it right up?"

"He was pretty sore at first, so I told him he could stay in my barn if that was a problem. One thing I take seriously is my cards. You place a bet, you better be prepared to pay. Hell, I even learned how to fly that plane. Lotta fun, but I guess you gotta have somewhere to go."

"Listen, Mr. Tanner, you seem like a swell guy, but…"

"But you want me to get to the point, huh?"

I nodded. "I can save you the trouble. The Prescotts have this crazy idea that I'm looking for a job, but I'm not. So I appreciate them talking to you, but…"

He smiled. "Gus, I didn't ask to see you to offer you any kind of job."

"Then what is it?"

He turned his back to me, walked toward the gun rack. "Nat tells me you were in the war, had some kind of trouble on a ship."

My stomach knotted. "Something like that."

"Was it bad?"

"Why do you ask?"

"I…I…just wanna know. I don't really know why, I just wanna know." I stepped closer, behind him. "Who are we talking about?"

His shoulders sagged. "My…my…son."

"Where?"

"I don't rightly know. Somewhere in the Pacific. Their ship was sunk by a Jap torpedo. None of 'em survived."

"Look, Tanner," I said. "I'm sorry. It was a helluva mess. Too many men died."

"Nat said he heard you went through something kinda like that. I know it must be terrible for you, but I want to know what it was like. I know I don't have any right to ask, but…"

I knew what he meant. I'd seen it in the faces of people who'd lost loved ones during the war. The uncertainty, no chance for good-byes. The thought of a man suffering, dying. The helpless, horrible feeling that you hadn't done anything. I touched his shoulder, looked over it into the gun rack. "The fellas on my ship were good men," I said.

It was like letting the air out of a balloon, real slow. I talked and talked, but kept my fingers tight on the nozzle, knew that if I slipped, it would all come out in one uncontrollable gush. I told him about the songs, games and bull sessions. I told him about wrestling the biggest sailor on the ship while his Navy buddies screamed for my head, doused me in beer when I pinned him. I told him about the cook sending cake and brownies down to the brig, men stopping down for a game of cards.

I told him about the torpedoes, the fire, oil and water. I told him about the men swimming around the floater net, dragging back stragglers. I told him about the hymns and the prayers—religion didn't matter, it was us looking for God, praying He was looking for us.

I didn't tell him about the cold and the heat and the sharks. I didn't tell him about the unbearable urge to drink the poison—salt water. I didn't tell him that some couldn't resist, went crazy, foamed at the mouth—we had to let them drift away, sink. I didn't tell him that I found out that there was one thing that God created that was worse than death. I didn't tell him that more than starvation, thirst or death, there was one thing that had terrified me. I didn't tell him because I saw that he was facing it, knew what I'd say. I didn't tell him that the worst thing that could ever happen to a man was being alone.

He turned around, tears filled his eyes. "If there's anything I can ever…" I threw an arm around his shoulder as he started to sob. "My son, my son."

WE FINISHED THE FIFTH OF BOURBON just before midnight, and by that time we were Gus and Luke. Luke scribbled his phone number on a scrap of paper—I jammed it in my wallet and told him I'd call him. Jerome, the Prescott's butler, had one of the security men drive Luke home while he guided me to the guest house. Sheila, he said, had turned in early—even in my own foggy state, I knew that she'd been over-served.

The guest house was a hundred yards or so from the main house. It was a single-level dwelling with one bedroom, a bathroom, kitchen, living room and breakfast nook. I'd stayed in it before, so I had no trouble navigating my way around after Jerome unlocked the front door.

I stripped, crawled into bed and fought the bed spins. After just a few minutes, I drifted into a fitful, light sleep. "Happy Mother's Day!" played through my dreams like the scratched Bix Bennett record. I saw

Lucas Tanner, guiding a sailboat across the ocean, searching for his son. I saw a colored gardener snipping at a bed of flowers—when he turned to face me, there were black holes where his eyes, nose and mouth should've been. I saw Sollie the Jew start to sink. I dove after him; the water was murky, salt burned my eyes. I saw a figure, swam to it. "Happy Mother's Day!" mouthed my mother as she rolled over in the water. Suddenly I saw her standing on the Michigan Avenue Bridge. She stepped off, fell into the water next to me. I reached for her, saw her face. "Happy Mother's Day, son," she said as I sobbed.

In and out of consciousness; booze, stress, exhaustion pulled me up, pushed me back under. I heard the voice: "Happy Mother's Day." I felt the cool hands run across my chest, stroke my cheek and hair. Warm lips brushed mine, gently bit my lower lip. Heavy breasts fell across my chest, legs intertwined with mine, a hand stroked me. I responded, wrapped my arms around her, pulled her on top of me. Suddenly I was inside her—we panted, moaned, pushed and tugged at one another. Our skin slapped like waves; I looked at her over the top of the swell. Virginia, Sheila, Gloria Blanchard, my mother. I drifted off.

The booze wore off at four thirty in the morning, jarred me awake. I dressed in solitude, left the guest house, walked through the main house, stopped in the kitchen. A pot of coffee boiled on the stove. I grabbed a big ceramic cup, filled it and wandered out to find my car. Someone had pulled it up front. It was parked right outside the front door, unlocked, keys in the ignition. I started it up, drove off, took a sip of my coffee. The cup was hot; it burned my lip. I ran my tongue over my lip and tasted blood.

## MONDAY, MAY 13

ONE HELLUVA HANGOVER JOINED ME in the driver's seat for the ride to Terre Haute. I stopped once to refill my cup of coffee, rolled the window down and drove hard. The cool air made me feel a little better; I forgot about the forty-mile-per-hour speed limit, pushed it to fifty. A hundred-and-eighty-mile drive gave me plenty of time to think.

Playback: I'd called the Kingdom Come Novelty Company the day before—some stiff in accounting refused to tell me the names of their customers, suggested I see the owner, in person. Another call—to the Federal Pen: I could see Sam at eleven—that gave me two hours to work the juke boys.

Questions: Why nothing in the paper about the killings? Why no call to the gardener's widow? Keeping the death of the colored man out of the paper was one thing, the attorney a different story altogether. The biggest why: Why would a simple gardener kill the attorney? None of it made sense, none of it paid my bills. Focus. Ed Jones, Ed Jones, I repeated the name, laid odds: Joe Batters, Paul Ricca, Sam Giancana—the Syndicate, even money. Why? Jukeboxes, policy, prostitution. It all ran through my mind, tweaked the hangover; I made it to Terre Haute in just under four hours.

THE KINGDOM COME NOVELTY COMPANY occupied a single-story industrial plant, but only a small sign on the parking lot gate announced that to the public. I pulled into the lot and saw that none of the empty spaces were marked for visitors, so I pulled to the back of the lot and parked in the corner, near the chain-link fence that surrounded the property. I walked back across the lot, followed the sidewalk to the front door and let myself inside.

The reception area was no wider than an average bathroom, and the dirty carpet and handprints on the wall showed that the few people that used it probably worked in the plant. I leaned over the counter, slid the little window open and asked the startled receptionist for the owner, Harvey Edwards. She must have been a temp: She led me into Edwards's office while he was in the middle of a conversation with another man. Edwards glanced up as we entered the office, shook his head. "Miss Christopher," he said, "can't you see I'm in a meeting? Please take this man back out to reception, and I'll call you when I'm done."

"Oh," she said, "if you'll follow me." She started back out the door, I didn't follow.

"Listen, Edwards," I said. "I'm a police officer, I called here yesterday. I just need to get a list of your customers. If you'll instruct someone in accounting to fork it over, I'll get out of your hair."

The temp stood in the doorway: "Sir, if you could please follow me back out."

Edwards looked at me. He was tall and thin and wore blue coveralls with the name "Kingdom Come Novelty Company" stitched over the left breast. The man in his office wore the same outfit but was older, short, frail and gray—he coughed and gulped water as Edwards questioned me.

"You can leave, Miss Christopher," he said. "Now, who are you, sir?"

"Name's Carson. I'm from Chicago, and I'm looking into the kidnapping of a colored man named Jones. You ever take an order from a guy named Jones?"

"No," said Edwards. "Can't say that I have."

"Ever talked to anyone named Jones about an order?"

"No."

"Pretty common name, I'm surprised you can answer so fast."

"He can answer so fast 'cause he's lying," said the old man as he coughed.

"Shut up, George!" yelled Edwards. He leaned over the desk and glared at the man.

"Shove it, Harvey. I'll tell this man whatever I want."

"Who're you?" I asked.

"George Ross. I'm the chief designer here. Got emphysema, maybe two months left, so Harvey and I don't play by the same rules."

"You're making a big mistake, George," said Edwards. "You're still an employee here, and you won't just answer to me!"

"You're making the mistake," I said. "Hindering an investigation is a crime. I find out you're holding back something from me and I'll run you in."

"C'mon," said Ross as he stood up. "Let's go out in the yard for a quick talk. That way we don't upset poor Harvey here."

Edwards cursed as we walked out the door. He led me out of the building, through the parking lot and around the side of the factory. A picnic table sat just outside of an overhead door. We sat down; Ross fired up a cigarette.

"Damn things are about all I got left," he said as he offered me a cigarette. I took one, lit it and thanked him as he put the deck of smokes back in his pocket.

His skin was sallow. He rubbed his eyes, temples. "Now, what can I do for you?"

"So you've sold to Jones?"

"No, but I know some colored guy named Jones has been calling around, talking about placing a big order for jukes. We didn't do business with him. Won't."

"Why?"

"Let's just say that all of our customers have names that sound like they belong on a menu."

"The old Capone gang?" I asked.

"Seems so. Albert Carpacci. Heard of him?"

"Yeah. He's one of 'em all right. Think your boss let him know that Ed Jones has been looking to get into the jukebox business?"

Ross bent over, slapped a knee, laughed. The laugh triggered a cough, he spit out a big glob of phlegm. "Shit, yes, he'll tell him, but 'boss'? Hell, in name only. That dumb son of a bitch couldn't build a decent machine if his life depended on it. And I can tell you, 'cause mine does. Only reason I'm alive now is to finish the thirty-five fifty-three. That's our newest model. Gonna have forty-eight selections. Full cabinet, chrome-edged. You oughta see her."

I bit. "Been here long?"

"Sixteen years, from Chicago."

"Any friends still live in Chicago?"

He cracked up. "Haven't seen today's paper!"

I laughed. "What brought you here?"

"Had my own shop in Chicago, but when my wife died, I moved here to help Harvey. Gave me a pretty good salary, told me he'd let me design whatever I wanted. We do jukes and pinball machines. Then the war broke out, and they had us make parachute equipment and machine-gun parts. Can you imagine that? I make games and music and they got me making parts for machine guns." He shook his head, puffed the cigarette. "Well, hell, we got an 'E' award for our war efforts, but we weren't making any new machines. All we was doin' was convertin' old pinball machines. You know, new color glass, playboard designs, bumper caps, scorecards. It's been fun, but it ain't like making 'em from scratch."

He stood up. "Come on," he said. "I want to show you something."

We both stamped our cigarettes out on the ground, walked across the yard to a small shed. He opened the door, stepped inside. I followed. "This here," he said, "is a genuine, brand-new pinball machine. This machine is going to revolutionize the business. I call it 'The Eternal Game.'"

I looked at the machine. It looked like any typical pinball machine—colored glass, lights, attractive women painted on the playboard and backglass—but it went further. The women were nude, and on both sides of the playboard were naked men, hands at their hips, erections posing as some kind of flippers. At the bottom of the board, where the ball spilled back into the machine, was a naked woman, lying on her back, legs spread wide.

"Well, what do you think?"

"Catchy."

"Catchy, hell," he grunted. "You, sir, are looking at history. This is the first pinball machine with genuine flipper bumpers. Now, the player doesn't just launch the ball with the plunger, he gets to bat it around with the flipper bumpers. Watch."

He pulled the plunger, launched the ball into the machine. Lights flashed as it hit the bumpers, numbers lit up the scoreboard. The ball descended, appeared ready to drop, but he hit a button and a tiny penis slapped the ball back into play. This went on for several minutes as he yelled, laughed and coughed. Finally he missed with a thrust and the ball slid between the woman's legs and disappeared.

"Well, now, what do you think of that?" he asked, eyes gleaming, a bead of sweat rolling off his nose.

"Sinsational," I joked.

"You bet it is. Know why I call it 'The Eternal Game'? 'Cause it's the eternal game—men get a sniff of quiff, start throwing their money around. And in the end, the woman always gets the money!"

I laughed. "That's great, Mr. Ross, but we were talking about the jukebox business."

"Yeah, I know. That Goddamned Harvey says he isn't going to market this. But I'm betting he's just waiting 'til I'm gone, then he's gonna bring out a bunch of 'em. Only problem is, he don't know how to make 'em and I'm taking the plans with me."

"The jukeboxes?"

"Oh, sure. Harvey told the colored fella that he wouldn't sell to him, wouldn't ever. He knows where the jukes end up and who's ordering 'em. Harvey called Carpacci and told him the guy was trying to buy machines, and you know what? He said Carpacci just laughed, told him nobody would sell to the colored man. No, mister, if them Italians are the ones that kidnapped that man, it weren't because of jukeboxes. Know why? They wouldn't have to. They control that racket like a Rockefeller. They sell you the machines, tell you what you got to play."

I thanked him. He walked me to my car, shook my hand. "Now, after I'm gone, you ever see 'The Eternal Game' on the market under some other name, you come out here and arrest Harvey."

I promised him. I watched him go back into the factory, could see Edwards yelling at him.

I pulled out of the lot, drove off. My mind wandered.

I thought about plants designed to manufacture games and then used to build weapons.

I thought about the different things that kept us alive.

I thought about Virginia Prescott and the eternal game.

TERRE HAUTE, FEDERAL PENITENTIARY: A guard led me down the hall toward the warden's office—it would be the first time I'd see a warden for a simple visit. It burned me; I wanted to get back home in time for a quick nap. I was already tired and was looking at one long shift.

The guard opened the door, let me in. A man sat in a brown leather chair, back to me. Cigar smoke pooled over his head. He didn't move as I sat down. I took off my trench coat, draped it over the arm of the chair. I noted the pictures of the warden's wife on the desk, President Truman on the wall. The man still didn't acknowledge my presence.

"Can we get this over with, warden," I said. No movement. "I want to see Sam and I haven't got all day."

"Blow it out your ass."

"What?"

He turned to face me, let out a puff of smoke. "I said blow it out your ass."

I shook my head. "How the hell...?"

Sam put out the cigar in an ashtray, moved around the desk and clapped my shoulders. I clapped him back. "Fucking warden's out at some meetings, so one of my guys worked me in here. I thought it'd be funny as hell to see the look on your face."

He sat back down in the warden's chair, opened a desk drawer. "I've already been through here. The fucking nance doesn't even have a bottle. Sorry. Not bad smokes, though. Want one?"

I shook my head. "Looks like you've already made yourself at home."

"Hey, they told me life and this is the life." He threw his hands in the air, gestured around the room.

I studied him. Still the widest son of a bitch I'd ever seen, save some joker who worked for Giancana named Lipranski. His gray hair crept back from his forehead in a prison crew cut, and he was clean-shaven. He had thick, dark brows that rose above eyes so brown they appeared black. He wore a dark bowling shirt and a pair of blue jeans. His massive arms bore tattoos—"Mom" on his left bicep, "Margaret" on his right—and were folded across his chest. I guessed Sam didn't believe in prison issue.

"Cut the bullshit," I said. "How're you really doing?"

"No bullshit, great. I can take this for another three to seven years."

"Three to seven doesn't sound like life."

"I got an ace up my sleeve."

"What's that?" I asked.

"Don't worry about it. What're you doing up here?"

"Working a case. Had to talk to some locals."

"Bullshit. I heard you got suspended."

I folded my legs, sat back. "Where'd you hear that?"

"Just because I'm behind bars don't mean I don't have my feelers out there. What happened?"

"Damnedest thing. I was at Mona's on Friday night, when some colored guy slipped in and shot this attorney. The hook got it, too. I got him just before he got out."

"Who's got it?" he asked.

"Jameson, McGuire."

"Couple a pricks. Who was the attorney?"

"Some guy named Don Cordell."

Sam clipped another cigar, whistled. "Whew. He's a big one. Know who he is?"

I shook my head.

"Works for the boys. Anything happens to Joe Batters, Momo, any of their boys, they call Cordell or his brother. He made me look like a knight in shining armor."

"Right."

"No bull," he said. "The guy was a bagman. Ran money from the boys to us, kept 'em outta jail, bribes, extortion, the worst."

"You killed a federal judge."

Sam flinched. "You don't have to get petty. Jesus, I'm just saying he was no saint. The nigger probably took the fall for one of his crooked deals, clipped him."

"His wife said he was just a gardener."

"What the fuck you doing talking to his wife?"

"I was in the neighborhood. Something just doesn't feel right. Jameson's already put it off as robbery."

He shook his head. "Keep your nose out of it. What'd I teach you?"

"To cover my ass. That's what I was doing. They hadn't even told the widow."

"Who cares? Drop the Good Samaritan act with me. Now tell me why you were down here."

"I told you. I'm working a case. Chief Hogan and a private citizen have got me looking for a kidnap victim."

"Who's the citizen?" he asked.

"Arvis Hypoole."

"Some rich fuck, *that* I know, but I don't know him."

"Kinda creepy and maybe a little delusional. He thinks if we find the guy who's been kidnapped, a colored policy guy named Ed Jones, we can stamp out policy."

Sam laughed. "Sure, and one of the guys here happens to get fucked up the ass, he's gonna have a kid. No miracles, Gus."

"I know, but if I find him, it's five C-notes to me."

"Chump change. What else?"

"A bump up the ladder."

He waved a finger at me. "Get more. It was me, I'd be looking for a couple of grand, upgrade to detective, maybe a piece of the racket."

"But he's gonna stamp it out."

"Sure. You got a system set up like that, nobody stamps it out. You guys ain't careful, you'll get stamped out."

"Enough about me," I said. "How about you?"

"You see it. I got my run of the place." He sighed. "But it's all bullshit. God, how I'd love to be out on the street breaking heads. Remember the time we broke up that transvestite party? Bras and panties everywhere. You made 'em strip and walk home. That fucking ward committeeman walks home, no clothes, lipstick and shit all over his face. His wife screams batshit." Sam howled, slapped the desk. "And the dumb son of a bitch hangs himself. Oh, fuck, I miss that action. Here, I got a bunch of creeps and cruds, but nothing much happens out of the ordinary. Just one ass fuck after another."

My stomach churned; the sandwich I'd grabbed in town refused to settle. "What's the matter?" asked Sam. "You don't look so good."

"Hungover."

"Where was the party?"

"Prescott's estate."

He raised an eyebrow. "You hanging out with that cooze again?"

"A little."

"Well, don't get used to it. She's from a different world. Now the mother, that's another story."

My stomach flipped.

Sam found a box of matches in the front desk drawer, struck one and lit the cigar. He leaned back in the chair, stoked the cigar, blew a pool of smoke over his head. "I knew her when she was just a kid. Tough broad, though. I didn't have any dough, so I used to push her around a bit, try to score. She wouldn't take an ounce of shit. Always ended up with the ritzy guys, doctors, lawyers, and she was no more than fifteen, sixteen years old. That's all that dame ever cared about, was money. I'd rather try to pull a steak out of a tiger's mouth than pry a nickel from her pretty little hand. Gorgeous, young, tough, and she ended up marrying rich. Can't beat that." He leaned back, further. "Yeah, she was one tough broad."

"Kinda like my mother."

Sam eyed me, searched for sarcasm. "Yeah, a lot like your mother, except the money part. Hey, you visit the graves on Mother's Day?"

"Couldn't. I was busy."

"Busy, shit!" screamed Sam. Ash from the cigar fell, landed on a stack of papers on the desk. "Do not forget that after your mother jumped, me and Margaret took you in. She loved you like her own son!"

"She only lived for three years after you took me in. Christ, I was seven when my mom died, ten when Margaret died."

"Doesn't matter. You remember. Margaret would've lived, things would've been different, for all of us." He tore open the bottom drawer of the desk, flung a stack of papers onto the floor. "Can't believe he doesn't keep one damn bottle in here."

"I haven't got much time," I said.

Sam sat up, stared at me. "How come you haven't come to see me before this?"

"Been busy."

"Horseshit. You get back from the war, no visit. What the fuck is it with you? I had to hear that you made it back from my cronies and not you? That's the thanks I get for raising you? Christ, I'm lucky you take my phone calls."

"Look, Sam, I'm sorry I didn't get down here before. I'll make it more often. Anything I can do for you?"

"You collecting the rent?"

I nodded.

"You check on Tommy Franks, make sure he's collecting at my other places?"

"No. He sending you the bank statements? That'll tell you."

"Check on him anyway. Also, get your ass over to Billy's pool hall and make sure he's keeping my package."

"Will do."

He pretended to study the cigar. "A C-note, I'll help you with your case."

"What can you do?"

"You know Ed Jones? Know what's up? I do."

I didn't have to think long. If Sam could cut my time, help me, it would be worth it. "All right. What do you know?"

"I know a C-note when I see one. Hand it over."

"I don't have that much cash with me. I'm good for it."

"Jesus, always carry a roll. All right. Who were you visiting here?"

"Kingdom Come Novelty Company," I said. "Jones tried to buy juke-boxes from 'em. I figured maybe they told one of their customers, he got burned, grabbed Jones."

"No. Albert Carpacci runs the jukes. Everybody knows who he's with. Nobody'll sell to the niggers. I'll tell you right now what's up, but the C-note ain't gonna cover it. I need a favor."

I was afraid to ask. "What?"

"Sid Pasqua."

"No."

"He's the only witness. I think he's in Phoenix. Take your time. I got three years left, minimum."

"No. Tell me what you know about Jones."

"Why? You don't help me, I don't help you. Jesus, if Margaret could see you now."

I smirked. "If Margaret could see you now, Sam. You aren't turning Jones over to me. The C-note's plenty."

"Motherfucker." He leaned back in the chair, drew on the cigar, exhaled. "All right. It's crystal fucking clear. Jones did time here. Tax evasion."

I waved cigar smoke away from my eyes. "And?"

"And, Sam Giancana was here, too. I figure Jones started shooting his mouth off about how much money he was making in policy, Giancana decided it was time for the boys to move in."

"If that's the case, there's gonna be a bloodbath on the South Side."

Sam slapped the desk. Cigar ash fell on his shirt. "And I ain't gonna be there, dammit. I'll tell you what, you grab a couple of Giancana's boys, nail their hands to a table and pull out a blowtorch, they'll tell you where Jones is stashed."

"They got him, he's probably dead."

"Nope. They want to take over the policy rackets, they'll need his cooperation. The niggers got a whole system set up—those baskets of coins don't just show up. You think those people are gonna just start doling out their money to the Italians? Think they'll trust 'em? No. There's gonna have to be a lot of cooperation, or a face man. The Italians are gonna need one dark, smiling face covering for 'em. Easiest thing for 'em to do is tell Jones either he cooperates or he dies. Pretty simple."

"Pretty simple," I agreed. "Where do you think they've got him stashed?"

"Anywhere. Break out the blowtorch."

"Where can I find Albert Carpacci?" I asked.

Sam shook his head. "You don't want to find him. I'll tell you this, you do cross him, you'd better kill him. He's got more sons than a Bible Jew and if you cross any of 'em, they'll come after you."

"Might make my job easier," I said. "Where?"

Sam shrugged. "They own a bawdy theater in the old Levee area. Remember that dump where we talked to Bravo Nunez?"

Louisville Sluggers and duct tape across his mouth; we painted the walls abstract. "Yeah, I remember."

"It's across the street from there. Emcee goes by Marvin the Magnificent—I busted him with a Joliet Josie a few years ago. Carpacci bought his way out. You're looking to cause him some trouble, there's always something going on there. The place is one of his cash cows."

I grabbed my coat, stood up. "Sam, I've gotta go. Thanks for the tip."

He stood up, came around the desk, put his hands on my shoulders. "You get your ass back here, soon, or I'll raise your rent. Bring the C-note next time and some booze. I'll ask around for you. You go see Albert Carpacci, you watch your ass. Tell him you're still with me. And think about Pasqua."

I shook my head. "Wouldn't help anyway. What's your ace in the hole?"

He pointed at the picture of Truman on the wall. "Right there. I'm getting a little package ready for him when he gets ready to leave office."

"What're you talking about?"

"Truman," he said as I opened the door. "His last official act is gonna be offering me a full pardon."

I TOOK THE DRIVE SLOW, MULLED OVER THE TRIP. Sam hit it: had to be policy. My jukebox theory was pie in the sky; Giancana and Jones shooting the shit made too much sense. Lincoln Johnson had said it— Jones made friends too fast. The key question: Where did they have him stashed? No blowtorches for me, questions and the threat of arrest would have to do. I figured I'd stop and check out the Carpaccis bawdy theater—step a little harder on their greasy toes. I figured if I could find some reason to shut the place down, take a little dough out of their pockets, the Carpaccis would come running. I figured I didn't have to be at Martha Lewis's house until six o'clock, so I stamped on the accelerator and shot back to Chicago.

Four hours later, I hit the Loop, took Grand Avenue and passed the limestone courthouse building. I crept by the squad cars parked all around the courthouse, found Clark Street and parked across from the Chelsea Theatre. It occupied the ground level of a three-story brick building. A black wrought-iron fire escape ran down the side of the building, behind a sign that simply read CHELSEA. The sign was vertical and unlit and a few of the red bulbs were broken, but the display window in front of the building made the theater impossible to miss. MARVIN THE MAGNIFICENT was stenciled in the window, and a picture of Marvin sat inside the case. Next to the picture was a large top hat that was at least four feet in diameter. The hat had been turned upside down, and a life-size cardboard cutout of a woman peeked out of it. She had curly blonde hair and big fake eyelashes and wore a pair of rabbit ears, dark whiskers and a black nose. Her arms were spread wide and the top of her ample bosom peaked out over the rim of the hat. Marvin the Magnificent's furry friend invited all to come in and check out the show. I stepped inside, nearly threw up when the ticket taker peered at me through his thick glasses and demanded five bucks. I forked it over, even more burned at the Carpaccis. They were costing me time and money.

I entered the theater lobby. A convenience stand was open—stale popcorn sat in a popper, untouched. A skinny, red-haired teen stood behind the counter, eyelids at halfmast. He drummed his fingers on the top of the counter, watched me move toward the theater. "Popcorn, mister?" he asked as I passed.

"No thanks," I said.

"It's always no," he said. "Soda pop for your flask?"

I shook my head.

"Always no," he said again. He reached inside the case, pulled out a Hershey bar, unwrapped it and broke off a piece. "Some glamour," he muttered. "I never even getta see any of the action."

I stopped. He didn't look any younger than most of the guys I knew in the service. "See some action before?" I asked.

He nodded. "Omaha Beach." He looked around. "Really made it, eh?"

"Other jobs out there," I said.

He shrugged. "And I got a few of 'em. Want some advice, mister? Never bet on the horses. My sure thing broke his ankle on the first turn. You know it's bad when they shoot your horse on the track."

"Hang in there, brother," I said.

"Sometimes I wish someone would put me out of *my* misery," he muttered.

I cast a finger at him and walked toward the maroon curtain that separated the lobby from the theater. As I pushed the curtain aside, I saw a huge, dark-haired man sitting on a stool. He looked to be my age and height, but heavier. His shoulders bulged inside his shirt, and his brow was so thick it looked like a hose ran underneath it. His shadow was set, permanently, at five o'clock, but his mind seemed to be on recess. He read a comic book in the dim light of the theater. He glanced up at me like I was the next sheep in line, decided not to count and looked back down at his comic book. I watched his lips move, slowly, as I turned and walked down the aisle.

A dark red carpet ran down the aisles, between theater seats arranged in three sections. The center section held a dozen rows of ten seats each, and the sections on each wing also had a dozen rows, but only went six across. There was a stale odor in the air that I didn't want to i.d., and there was a crowd of about thirty men scattered throughout the seats. I figured traders and tradesmen: It was four-thirty in the afternoon, too early for most businessmen.

I grabbed an aisle seat in the fourth row of the center section, sat down. The fabric on the chair was worn and the seat fell too far. It left me leaning forward. I ignored it, set my arms on the wood armrests, looked around.

The stage stretched from one side of the theater to the other. It was brightly lit and a five-foot catwalk stretched out toward the audience; the four seats on either side of it were occupied. The house comic was finishing his act. He was a tiny, bald man in a bright green sport jacket that hung nearly to his knees. "So my wife says to me, 'Honey, I'm gonna take a cue from the government—I'm gonna ration the quiff.' I look at her and says, 'Don't tell me, tell the milkman. He's the only one around here offering a daily delivery!' Get it? The milkman..." His voice trailed off, he tugged on his coat sleeves, straightened his tie.

I ignored his shtick, looked around. Most of the men in the crowd sat by themselves; occasionally I'd see two heads turn and one man would move into a seat next to another. I didn't even want to think about that, so I did some quick math. An audience of thirty at five bucks a head and five shows a day put seven hundred and fifty bucks in the Carpaccis' pockets before paying the talent. A lot of dough—if I could take it out of their pockets for even a few days it would give them a reason to hunt me down. Then, with some luck, I could get some answers. But I couldn't smash the place up for grins; I had to find something that even the cops on the take couldn't ignore. I crossed my fingers and looked toward the stage as it started to echo in my head: Give me a reason, give me a reason, give me a reason.

The comic finished his act. "You fuckers have been great, just great," he said with all the enthusiasm of a judge issuing parking fines. "Anyway, get ready for the one, the only, Marvin the Magnificent."

The comic walked off the stage as Marvin the Magnificent burst through the curtains. He wore a black top hat, black tux with a white handkerchief tucked in the front pocket and a long, black cape. He was tall and sick skinny; his Adams apple bulged in his throat. His skin looked jaundiced, and his dark eyebrows nearly grew together over his long nose. He had no moustache but wore a long, brown beard. His hollow eyes read "junkie." I figured if I pulled up his sleeves, I'd find his arms held more tracks than Union Station.

"Thank you, thank you!" yelled Marvin to the silent crowd. His voice surprised me—it was deep and strong. "It's always a pleasure to be here. Tonight I will start with a few simple tricks."

"Bring out the cooze!" yelled a customer from the back of the auditorium.

Marvin lifted his head, pretended to glance toward the back of the room. "Aah, if only I knew a spell to make the assholes disappear, we'd all be better off."

"Cooze!" someone yelled again.

Marvin ignored them, went on with his act. "Now where the heck has my wand gone? I've forgotten my damn wand. Gentlemen, help me, please. If you'll whistle loud enough, my wand should come through that curtain." He gestured to the curtain to his left as a few of the audience members began to whistle. "Cooze," yelled the man in the back, again.

The whistles grew louder as Marvin egged them on. He threw his arms up and down like he was shaking a rug, and after a few moments the wand peeked out from behind the curtain. It was held, shoulder high, by a woman's hand, which extended from a long, fleshy arm. The whistles grew louder, and the woman stepped through the curtain.

"Gentlemen…and ladies…may I present," shouted Marvin, "my assistant, Zelda."

Zelda walked to the center of the stage, turned toward the audience and bowed. She was the woman from the picture in the display case, and she was a tall, pale-white blonde with a thick waist and legs. She wore a gold-sequin one-piece that covered most of her ass and about half of her bosom. As she bowed, her breasts fell out of the top, and she stood up and tucked them back in with exaggerated effort. The crowd went bananas. "Take it off, take it off!"

Zelda smiled, sucked in her gut and curtsied. She smiled at the crowd, again, and I noticed that there were deep, dark circles under her eyes. I pegged her another junkhog, late forties, going on toothless and babbling.

Zelda stood next to Marvin, handed him his wand. He thanked her. "But let's see if my wand truly works," he said. He shook the wand at Zelda, said, "Fuck us, ruck us!" Nothing happened. "No, that's isn't it," he said, scratching at his beard. He shook his wand at Zelda, again. "Hocus, smoke us!" Still nothing happened. He stamped his feet, cursed the wand and implored the audience to help him with roars and whistles. "Aaah, now I remember," he said as he stepped toward Zelda. "Poke us, bofus!" He flicked the wand at her, caught a button in the middle of her outfit and her top flew open, exposing her breasts. She screeched, ran toward the front of the stage, took off the top and twirled it like a lasso.

The crowd screamed as Zelda pranced about the front of the stage, walked out on the catwalk, got down on her knees and nuzzled the men next to the stage. She grabbed one man's head, put it between her breasts and shook them. His glasses fell off as she rumpled his hair and shook.

"Zelda!" screamed Marvin. "Zelda!"

Zelda jumped up and scurried back toward Marvin; she shuffled backward so the audience could watch her breasts shake, and the crowd booed when Marvin asked her to go offstage and get the "apparatus." The apparatus, he explained, would be used in conjunction with a volunteer from the audience.

She returned a minute later pushing a rolling table set on casters with a yellow and green box on top. There were holes at each end of the box, and MARVIN THE MAGN. was printed on the front. I figured he needed either a longer box or shorter volunteers.

"And now," he said as he approached the front of the stage, "we'll need a member of the audience to help us with our first trick. And trick is the operative word." He peered out into the audience; two spotlights spat light from the rafters and smoke curled in the light. Marvin walked back and forth across the stage, finally leaned forward and pointed to someone in the front row. He reached out and grabbed a hand, yanked someone up on stage.

The audience member he'd selected turned out to be a young girl. She wore her blond hair in pigtails and a few freckles dotted her cheeks. She was just over five feet tall, but her knees were knobby, legs spindly and white, and her polka dot dress hung loosely over a lanky frame. I figured her fourteen or fifteen, felt the hairs on the back of my neck stand up straight.

"And what is your name, young lady?" asked Marvin. He put a hand on her shoulder, caressed it.

"I'm, uhhh, Tammy," said the girl.

"Well, Tammy, would you like to help us with a trick?" asked Marvin. He lifted his head, leered at the crowd.

"Sure!" she yelled. "Waddo I do?"

"Zelda, help our friend Tammy into the apparatus, please," said Marvin. Zelda, still topless, walked around the table to catcalls, took the young girl by the hand and pulled her behind the table. Marvin lifted the back of the box, and the hinges on the front creaked as he pushed it overhead and Zelda helped the young girl into the box. They closed the lid over the top of her and Marvin walked around to where her head poked out, face up. He stroked her hair. "Now, Tammy," he said, "you just relax."

He reached under the table and stood up holding a long handsaw and when the young girl saw it, she screamed. "Hold on, now, Tammy," said Marvin. "I've performed this trick a hundred times and I haven't even lost half of the volunteers."

"No," she screamed, "I don't want to . . . Let's do another trick."

I bit my tongue, felt the sweat start to gather on my brow, felt the muscles in my neck start to fill. Marvin looked at the audience, arched his brows. "Another trick? Hmmm. What do you say, audience. Another trick?"

"Cooze!" yelled the man in back.

A few more shouts came from all parts of the audience. "Another trick."

Marvin clapped his hands together. "Well, another trick it will be. Zelda, if you'll help me, please."

Zelda nodded her head, and they each moved to one end of the table. Marvin started chanting as they moved the table around in a circle. "Hocus, bofus, ripus, chokus. Tease us, Jesus, let her please us. Rookie, nookie, let's see her cookie!"

They stopped the table, and Zelda slid down toward Marvin's end. They each grabbed one side of the box and pulled it apart, exposing the young girl's bare legs. They hit two latches and the sides came off, leaving the young girl trapped in the upper half of the box, her nude lower half exposed at the bottom end of the table.

The young girl screamed as the audience began to shout and whistle. Marvin the Magnificent and Zelda each grabbed one of the girl's legs, spread her wide and began to parade her around the stage. The casters squealed as they dragged the table to the front of the stage. They turned so that the girl was spread toward the audience, and Marvin used his free hand to slap her bare ass. He took his wand and touched her between her legs, laughed when she twisted and shook. He nodded at Zelda, and they moved her in front of the catwalk.

"And now," he said.

I squeezed the right armrest, balled my left hand into a fist.

"For our next trick."

The muscles in my neck and jaw went rigid.

"I'll use my real magic wand!" He stepped back, unzipped his pants, exposed himself, gave me the reason.

I tore the armrest free, lunged into the aisle as Marvin stepped toward the girl. I leaped up on the catwalk, barreled forward, swung the armrest and caught Marvin flush on the ear.

Blood spurted and Marvin flew toward the back of the stage. I stepped on his hat, tossed the armrest to the side. I jumped on him, drove his head into the floor, punched his face. Suddenly I felt fingernails in my neck as someone jumped on my back. I grabbed the figure with my free hand, tossed it over me. The young girl rolled, sprang to her feet. Her skirt was rolled up over her waist—bobby pins held it in place. She was still nude from the waist down, except for her shoes, and she tried to plant one in my ear. "Stay away from my daddy, asshole!" she yelled.

I grabbed her face, pushed her away, slapped an open palm on both sides of Marvin's face. "Sick freak," I said. "I'm a cop. I oughta take you to jail."

"We pay!" he gasped. Blood soaked his beard. "We pay every day. You must be in the wrong joint!"

I heard a roar, and I saw the big man who'd been reading the comic book come running toward the stage. I jumped up, took a step forward, caught him with a straight right to the forehead as he leaped up the cat-walk. The punch buckled his knees, but he staggered forward, caught his balance with a hand on the stage, tackled me.

We went down in a flash, but I rammed my elbows into the stage, spun on top of him and slapped my hands over his ears. He screamed in pain as I drove a fist into his throat. His eyes bulged and he gagged, gulped for air. I stamped on his stomach, forced all of the air out of his system, gave him a donkey kick in the balls to make sure he was done. I turned around and caught Marvin the Magnificent by the back of his collar as he tried to run from the stage.

I reached into my jacket, pulled my badge and told Zelda and Marvin's underage daughter to stay put. I jerked Marvin toward the stage stairs, watched the audience flee. I dragged him down the steps, up the aisle and through the curtain. The kid sneered from behind the popcorn stand as I pulled Marvin into the lobby. "Finally, some action," he said.

I yanked Marvin across the lobby, used his head to push open the front door. "You don't know who you're messing with," he murmured. A stream of saliva dripped from his mouth. "You just don't know."

"Sure I do," I said as I lifted him over my head, threw him through the display-case window. Glass shattered, the cutout Zelda disappeared and he landed face first inside the huge top hat. I looked at his shredded pant legs as they popped out the top of the hat, then slumped. "You're Marvin the Magnificent."

I EASED MY CAR DOWN THE STREET, took deep breaths. The sick father and dullard doorman deserved it, but I'd stepped over the line. I'd stopped by to let the Carpaccis know I was on their case, not to revisit my past. Too many men in the ocean, Francisco Juarez's voice in the night. Fires I didn't need to rekindle, stoke. I concentrated on the road, tried to ignore the juice. I bit my tongue, hard, to stop it.

TWENTY MINUTES LATER, just east of Wentworth Avenue in Bronze-ville, a row of tall houses with steep wood steps, one in the middle without them. It was a two-story, off-white jobber with green-and-red-striped awnings above the windows, and the address told me it belonged to the subject. Two car lengths away, Art McGuire sat, slumped, in his light blue Ford, snoozing. I parked in front of him, stepped out and rapped on the driver's window. He sat up quickly, rubbed his eyes, righted his felt hat. "What's the big idea?" he said as he rolled down the window.

"Relax, I'm here to relieve you."

"About time," he said, as he straightened up, pulled his shoulders back. He was in his mid-forties but had a boyish face. Brown hair peeked out from under his hat, which pressed out a pair of big ears. He sat low in the saddle; he couldn't have stood more than five feet four inches, and he tried to balance his tiny body with a big attitude. "It's six fifteen, asswipe. I've been here since six this morning with no break."

"Sorry to interrupt your sleep, Art," I said. "What's the deal here?"

He gestured toward the house: "It's the one with the striped awnings. Girl lives on the first floor with her kid; some woman lives above them. The girl left about seven this morning in that green Plymouth back there. She came back for lunch, right at noon, then left again. She just got home. The woman came down and watched the kid while the girl was gone. No sign of Jones, nobody else showed up. Christ, I shoulda brought more coffee and food. I'm starved."

"You have any contact with any of them?"

"No. Only person I talked to was a guy delivering coal. I offered him fifty cents to run get me a sandwich. Asshole just laughed. Anyway, I'm outta here, big boy. See you in the morning."

"Art, what've you guys found out about the shooting?"

He fired up his engine. "Not much. Robbery. I'm taking vacation this week so's I can make a couple of extra bucks watching this colored dame. Jameson's covering it. He said the shine must've followed Cordell there, waited for his chance and gone in."

"How can it be robbery? They found Cordell's wallet."

"We figure you must've scared him off."

"No. He didn't hear me until he hit the stairs."

He snarled. "The guy had an arrest record—burglary convictions."

"Burglary ain't robbery and those convictions were juvy—that was years ago."

"People don't change."

"Sure they do."

"Why do you give a shit? Griffin's just making an example of ya. You'll be back in no time. Say, what're they paying you for this?"

"Not much, how 'bout you?"

"That don't answer my question. I'm getting fifty bucks a day."

"Assholes," I muttered.

"Hah, I knew it," he said. "Taking advantage of a dumb kid. See you tomorrow, sucker!" He drove off.

I chuckled as I walked back to my car. I hopped in the driver's seat, fired it up, threw it in reverse and rolled back into the spot McGuire had vacated. It was still light out, so I leaned back in my seat, tipped my hat down over my eyes and looked toward the front window of the house.

The drapes were drawn, and I could see the woman working in her tiny dining room. She appeared to be of medium height, slender, with short, bobbed black hair. Her hands moved quickly and after a moment, I realized she was knitting. Suddenly she set down her knitting needles and moved toward the window. She stopped a few feet short of the window, reached down and came up holding a young child, clad in a tiny pink jumper.

The child was small, probably a couple of years old—I assumed it was a girl. The woman lifted her and pulled her to her chest, but the child didn't wrap her arms around the mother. The woman walked to the center of the room, set the child down and bent over her. They dropped below the window-line, so I couldn't see what she was doing, but whatever it was, she labored at it for an hour. Finally, as night fell, the woman picked up the child, walked toward the window and closed the drapes.

I sat in the car, my eyes trained on the front door, my windows cracked so I could hear the night sounds. I made a mental note to bring a thermos of coffee the next night, a couple of sandwiches and a deck of cards. I could play solitaire and still keep an eye on the house. Five hundred reasons kept me awake. An eternity later, Art McGuire showed back up. I gave it to him quick—nothing had happened—drove off and got home at six-thirty in the morning. My eyelids felt like they were made of lead. I opened the door to my place, saw the dress and shoes on the couch, walked into my room and saw Sheila, sleeping in my bed.

She heard me walk in, rolled over and held her arms out wide. "Come to bed, lover boy," she mumbled, eyes half shut. She threw back the covers, exposed her naked body. I slipped out of my clothes and joined her.

## TUESDAY, MAY 14

NOON: The telephone pulled me out of a deep sleep—Sheila wrapped a pillow around her head. I lurched out of bed, rubbed the sleep from my eyes, slipped into the front room and answered the phone. "Carson."

"Gus, it's Arvis Hypoole. What have you learned so far?"

"I've learned that I'd better take the phone off the hook—I've only been asleep a few hours."

"I'm entitled to information when I please. You *are* in my employ."

The door to the bedroom was ajar—no reason to involve Sheila in police work so I talked quiet. "You must've got plenty of sleep. I didn't. I can't talk now."

"I simply want to know what progress you've made."

"You don't listen too good, Mr. Hypoole. I said I can't talk now."

"Then stop by here on your way to work. I want an update."

"Will do."

I hung up the phone, walked back into the bedroom, past the clothes I'd thrown on the dresser and climbed back into bed. Sheila rolled over, wide awake, grinning. "Was that *Arvis* Hypoole?"

"Vacuum cleaner salesman."

"How many vacuum cleaner salesmen do you know named Hypoole?"

"None."

"See."

"No. Fact is, I don't know any vacuum cleaner salesmen."

She climbed on top of me, put her hands on my chest. Martini glass nipples popped. "Are you going to be serious?" she said. "Was that *the* Arvis Hypoole?"

"Yeah."

"What did he want with you?"

I tweaked a nipple. "What do I want with you?"

"Stop it," she said. "I'm serious. Mother was just talking to Mr. Hypoole the other day."

"What about?" I asked as I ran my hands over her breasts.

"He's a leader in the Republican Party. They're planning a huge party for May twenty-ninth in Bloomington. They're going to celebrate Abraham Lincoln's lost speech and kick off the campaign."

"Campaign for what?"

"Office! Mayor, governor, president. Daddy says that the president doesn't have a prayer of winning."

"Only race I'll care about is mayor. The papers say Kelly's out. I say it doesn't matter who replaces him, as long as he's gone."

"Mother says that Mr. Hypoole might run for mayor."

Hypoole for mayor—seemed Chief Hogan wasn't the only one with ambition. I gave her something to chew on while I thought. "What's this about Lincoln's lost speech?"

"Lincoln was just getting back into politics. At the meeting, they decided to name the party Republican because they disagreed with the politics of the Whigs. Anyway, Lincoln is supposed to have given one of the great speeches of all time, but everyone there was so enthralled with it that they failed to make record of it or even take any notes."

"Wish they were that way with Mayor Kelly. What else does your mother say about Hypoole?"

"That he used to be rich. He's social-minded, sad."

"Why sad?"

"His wife died a few years ago. He's lonely. That's why he puts so much time into the politics."

"What do you mean, 'used to be rich'?"

She shrugged. "His father made the family a lot of money in real estate, but Mr. Hypoole took it out and invested it in the stock market right before the crash. But Mother said he's back into real estate and doing fine, just not like before."

I did the math: Hypoole said his father died in thirty-one, just in time to see his son lose the family fortune. One shitty send-off—the kind that left a man with a yearning that would never go away. Hypoole decides to run for mayor after the old man is gone—obviously never got the blessing while he was alive. The father: the Republican kingmaker. The son: a financial flop with visions of Republican grandeur. Daddy's silence spoke volumes—in his eyes, Arvis Hypoole didn't rate.

"Your parents know him very well?"

"No, just through the Party. They do fund-raisers together and things like that. Daddy's always found him a bit of an extremist."

I pushed her off, started to get up. She was on me like an alley cat after the last drop of milk. She kissed my neck, ran her hands over my chest. I turned around, grabbed her by the waist and lifted her straight up. I looked between her legs, up into her eyes. I gave her some Teddy Roosevelt and listened to her sing.

ONE O'CLOCK: coffee boiled on the stove, Sheila finished her shower while I dried off and dressed. Anticipating twelve hours in my car—I threw on blue jeans and an old, white cotton shirt; surveillance in comfort. I went into the kitchen, poured a steaming cup of joe, called Burt Cordell. His secretary answered on the first ring, put him on the line.

"Burt Cordell."

"Mr. Cordell, Gus Carson. I'm a police officer. I'd like to talk to you about your brother's death."

"I'd like to talk to you, too" he said. His voice was as deep and loud as an engine's backfire. "My lunch canceled. Know The Kitchen?"

"Sure? What time?"

"Twenty minutes."

I didn't get a chance to tell him that was pushing it; he hung up.

I rapped on the bathroom door. "Sheila, sorry, but I've gotta run. Let yourself out."

The door opened, steam escaped. Sheila leaned out, a towel wrapped around her waist, another around her hair. "Gus, I was hoping you could run me home."

"Can't, I'm late for an appointment."

"You didn't have any appointment a little while ago."

"Just came up."

"Sounds familiar. When am I going to see you again?"

"Don't know. I'm running on empty. And don't sneak in here tonight; I need sleep. Say, how did you get in, anyway?"

"One of the children from upstairs let me in the front door. The door to your apartment was unlocked. Some cop."

"Oh well, I'll call you. And say thanks to your parents for the party."

Sheila leaned out, closed her eyes and puckered. I gave her a quick kiss, headed for the door. "I'll say thanks, all right," she said. "After all, it was Mother's idea that I invite you."

I PARKED ON THE STREET, crossed under the el tracks and stepped inside The Kitchen. It was a diner, set in the heart of the Loop—dirty linoleum floor, a long counter with cracked stools. Red vinyl booths with tan, spotted tables lined the walls. Similar four-seaters were scattered throughout the center of the room. One thirty in the afternoon and every seat was still taken. A squat, fleshy man signaled at me from a corner booth by the window.

Burt Cordell looked exactly like his brother, save the blood and holes. He had a huge melon with thick, dark lips, puffy, squinty eyes and a purplish face. He tore a piece of bread off of the fresh loaf as I sat down.

"You're late," he said, between bites. "I said fifteen minutes."

"You said twenty, and you hung up before I could tell ya your clock was broken. I got here as quick as I could."

He didn't offer a handshake, kept filling his mouth with bread. Crumbs sprayed as he talked, gathered on his dark suit, red tie. "What are you doing bothering my clients?"

"What?"

"Albert Carpacci called me this morning to tell me you've been interfering in his business."

"I asked a few questions about him. That's all. Free country."

"You fit the description of the joker that just busted up one of his joints. That's hardly asking a few questions. I made a couple of calls. You're suspended. You've got no reason to interfere. Let me tell you something," he said as he grabbed another piece of bread. "I know all of these stupid rumors going around about Albert. He's got nothing to do with gangsters. He's a reputable businessman and wants to remain that way. That's why he doesn't want people like you spreading any filth about him. So, stop it, right now."

"I didn't say boo about your client, Counselor. So I checked into the jukebox business? Your client happens to be a big buyer. That doesn't mean I'm trying to implicate him in anything. And he's lucky I stopped by the Chelsea. One of his employees was about to perform a lewd sex act. Your client may have bought a little protection for his show, but incest with a minor? Can't buy protection for that."

He pursed his lips, went silent. A moment later he exhaled, spoke in a hushed voice. "I know what you're looking for, so maybe I can help you with that."

"I'm all ears. Give me something and maybe I won't call in a beef on the Chelsea."

"Call in anything you'll be sued for harassment, personal injury and damage to property," he said. "You want to hear what I think or do you want to go on with these ridiculous threats?"

"Fire away."

"This Ed Jones you've been asking everyone about. Now, I don't have any personal knowledge of the man, only what I've read in the papers. But I know colored men. They've got a nose for the quiff like cops have for graft. So this guy sets this whole thing up just to take some time off from his wife. You watch—he'll be back in a couple of days."

A heavyset, red-haired waitress stepped up to our table, looked down at Cordell. "Welcome back."

Cordell didn't answer, broke into his order. "Give me the spaghetti, extra meatballs, a salad up front—oil and vinegar, black coffee."

"Finally had enough of our meatloaf?"

"What?"

"The other day, you had two orders of the meatloaf, said it was the best you ever had. That old, skinny fella that couldn't drink his milk was with you."

"Wasn't me," he said. "Must've been my brother."

"Oh, well, sorry. Ask him how he liked it."

"Can't do that."

"Why?"

"He's dead."

The waitress put her hand to her heart, batted long, fake eyelashes. "Oh, my, I'm so sorry. What happened?"

Cordell wiped his face with a napkin, looked her straight in the eye. "I think it was your meatloaf."

The waitress's eyes widened, mouth fluttered. "Well, I..."

"As a matter of fact," said Cordell, looking at me, "bring him an order."

"No, club sandwich," I said as the waitress scurried off with the order. "You're quite a sensitive guy, Cordell. Your theory on Jones is a joke, but I didn't expect anything from you, so let's move on. You obviously know I was there the night your brother was killed."

He nodded. "I also know you took down the shooter."

"Well, it doesn't add up. Got any theories?"

"Police say robbery. Why wouldn't I go along with that?"

"Because you're too smart. The perp hadn't been arrested in years, and all of a sudden he decides to follow your brother into a brothel, rob him and kill him? Sorry, doesn't add up."

He closed his eyes, rubbed his nose. I grabbed the last piece of bread. He opened his eyes, reached for the basket, burned when he saw it was empty. "I can't help you, Carson. My brother and I were partners, and I can tell you, we had virtually no dealings with the coloreds. Wasn't planned, just happened that way. Our clients would've frowned on it."

"Gangsters, bookies, murderers. You've got some clientele."

He snorted. "I won't even ring those up as accusations. You're a dirty, violent, suspended cop who's pals with South Side Sam and you have the audacity to question my business ethics? That's rich, that's really rich."

A different waitress brought us our order. "You should've sent the salad over first," said Cordell. He pushed the plate of spaghetti to the side, tore into the salad. I dug into my club sandwich.

"What I'm getting at is this, Cordell," I said, between bites. "You don't exactly represent the pillars of society. Was there anything you're working on that could've provoked the coloreds?"

"No. We handle criminal-defense cases and advise our clients on legal matters, but we don't get involved with their business. Don carried a big roll around. I'll bet he stopped for a drink somewhere, flashed his cash and the Negro saw him, followed him to Mona's and robbed him. Don probably threatened him—maybe even used some of our clients' names and spooked him. The man shot him so he couldn't turn up the heat. Sad but simple."

"You don't seem too broken up about it."

"I was damn mad, but what good does that do? You took care of the shooter. Case closed."

"An innocent girl was killed, too."

"And my brother wasn't innocent? To hell with you, Carson. Just because I'm not sitting here crying in my spaghetti doesn't mean I don't grieve. All I meant was that it's no good stirring up ashes. And you know something? That girl took a job filled with risk—syphilis, gonor-rhea, violent drunks, crazies...she made the same decision you made when you became a cop; she thought the reward was worth the risk. Well, is it?"

I finished my sandwich, wiped my mouth, popped my knuckles. "I don't like where you're going with that, Cordell, but I'd rather be com-pared to a two-dollar whore than a man like you any day. Something stinks and it ain't the meatloaf. You're not helping me because you know who killed your brother and why. Got something to do with the guineas taking over policy?"

He lowered his head, took a last bite of spaghetti, washed it down with a swig of coffee. "You think you're smart, think you're tough, eh? Well, you're barking up the wrong tree. My clients have nothing to do with policy and won't. It's a colored game in the colored part of town, and that's the way it's gonna stay. You want to start throwing around accusations, stirring up trouble, then get ready for the same. I don't think your superiors are going to appreciate you bothering legitimate businessmen or strong-arming a licensed attorney whose brother has recently been murdered. Matter of fact, my friend Dally Richardson down at the *Daily* just might give you a nice plug in his column, what do you think of that?"

"I think I must be on to something. Otherwise you wouldn't be turning up the heat. Momo shared a cell with Ed Jones and now Ed Jones is missing. Smells like an APB for your top client."

"Try it. You'll find your suspension lasts forever."

"Is that a threat, Counselor?"

"No. You want to hear a threat? Here's a threat for you. We had a nice lunch with a nice window seat. Plenty of eyes along the counter, at the other tables and outside. A lot of those eyes were trained on you, Carson. I don't know why you're hunting for this Ed Jones or why you're throwing my clients' names around, but it's going to stop, or someone's going to stop you."

I gripped the seat to stop from going over the table. I stared into his puffy eyes and thought about his brother, the whore, lying on that bed. "Cordell, you can make all of the calls you want and I don't give a damn. Wanna know something? You're the second guy to threaten me in the last couple of days and I don't like it. I took this case to make some dough, but now you've gone and made it personal. Momo, Big Tuna, they just might remember me. You tell 'em I'm looking for Ed Jones. You tell 'em I'm gonna crush policy. You tell 'em the next time someone tells you to threaten me, I'm gonna haul you in. My suspension lasts forever? Just more time to screw with you."

He stood up, grabbed his jacket, slid out of the booth. "You'll forgive me if I ask you to pick up the tab, Officer. I don't carry the wad my brother did. Too dangerous."

"Too dangerous," I repeated. "Cordell, I'm gonna get to the bottom of this, with or without your help."

He looked at me, shook his head, muttered as he walked away. "You're gonna get to the bottom all right," he said. "But you're lucky. Lake Michigan's just starting to warm up."

I watched him walk out, peered around the room. No one was looking at me, no heads turned when he walked out the front door. I looked out the window, watched him head north. I turned back toward the counter and the second waitress approached with the bill. "That'll be a dollar seventy-five," she said.

I handed her two singles. "Say, would you send our first waitress over?"

"Can't," she said. "I don't know what that other fella said, but she left for the day, said he gave her the creeps."

"Her and everybody else. She work every day?"

"Lou Ann? Every day and most nights. She'll be back tomorrow."

"Okay, I'll stop in later this week, apologize for my friend."

"Oh, don't worry about it," she said. She lifted the two singles, looked at the cash register.

"Nah, keep the change."

"Thanks," she said. "You have a nice day."

I picked up my brown leather jacket, slid out of the booth, slipped it over my shoulders. I glanced around the room one last time and promised myself I wouldn't leave home again without my .38.


BURNED, I LEFT THE KITCHEN. Cordell knew a hell of a lot more than he was letting on and I needed to sort it out. I pushed the pieces: His clients ran the jukeboxes, gambling, prostitution. Ed Jones did time with Giancana, opened his big mouth to the tune of "I own villas in Mexico, France." Putting cheese in front of a rat; the dagos wanted policy—a colored cash cow. They snatched Jones, were probably convincing him with a blindfold and garden shears snipping at fingers. Garden—where did the gardener figure in? He didn't, that didn't play. The Cordell connection a fluke? Possible bordering on probable. My shitty Friday night, the Negro killing Cordell, me killing him—a separate puzzle. I'd sort out those pieces in a week, when five C-notes greased the wheels.

I drove by Tommy Franks's place; he said he sent Sam the bank statements once a month—Sam was just busting my chops. Ditto when I stopped by Billy's Pool Hall—Sam's package was safe and sound. Billy would save it for life, his or Sam's.

Four o'clock and I needed coffee and sandwiches, a side order of information. Harry's fit the bill. I parked, stepped inside—just me and Harry, no jukebox tunes to tweak my nerves.

Harry sat at the bar, studied figures on a piece of paper, tapped his fingers against his thumbs—counting. "Bookie fingers still work, eh?"

He looked up. "Old habits die hard; I can't afford an abacus. Say, you going shopping?"

"No," I said as I sat down next to him.

"Then why're you carrying those bags around under your eyes?"

"This suspension carries too much work. Hey, you got any of that coffee you make?"

"My stuff? That'll keep you up all night."

"Perfect. A thermos full—I'll bring the thermos back—and a couple of sandwiches, eh?"

Harry went back into the kitchen, came back out with his low-rent chef. "Just tell Ernie what you want."

"Couple of ham and cheese on white, horseradish, red onions and any kinda peppers you got."

Ernie nodded and went back into the kitchen. "Some appetite you got there, Gus," said Harry. "You're gonna be up all night with a stomach full of coffee, peppers and onions. Ouch."

"Gonna be a long night. Gotta have some kinda entertainment. Harry, who did you buy your jukebox from?"

Harry folded the paper, tucked it into his pocket, put the pencil behind his right ear and spun on his barstool to face me. "I thought we never talked business."

"We don't. You buy it from Albert Carpacci?"

"Army buy its jeeps from Ford?"

"And the tunes?"

"You're pushing it, Gus," he said. "I don't really feel like discussing my business with a police officer."

"Not one sitting here. I'm suspended, remember? This is just one friend asking another."

He ran a hand over his face, stroked his chin. "This is the deal, see. You buy your jukeboxes from him, they push some tunes. All part of the same racket. It shouldn't surprise you that I pay a bit of protection money, either. How do you think I keep the Bing and twenty-six games going? I had that robbery last year—you think the cops found them? Albert Carpacci's boys found the guys, beat 'em silly, and I haven't had a problem since."

"Get your money back?"

"Small price to pay for peace of mind. Hey, I wish I didn't pay protection, but this is Chicago. My old man paid it, his old man paid it and, God help me, if I ever have a son, he'll pay it. Takes a lot of coin to keep the wheels of democracy turning."

"More rackets here than a tennis tournament. You know Carpacci's lawyer, Burt Cordell?"

"No. Guy has funny business with them, they don't exactly send their lawyer. The kinda suit they bring is the kind you wear in a hearse."

I laughed. "Fits forever. How's business?"

"Quick change of subject. Good. I don't like dealing with those guys, and I like talking about them even less. Business is fine. Bar business is always good. The Depression—people drank, prohibition—people drank, war—people drank, times are good—people drink. I make sure the beer's cold, the food is good and the help's friendly. I shake a lot of hands, dole out the free drinks like a Jew on a budget and I'm fine."

Ernie came out with my sandwiches, a large thermos of coffee. I gave him a single and told him to keep the change.

"Big spender," said Harry. "You got a big payday coming?"

"Could be. Harry," I said. "I need you to do me a favor."

"What's that?"

"They come to collect their money, I want you to tell 'em I was asking about 'em."

"Jesus, Gus, that's one favor I can't do. Why in the hell would you want guys like that on your case?"

"You ever play hide and go seek when you were a kid?"

"Sure."

"Well, I didn't. But I always figured, if I ever did, I wouldn't seek any of 'em. I'd just make enough of a ruckus that they'd come out of hiding just to see what was up. Tell 'em, Harry. Tell 'em Gus Carson's the guy making the ruckus."

ARVIS HYPOOLE sat in a high-backed overstuffed blue chair and sipped a cup of tea. I noted that the age spots on his hands matched the color of the design on his china. I leaned back into the couch, tried to pick up my cup of tea. My finger was too thick to slip it through the handle, the way Hypoole's did, so I wrapped my mitt around it and drank from it like I would a shot glass.

"Like I said, Mr. Hypoole, there are a lot of variations of the numbers game. I told you about Busy Jackson's, but with some wheels, you've only got to pick three numbers out of twelve that are drawn. Sounds good, but when they draw a dozen numbers out of a hundred and you've got to pick three out of that twelve, the odds are pretty low.

Other wheels are tied to stock-market numbers, horse-race winners, all sorts of stuff, but the odds of winning are still really low."

"But people play," he said.

"That's right. A mother will damn near play her numbers before she buys her kids food. They call it policy because they look at it like some kind of insurance policy, but it ends up as an insurance policy for the operators. Those pennies, nickels, dimes and quarters add up pretty fast. And it's kind of interesting; they have all sorts of names for the wheels, like Gold Rush, Klondike Express, End of the Rainbow, Lion's Luck.... You know, there are probably a hundred wheels operating on the South and West sides."

"Thank you for the primer," said Hypoole. "And I mean that, sincerely. But allow me to summarize your activities. You've visited with some of the Negroes in the numbers game and they've convinced you that Mr. Jones wasn't kidnapped by a competitor. Your jaunt to Terre Haute has convinced you that it has nothing to do with the jukebox racket, but you are confident that the Syndicate is involved. And now you're led to believe that the Syndicate has kidnapped Jones so that they can break into the policy racket? Is that about right?"

"Words like 'convinced' and 'confident' are probably too strong, but that's about right. Once I found out Jones did time with Sam Giancana, it seemed pretty logical."

"Have you confirmed that?"

"No, but I will."

He sighed, leaned back into the chair. "Well, Gus, it's already Tuesday and you only have until Saturday. It seems like you're diddling around a bit."

"I wouldn't say that."

"Then what would you say?"

"I'd say that finding Jones is like finding a needle in a haystack. Our chances hover between slim and none. But five hundred dollars has me betting on slim. You know, if people were open and honest all of the time, police work would be a lot easier."

He leaned forward, fixed me with a look. "What is that supposed to mean?"

"Nothing, Mr. Mayor."

He set his cup down on a saucer on the coffee table. "Oh, so that's it." He stood up, walked to the window, gazed out. "I fail to see what my aspirations have to do with your finding Mr. Jones, but I guess I owe you an apology. I have considered making a run at mayor."

"And you think finding Jones helps your chances."

"Yes."

"Why?"

He turned to face me. "Because I believe in the spirit of the people of Chicago. They are as sick and tired of graft and corruption as I am. They will vote for a man who helps curb policy. They will support a mayor who will not tolerate such activities."

"You must know different people than I do. But let's just say you show up at a Grand Jury with Jones, he talks, and the department starts really cracking down on policy. You may be the guy to show up at the press conference with him, but I know Mayor Kelly and his men. Somehow, some way, they'll end up with the credit. They'll stamp out the policy rackets and your shot at mayor in one fell swoop."

"Follow me, Gus," said Hypoole. We left the sitting room, walked across the foyer, up a set of stairs and down the hall toward the master bedroom. We passed a study—its door was open. There was a large, arched window in the center of the back wall, but dirt had caked onto the outer side of the glass and only a few slivers of light pierced through cracks in the dirt, sprayed across the floor and into the hall.

At the end of the hall was the master bedroom. It was large and dark, and it had that musty old-man smell. A king-size bed under a white canopy filled the center of the room; a mahogany dresser sat against a wall, and matching nightstands stood on either side of the bed. Hypoole stepped quietly to the far side of the room, lifted a portrait of a woman off the wall and spun the dial of the wall safe. He opened it and pulled out a letter-size envelope.

"Gus, I'm about to take you into my confidence," he said. "I need you to assure me that my confidence will be well placed."

I nodded. "It'll be more well placed than your wall safe, Mr. Hypoole. That's the first place a burglar would look. But sure, yeah, I'll keep your deep, dark secrets."

He sighed. "The deep, dark secrets aren't mine, Gus. They belong to your department."

He stepped forward, lifted the envelope to one side of his head and held it like a bottle of Bay Rum he was ready to dump on his hair. He wagged the envelope as he spoke. "Gus, in this envelope are twenty-seven names. I will refer to them as the twenty-seven martyrs when I'm in front of the Grand Jury. These are the names of twenty-seven officers that have been transferred over the past three years—twenty-seven men who failed to stop smashing policy wheels or arresting operators. These men were transferred because the corruption in the police department runs deep enough to have their efforts simply erased. I am going to parade these names and these men in front of the Grand Jury when I present evidence that the policy kingpins, including one Mr. Edward P. Jones, have bought staggering influence within the department by giving millions to the Democratic machine that runs it."

"You've been rehearsing that speech for a while," I said. "Look, I didn't know that guys were getting transferred, but you're not the first guy to figure out that the rackets are sending a lot of money our way. Sam collected so much that he probably rivals you as a real-estate baron, although he's more along the lines of a slumlord. What I'm telling you is that these aren't exactly startling revelations."

"Not to you, maybe, but when the average citizen is confronted with irrefutable evidence of that kind of corruption within the department, he simply won't stand for it."

I smirked. "You're sure of that."

"I'm sure enough. Your job is to find Mr. Jones, not pick apart my political aspirations. Now what do you intend to do to find him?"

"I've already done a lot."

"You've tested theories; you haven't actually searched for the man."

"Real police work isn't like the movies—we don't find the secret room or the hidden key or the diary that explains everything. You know how we catch people? We talk to people. Sooner or later, somebody spills their guts."

"What does all that mean?"

"Mr. Hypoole, you want to find the rats, you start kicking the cans. I've kicked the shit out of cans for the past two days, and my bad rep is getting worse, thanks to you. What I could do without is the night watch at the colored girl's place. That's a dead end."

He shook his head, violently. "No, no, no. The same source that told me about the kidnapping convinced me that would be the first place he would go, should he escape or be released. You have four more nights, maximum, so I suggest you stick it out."

"The only thing that's gonna be sticking out is my tongue, 'cause I'll have gone crazy from a lack of sleep."

"You'll be fine," said Hypoole as he returned the envelope to the wall safe, spun the dial and replaced the picture. He stepped back to admire it, and I gazed at it, over his shoulder. It was an old oil portrait—a plain woman with brown hair pulled back from her thin, long face. Her features were gaunt and appeared at odds with the color of her skin. My money said the artist knew where his paycheck came from, added the pink hue to pad his pocketbook.

"Your mother?" I asked.

Hypoole didn't turn around. "My mother died during my birth. That is my wife, Mildred. She was a remarkable, remarkable woman."

I pulled my shoe out of my throat. "When did she pass?"

"She passed on in forty-two, heart trouble. She was never very healthy, physically, but she was an intellectual giant. She could've been another Eleanor Roosevelt—except for the party affiliation, of course. Such a way with people. I miss her every day of my life."

"Any children?"

"No, she was incapable. Just as well. If I had to see a part of her every day and know that I couldn't be with her, it would break my heart even further."

He turned, raised his eyebrows. "A wife can be a wonderful ally in trying to help our fair city. This would be a much easier task were Mildred still alive." He paused, lost in thought, then looked at me. "How about you, Gus? Have you got a steady?"

"Not really. Sampling the goods."

He chuckled. "A man who's been through what you must have deserves a few years of carousing. But when I'm mayor, it might behoove you to settle down, work on your career. It's not often that a young man gets the opportunities that you're receiving."

I smiled. "Yeah, I've got a long list of opportunities."

"Find Ed Jones and you will."

We left the bedroom, went down the stairs, walked to the front door. The foyer was dark and cold, and our voices echoed as we said good-bye. "One last thing," I said. "Have you ever heard of a couple of brothers, lawyers named Cordell?"

"I can't say that I have. Why?"

"Chief Hogan must've told you about why I was suspended. The guy

I shot killed this attorney named Cordell and a prostie. I met Cordell's brother today, and he started in on me about rattling his clients. Seems he works for the boys. So you just might want to be careful about who you tell I'm working for you."

He opened the door; I stepped outside. "See, Mr. Hypoole. Like I said, I've been kicking the cans. And the rats are coming out."

TWO DAYS INTO THE ASSIGNMENT and we already found it routine; Art McGuire sped off in his light blue Ford the moment he saw me round the corner. No report on the shootings, surveillance—I'd have to surprise him to get any info. I parked on the opposite side of the street, in front of the house, just beyond their light green Plymouth. I looked past the car, trained my eyes on the house and got comfortable. I slipped my jacket off, dropped it in the back seat, unscrewed the lid of the thermos and poured myself a cup of hot mud. I tasted the coffee— bitter and strong. Steam from the thermos fogged the windows—I wiped the driver's-side window, watched the house.

It was still light outside and the drapes were open. The woman I took for Martha Lewis walked through the room, holding the infant I'd seen the night before. She stopped in the center of the room, set the girl down and started to do whatever the hell it was she did. I cursed the window-line, unwrapped a sandwich and ate.

My level of attention fell with the night. By the time it was dark, I saw the woman rise up, walk out of the room—I noticed but didn't note. Moments later the tap on the window caught me by surprise.

The baseball bat rapped lightly against the passenger-side window again. I bit my tongue to stop myself from screaming—fool me twice; I'd decided against stopping to pick up my .38. My chronic gambler's luck. I leaned across the seat, rolled down the window, stared into a large, dark face. "What's the deal, Mac?" I asked, harsh.

A large, angry colored woman swayed back and forth. She wore a heavy, dark overcoat, and her fleshy cheeks shook as she slapped the baseball bat into her hand, yelled at me. "Don't you go calling me Mac, mister. Jest what the hell do you think your doin' hangin' outside our home, starin' in my daughter's winda?"

I stepped out of the car, stayed on the driver's side, looked over the roof. I held my badge up, gambled. "Police."

The woman leaned over the roof and grabbed the badge, eyed it and handed it back to me. "What the hell the po-lice doin' 'round here? We ain't done nothin'."

"Didn't say you had. Routine surveillance."

"The hell," screamed the woman. "I'm gonna go call the po-lice, find out why you's sittin' out here. You ain't with the police, you better be gone by the time I's back."

"Do what you've got to do, ma'am. You may or may not get any confirmation from the station, but I can promise you two things: I'm a cop and I'm not going anywhere."

"We'll see 'bout that."

I watched her go back into the house—she used a door in the rear. Seconds later, she appeared in the window, talked to the other woman, pointed in my direction, pounded the bat in her hand. Suddenly she opened the front door, stepped out and waved her hand like she was fanning herself. "Come on," she yelled. "Git yourself on up here."

No contact with the woman, Hypoole had said. No contact had given me no results—Ed Jones could wash McGuire's windshield and he wouldn't notice. Up to me. I played a hunch and approached the house.

The big woman stepped back inside; a smaller, pretty colored woman leaned out, asked to see my badge. I showed it to her. "What are you doing here, Officer?" Her voice was soft, smooth, educated.

"I've been asked to watch your house, that's all."

"Why?"

"By my employer—it's a side job, non-police sanctioned."

Her eyes widened. "Who?"

"Private party," I said. "It's not really about you—you don't need to be worried."

"…don't need to be worried," she muttered. Her voice rose. "I'm going to have to ask you to leave. You're frightening my mother and me, and we won't have it."

"No reason to be frightened, ma'am, and I'm not leaving."

She glared at me, looked over my shoulder at the car. "If you tell me what you want, maybe I can help you. Then will you leave?"

The hunch might pay off; I doubled the bet. "Give me a few minutes, some straight answers, and I might be able to go. I don't want to be here any more than you want me here."

She stepped back into the house. "Then let's get this over with. Come in."

I stepped inside, onto the hardwood floor, heard the woman lock the door behind me. The lights were low. She closed the drapes and turned on another lamp. The older woman sat on the far side of the room on a cream-colored, flowered couch. The bat rested in front of her on a cherry coffee table. A rocker sat to one side, as did an easy chair. In the center of the room was an oval throw rug and in the middle of the rug sat a medicine ball. On top of the ball lay the infant girl.

"Martha Lewis?" I asked.

The pretty woman nodded. She wore a white, long-sleeved blouse and a tan skirt. Her hair swept back from her face and was held back with a red cotton scarf that she'd rolled and tied around her head. She had high cheekbones, big, expressive brown eyes and a short, broad nose. Her skin was a dark brown—not as dark as her mother's but a shade darker than her daughter's. She kneeled down behind her daughter, began to roll the medicine ball. The infant cooed when she dipped forward, over the ball. "What do you want?" asked Martha.

I played it straight. "I'm looking for Ed Jones. Someone thinks he might turn up here."

The big woman sat up straight, put her hands on her knees. "Don't you try an' go sayin' stuff 'bout my daughta and Mistuh Jones. They's friends. We's all friends."

"That right?" I said, looking back at Martha.

"Yes." She turned to her mother. "Why don't you draw Grace's bath water, Mama?"

"I'll do that all right, but I'm gonna take the bat with me. You just yell, something happens." The woman got up and left the room.

Martha motioned for me to sit down on the couch. I obliged. "Mr. Jones is a friend of the family," she said as she continued to move her daughter around on the ball. "I don't know where you heard that he might turn up here, but it isn't true."

"Any idea where he might be?"

"Of course not. Just because he's a family friend doesn't mean that we know anything about his business."

"Has he tried to contact you?"

She stopped moving the ball, pulled her knees up under her, lifted her daughter onto her lap. "Of course not. You seem to think that Mr. Jones has a tight relationship with us, but that's just not true. We see him *and his wife* on some social occasions, and they've been over here for dinner, but that's it. If he's released or escapes, he's not going to come here. I imagine he'll go home."

"So you know about the kidnapping."

"I'm not deaf and blind. The papers are full of it, and it's all anyone's talking about."

"What're they saying?"

"They're saying that it's horrible. First the dimout and factories forced to cut work, and now Mr. Jones is kidnapped. They're saying there are bad things in the air."

"How do you know Ed Jones?"

"My mother used to work for him at the Ben Franklin store."

"He socialize with most of his employees?"

She glared. "I wouldn't know."

"But he socializes with you?"

She snorted. "He and his wife are friends. You keep trying to make it seem like there's something wrong with our friendship or that there's more to it, but there isn't."

I looked at her daughter, noted that she had her mother's eyes. Saliva leaked out the side of her mouth and her mother wiped it away with her sleeve. I nodded at the infant. "Who's the father?"

Martha's voice rose. "Who's your father?"

"I don't know."

It threw her, but just for a second. "Well, someone didn't teach you any manners. Ed Jones is not my daughter's father and don't you ever say anything about her again. I can't help you find him and he isn't coming here. My neighbor is a sergeant with the police, and if you don't leave, I'm going to call him and have him come over here and arrest you."

I held up my hands. "Whoa. I'm sorry. I'm just trying to get some information. I'm a cop, remember? I'm used to people holding back. I'm sorry."

She shook her head. I looked back at the infant. She hadn't moved— at all. I was so caught up in asking Martha about Ed Jones that I hadn't paid much attention to the young girl. It hit me like I'd stepped on a rake. "Does Ed Jones help you with your daughter?"

On cue: The mother came back into the room. "Can you bathe her, Mama?" asked Martha. "I won't be much longer."

"All right, dear." The big woman scooped the child into her arms, lifted her elbow as the child's head lolled to one side. "Come on, precious, time for your bath."

Martha stood up, joined me on the couch. "Listen," I said, quietly. "I'm not trying to pry here. Someone thinks that Ed Jones has enough of a tie to someone in this home that this will be the first place that he goes. I'm just trying to figure out why."

"Who told you that?"

"I don't know. I got it secondhand from my employer."

"Well, maybe you should find out, because they're wrong."

"You're probably right," I said. I went silent, looked around the room, noticed the books, newspapers stacked on an end table. A radio sat in the corner of the room. It wasn't playing. I let the silence continue. Finally I smiled at Martha, leaned forward and dropped my head into my hands. "Oh, boy," I said. "Sometimes I hate this job. It's supposed to be about protecting people and making the streets safe, and too many times it seems like we're either hassling people or we're just too late. Miss Lewis, I'm just trying to find Ed Jones before it's too late. I've run into a lot of people in the last few days who wouldn't mind finding him before me, and if they do, it's not gonna be good for Mr. Jones." I stopped, slowly lifted my head. "Can't you help me?"

She sat still, bit her upper lip. She stuck the tip of her tongue out from between her teeth, wiggled it. "I'd like to help you find Mr. Jones, I really would, but I don't know anything."

"Then just tell me why someone would think that this would be the first place he'd go. Is it you? Your mother? Your daughter?"

She shook her head, slowly, pursed her lips. "They call Mr. Jones the Negro Santa Claus, did you know that?"

I nodded. "I've heard."

"When Gracey was born, two years ago, there were problems. Mr.

Jones found out, came over right away. We used to live in this tiny house, Mama and me. Then, after Gracey, Mr. Jones helped us move here. He said it would be better for us, since one of us would have to stay at home with Gracey. It's too hard for Mama to be on her feet all day, so she stays here with Gracey during the day and I go to work. One of us has to work, of course, but I make sure I'm home for lunch every day and I spend time with her at night."

I nodded my approval. "That's nice. Where do you work?"

She sat up straight. "I clean homes."

"Good work. But you sound educated. Did you...?"

She cut me off. "I was studying to be a nurse before Grace was born. That changed things. Hopefully, in a few years, I can go back."

Odds weren't looking good; the kid was going to take a lot of time. "What are Grace's problems?"

She started to tell me that it had nothing to do with Ed Jones, stopped, resigned. "Cerebral palsy."

"What's that?"

"She lacks motor control. It's like there's a short in the system. The brain tells the body it wants to move, but the message doesn't get to the body."

"Will she be able to walk?"

"Maybe."

"Talk?"

"Maybe."

"And you're working on turning those maybes into probablies."

A smile crossed her face for a brief moment. "That's right. That's why Mr. Jones had one of the boys bring over the medicine ball. We lay Grace on the ball and roll it around to get her body used to moving. Hopefully, something will click."

"And Ed Jones has helped you?"

She saw right through me, digested it, continued. "Yes, Mr. Jones has helped us. He's done a lot of little things, some bigger things, like help-ing us with the house. He's been nothing but good to us."

"Why's that?"

"What do you mean, 'Why's that'? Does there have to be some kind of ulterior motive when someone does something kind?"

"In my world, yes."

"Then I wouldn't want to live in your world. Mr. Jones helps us because Mama worked for him for a lot of years and we all became friends. Someday I'll be able to do the same for someone else. Have you helped any of your friends lately?"

I thought about Sam, chuckled. "Believe it or not, I have, but it's sure not worth talking about. Now, come on, Martha, why would someone think that this would be the first place that Ed Jones would visit?"

She studied me, began to rock, slow. "You know how people are," she said. "When Mr. Jones found out about Grace and started to spend more time with us, people talked. It really hurt Mama. She'd worked for him for all of those years, and people forgot about all of that and started saying that he was helping us because he and I were doing something. Well, he knows and his wife knows and I know that nothing has ever happened and nothing ever will. He's a good man."

"If you're not seeing Ed Jones, who do you see?"

Her eyelids lifted slower than garage doors. "Why do you ask?"

"Just trying to complete the picture. I imagine you've got to fight them off."

She didn't blush; she cringed. "I don't see anyone." She beat me to the punch. "I don't have the time."

I dropped it, stood up. "Miss Lewis, I appreciate your time. Now, I'm going to have to sit out there tonight and every night for a few more nights, so I'll apologize in advance. Just look at it as free police protection."

"You're wasting your time."

"I may be, but I've got to do it. Now the other man, the one that sits here during the day, he won't bother you either. He's not someone you'd want to get to know, but at least he's lazy and uninterested. He'll just sit in his car and wait for Jones to knock on the window."

"The light blue Ford? Mama saw him. She was going to go see him, but you took his place."

"He's not going to be a problem."

We walked to the door. "What was your name, Officer?"

"Carson," I said. "Gus Carson."

"Well, Gus Carson, I wish I could've helped you more."

"You can," I said. "If Ed Jones contacts you, tell him to see me. I'm his best chance of getting out of this alive."

THE NIGHT FLEW BY—I thought about Martha Lewis and her daughter, the kind of man that could leave them. I got a mad on, revived it whenever I started to doze off. Hard to work one up for Ed Jones, so I thought about the war, Mayor Kelly and my faceless father.

1916: Marilyn Carson—voluptuous blonde B-girl, a diet of whiskey and cigarettes, more men than the military. One of 'em knocks her up— no one stakes a claim. Marilyn left to raise the kid on her own, she passes on the family name, christens me "Gus" with a shot of Old Grand-Dad— a drop on my forehead, the rest Mommy's post-birth reward.

Our humble abode: one room above Clancy's Saloon. My childhood memories: the barkeep, B-girls, whispers in the night. The stairs creak, Marilyn out for the night, saloon noise nursed me to sleep. Mother wakes me in the morning, Marilyn goes out at night. One and the same, but nothing alike, my mother and Marilyn.

Seven years old: Mother doesn't wake me up. Marilyn never comes home. I wander the saloon for two days, cry at night. The barkeep makes some calls. That night, the bogeyman takes me home to live with him and his wife. "Your mother called it quits," he says. "Jumped off the Michigan Avenue Bridge." His wife tucks me to her breast, calms me, quiets him with a shake of her head.

Three years later, she goes, too. Just him and me left—South Side Sam and his make-believe son. Groomed to be a cop/co-conspirator. No stones left unturned, I learn to hurt with the best of 'em. Brass knuckles, saps, the butt of my gun; feet, knees, groins, throats, choppers, eyes. Sam says hit 'em, Sam says hard.

The years roll by. I join the force, Sam rigs our partnership. Sam needs muscle, Sam needs an enforcer. I make the grade on Clubber Jones. Everyone's afraid of me. Just the way Sam likes it. We're partners. We're friends. We're family.

Business too good: Bag money leads to real estate, pool halls, a bowling alley. Sam sitting pretty, but too wild to sit. He fucks up—the cookie jar is in the evidence room, heroin with a street value of the budget for the State of Illinois. Sam swipes it, gets caught. The judge plays hardball, no deals—fucks up himself by setting bail. Sam springs himself with a duffel bag full of cash. He tracks down the judge, beats him to death in his own garage. Witness, passerby, Sid Pasqua i.d.'s South Side Sam; the instrument that does him in—a bowling pin from his own alley. Sam's final strike: Terre Haute for life.

I kicked back in the car, let the memories ride. Six a.m. couldn't come too soon—I peeled out when I saw Art McGuire's Ford round the corner.

## WEDNESDAY, MAY 15

TOO TIRED TO BREATHE: I slid between two cars parked in front of my building. I turned off the ignition, grabbed my coat from the back seat, stepped out and dropped an arm behind my back to slip into the coat sleeve. Suddenly I felt someone grab my arm by the wrist. I started to turn—something hard slammed against the side of my face. The world went dark as I went face first onto the street.

THE ROAR OF AN ENGINE, exhaust fumes, bumps interrupted my tire-iron nap. Hands dragged me, my head dropped, hit, hung. Something lifted me to my feet, held me. It let go, I hung, perched. A motor growled; I felt myself being lifted, lowered, lifted again. Voices called; I fell back, tilted forward. I dropped, stopped hard, rose again.

Francisco Juarez: "I'll kill you, Carson!"

I heard it again. "I'll kill you, Carson!"

It got louder. A no-sleep nightmare. I opened my eyes, focused, closed them and opened them again. Wood everywhere. Large wood containers, stacked in rows, held together by metal clamps. Row upon row, stacked nearly to the ceiling. The voices. Suddenly I started to fall again. I looked down: sixteen feet below me Lincoln Johnson and a group of colored men screamed at me.

I came to an abrupt stop around eight feet from the ground. I stood on the forks of a forklift, my hands tied behind me—over my head, fastened to the lift. The knot was tied tight, but I could feel my hands.

Lincoln Johnson yelled at the forklift operator: "Knock him off, Gravy!"

The lift dropped, suddenly, and I pushed my heels against the forks to stop from slipping. It didn't work. My legs went out from underneath me and I fell. My arms snapped straight, shoulders tried to tear their way out of the sockets. I hung like a too-ripe tomato, nose to nose with Johnson.

"Why did you do it, Carson?" yelled Johnson.

I had no more idea what he was talking about than if I'd been listening to a Kraut interrogator. "What?"

"Why did you do it, Carson?" he yelled again.

"Johnson, I don't have any idea what you're talking about," I said. My voice was hollow and weak, my head hurt and I couldn't see out of my right eye. Whoever had clipped me had done a good job.

"Lift him, Gravy."

The lift reeled back, rose. I pulled myself up, swung my legs over the forks, scrambled to my feet. The lift rose higher and higher until I was only a few feet from the ceiling. I looked over the rows of large, wooden storage crates, saw the walls, realized I was in the back of a warehouse. A stamp on one of the containers: Blue ink said, JACKSON CARTAGE, HOUSEHOLD GOODS. The same warehouse I'd visited a few days ago—a different room. Suddenly I fell.

"Shiiiiiiiiiiiiiit," I yelled as I fell. The ground came up fast, but I slowed a bit and my knees buckled as the forklift operator stopped my descent. A few more feet and I'd have hit the ground—my spine would've snapped like a twig.

Lincoln Johnson strode forward. He wore his customary dark three-piece suit, but the necktie was missing, and there were dark brown stains on the front of his white shirt. "Gravy here is a wizard of a mechanic. He rigged this lift just for you. I say the word, that lift falls brake-free."

"Great," I said. "Mind having Gravy take a look at my car? The brakes squeal like a shine hitting a gig."

No laughs. "You're a very funny man, Carson. First you tell me you're looking for Ed Jones, then your fellow cops knock over twenty of my policy wheels and now this. You people don't know what's good for you, do you, Carson?"

My head fell forward. I spit blood that dripped from my tongue—I'd bitten it during a free fall. "I don't know what the hell you're talking about, Johnson, so just let me go and we'll chalk it up to a misunderstanding. You don't, I'm gonna kill you."

Johnson laughed, turned to the other four men standing there. They all wore coveralls and wool caps. They were big and stout, and they didn't laugh. "Did you hear that?" said Johnson. "This boy's been flopping around here like a yo-yo and he's threatening me."

The men forced a laugh. One of them said, "Jist let me play with that yo-yooo for a while. See how much he likes that."

Johnson turned back to me. "You are in no position to be threatening me, sir, but I guess on your last day, you can say about anything you'd like. You want to make this quick, you'd better answer me."

"I don't know what the hell you're talking about," I said. I flexed the muscles in my forearms, touched my hands against the material that was used to bind my arms. I figured Johnson's necktie: strong enough to hold me, but if it broke, they wouldn't care—if I was high enough, I'd plunge to my death.

"Gravy," said Johnson. He pointed up.

The lift rose, then dropped. This time the operator let it fall even farther; my knees buckled hard and I barely stopped from slipping off the forks. "One more time. Why did you do it?" I was face to face with John-son, pain shooting through my arms.

"If you want to know so bad, why don't you let me know what I did?"

Johnson motioned to the operator. He leaned out so he could see in front, and followed Johnson between the rows of storage crates. We came to an aisle and stopped. Johnson stepped up close, looked me in the eye. "Not looking so good, Carson. You think we're going to simply let you take policy? And to think, I really believed your story. You were with South Side Sam; I should've known you're working with the Italians."

"That's crazy."

"Crazy? What's crazy is me listening to you the first time. If you're not working for the Italians, who are you working for?"

No good reason to tell him—they were set to drop me. I had to figure out what he wanted to pin on me, fast. "Can it," I said. "I'm not telling you squat until you tell me what this is about."

Johnson frowned, looked at the forklift operator out of the corner of his eye. "Slow turn, Gravy."

The operator began to turn the lift; the tow motor spun slow and easy. Johnson followed me around, watched me, eyes trained on mine. I jerked my head, avoided his gaze, looked around the room. The forklift slowed, dropped slightly. I fell forward—my arms strained, my hands slipped through the tie, caught at the palms. Just a few feet from the ground, I lifted my head and saw the body.

Busy Jackson wore the same suit that I'd seen him wear two days before, but the dent in his skull was new. He was seated, slumped over; he'd hit the crate behind him and slid to the floor. His head fell to the side, and his eyes shot up at the rafters, like he was trying to read the name on a storage crate in a far corner. Blood covered the side of his face, his clothes and a few square feet of floor space. He looked like a fresh kill.

"Not so busy anymore, is he?"

"Damn!" Lincoln Johnson slammed a fat fist into my stomach. It didn't catch me off guard, so I didn't lose much breath. "Show some respect, please," he said.

"What's wrong?" asked the forklift operator.

"I was watching his eyes," said Johnson. "He was as surprised as we were when we saw him. The man didn't do it."

"I'm glad you see things my way," I said. "Now let me off of this so I can find you a seat next to him."

"Not so fast. Who did you tell about your visit to Busy's?"

"No one. I'm only paid if *I* find Jones, not if I lead someone else to him. That's my business."

"And this is my business. Like I told you, the police hit twenty of my wheels today. All the papers cry out against policy and it's all because of Ed Jones. You know something? I can tell you what's going to happen. Ed will be released. He'll spend a few months setting up the Italians with his games and then, poof, he'll disappear. And he'll leave the rest of us vulnerable. So now, you see, I've got to know your role in this. If you're aiding them in any way, you're dead."

"And if I'm not?"

"You're still dead, but I'll just let Ronnie plug you in the head. Otherwise, we're gonna drop you over and over, let you hit the ground every time. By the end, you'll look like one fucked-up accordion."

"You'll be making a big mistake," I said.

"Why's that?"

"Because I'm getting closer to Jones. You don't want him turning over his wheels, you want to find him, stick close to me."

"And what makes you believe that? Have you been in contact with the Italians?"

"Yeah," I said.

"And what are their plans?"

"I think you've got it right. Jones and Giancana did time together. They'll give Jones a little better offer than you just gave me. He'll turn over his games and hightail it to one of his villas."

Johnson frowned, shook his head. "Thank you for telling me something I already knew. How do you expect to find him?"

"I don't. They'll find me. I've got the word going around that I'm looking for Jones. I've been pushing their buttons."

"You obviously haven't been pushing that hard—they haven't come after you yet. I think you're overestimating yourself, Carson. Why should they worry about a man like you?"

I spit a glob of blood on the floor, rolled my head. "They know I'm suspended. They know I know Sam—I don't play by the rules. They know that if I can't find Jones, I'm gonna knock on all their doors. They know something about me that you don't."

Johnson laughed, yelled for the rest of the men to join him. He pointed up and the forklift operator lifted me straight up in the air. He stopped me a couple of feet from the ceiling. I was only three feet from the top of a storage crate, some eighteen feet in the air.

"And what is it, Officer Carson?" he yelled. "What is so special about you that the Italians know but we don't?"

"I should've died a loooong time ago!" I yelled as I snapped the necktie and dove for the crate.

I CAUGHT THE CORNER OF THE CRATE, scampered on top. The lid was covered in dust, it flew, caked to the blood and sweat on my face. I lay still, listened to them scream. Suddenly the forks appeared like an alien sticking its head out of a spaceship. They were spread across the lift, my feet must've knocked them loose. Held in place by pure physics, I could pop them off with one hand.

The forks moved forward, swiped at the air. The operator moved the tow motor too close to the crates, I felt them shake underneath me. The forks stabbed, swiped, stabbed again. I caught one near the back of the lift, popped it loose, jerked it free. "Son of a bitch," yelled the operator.

I poked my head over the front of the crate, saw the men look at the forklift. Their attention held for a moment, I dropped the fork. It fell silently, landed square on one guy's shoulder, ripped open another's neck, clanged loudly on the floor. War paint more like wore paint— blood covered the group. Four left, including Johnson and the forklift operator. I scurried across the crate, on my knees, flung myself to a crate atop the next row, repeated the leap to the row behind.

"You're dead!" screamed Johnson. "You are dead!"

Shots rang out as they searched for me. They couldn't see me on top of the crate, had to guess where I'd gone. I heard the tow motor move forward, watched it smash into a row of crates; they toppled—domino style; the entire row fell. Rats scampered across the floor like soldiers searching for foxholes.

Four feet between rows, I leaped toward the back, caught the edge of a crate, pulled myself on top. Someone saw me, a shot rang out. Two men ran underneath the stack of crates where I hid, shot up the edge. I looked up, saw the clamps straining on both sides of the top; the front of the crate bulged, pregnant. I slid forward, pried my fingers under the edges of the clamps, popped them loose. I scrambled back and dove to the row behind me as the cover of the crate blew off, spit boxes and fur- niture on top of the two men. A credenza knocked one across the room; the other man's arm peeked out from under a pile of boxes.

Just Johnson and the forklift operator: I scanned the rows, searched for the overhead door. Caught off balance—the forklift smashed into my stack, spilled me off the crate and onto the top of the stack behind me. I landed hard, nearly rolled off—the stack was only two crates high, and the forklift operator saw me land. The fork stabbed at me like a spear attacking fish. I rolled right; it tore into the top of the crate. Splinters flew: My head came up and I saw the window. Overseas crates peeked in through the window, piled high against the side of the building—my escape route mapped in a frenzy.

The fork swung, jabbed. I grabbed it, yanked it free, turned and flung it through the window. The glass exploded. I dove through the frame, felt shards of glass rip my back. The wet, rotten-wood crate burst as I landed on it, spilled down the pile. I hit the ground and came up running.

Lincoln Johnson rushed out a side door, took a potshot, missed badly. I scrambled over a steel-mesh fence, weaved through a junkyard, came out on a busy street. I stepped into the street, held my badge high—a gray Packard stopped inches in front of me. I moved around to the driver's-side window and told the driver to move over.

"Police," I said as I tore open the door and forced my way inside the auto. A white-haired man screamed, moved to the passenger side. His lips quivered; he asked to get a better look at my badge. I shut him up with one look, sped off. I saw Lincoln Johnson in the rearview mirror. He shot up the crates in frustration.

I DITCHED THE RIDE two blocks from my place, handed the old man a half and told him to never stop for strangers. I moved between buildings, slow, watched for the stakeout. No one around. I slipped into my building, my place, grabbed my .38 and rushed out the door. My machine hit thirty miles an hour before I took a breath.

One good eye: I headed north, realized I was homing in on Lake Forest, fought the pain and fatigue. Busy Jackson was dead, possibly three others. Accountable or unaccountable, the three were mine. Busy belonged to someone else. I spotted a phone booth, stopped, stepped in and dialed. I got Sally Rand, asked for Chief Hogan; he answered quick.

"Hogan."

"Chief, Gus Carson."

"Why the hell are you calling me here, Carson?" he whispered. "Give me your number; I'll call you right back."

I looked at the phone, read him the number. He repeated it, playacted. "No, Carson, I cannot help you with your suspension. Captain Griffin is your superior officer, so I suggest you talk to him." He hung up hard.

Five minutes later, I grabbed it on the first ring: "Yeah."

"Sorry about that, Carson," he said. "Too many open ears around here. What do you want?"

"A hospital bed, a cold beer, about twelve hours of good sleep."

"What have you done?"

I fought anger. "The department decided to crack down on the wheels, somebody tied it to me. I've been yanked around like a puppet, and I don't mean just by you and Hypoole."

"Watch it, Carson. What're you getting at?"

"What I'm getting at is this: Nobody's playing straight with me. First, Hypoole accidentally leaves out his mayoral plans, tries to play the good citizen. Now, the day after I tell him about my talk with Lincoln Johnson and Busy Jackson, someone pays them a visit and they return the favor. At least Johnson did."

"What happened?" asked Hogan.

"You oughtta know. The department jumped on twenty of Johnson's wheels. Somebody jumped on Busy Jackson's head. They thought it was me, so they jumped on me."

"What do you mean someone jumped on Busy Jackson's head?"

"Split him open like a melon. He's dead. A few others might join him. I was you, I'd send a couple of squad cars over to the Jackson Cartage terminal, pronto."

"Right away. What does all of this have to do with finding Ed Jones?"

"Jones was a competitor. Johnson thinks I'm working with the Italians. We all think the Italians want to take over policy. I didn't have to watch the girl, I'd be a lot closer to Jones."

A pause; Hogan's voice went soft, confused. "What girl?"

Gut punch. He didn't know. Hypoole ran his own game, Hypoole had the money. Hogan was a stooge, played to offer up bodies. McGuire, me, lined up by the ambitious chief—just a flunky. "Kidding. What else has the department got planned, policy-wise?"

"More wheels are going down. It'll be a temporary thing. The mayor called in the captains of the four districts where policy's rampant—Wabash Avenue, Pekin Inn, Warren Avenue and Stanton Avenue. Told 'em he didn't want a single wheel running by the end of the week. He's just reacting to the newspapers. You seen 'em? The kidnapping's all the rage."

I grunted. "Tell me about it. What about the Jones kidnapping? Anything?"

"Wife's been interviewed, nothing. We're watching the house. His brother's back in town, said he hasn't heard from the kidnappers. No ransom demand."

"Believe him?"

"Hell no, but there's nothing else to go on."

"What're you guys doing?"

"Cursory stuff: knocking down doors, talking to stoolies. Those guys' lips are like nuns' legs—shut tight. We haven't had much luck."

"What about my case, the shooting?"

He sighed. "Dead. Filed, locked away. We closed the whorehouse—Mona's."

"Jeez, I hope she lands on her back. Anything on my suspension?"

"This thing's over, I'll talk to Griffin personally. You'll be back in no time."

"What if I don't find Jones?" I asked.

"Keep trying. I'll play some angles, internally. And, Carson, you've got until Sunday morning."

"FBI deadline is Saturday."

"Not what I mean. I can hold off for a few days, but Sunday morning I want you here to fill out a report on the incident at Jackson Cartage. There'll be a squad car there in a few minutes. and it sounds like there'll be plenty of questions."

"Maybe, maybe not," I said. "I wouldn't be surprised if it's broom clean by now. Put out an APB on Lincoln Johnson—his prints and picture should be on file. I'll fill you in on Sunday morning. And while you're at it, spread word around the department that I'm closing in on the kidnappers. Tell 'em to keep it confidential. The rats hear that, they'll be calling Giancana himself."

"You're setting yourself up, Carson. Be careful."

I didn't tell him I agreed. A setup all right, but not by me. I didn't tell him I knew he and Hypoole were playing different games; one of 'em needed me more. I didn't tell him I was having second thoughts: The Grand Jury might get more than the bargain. I told him I'd be careful, hung up the phone and took off for Lake Forest.


NINE O'CLOCK IN THE MORNING, twenty-one sleepless hours, my right eye area turned to mush. My back stuck to the seat, courtesy of window glass. Traffic was slow—I rubbernecked every car that passed, watched the rearview for vindictive shines. Pain and no sleep meant delirium: I concentrated on the road, fought off nagging thoughts.

Playback: Bunny to Busy Jackson to Lincoln Johnson. Johnson says the Italians. Johnson says jukeboxes. Johnson threatens Jones, threatens me. Johnson doesn't have Jones. Jackson's dead, Johnson's threat a promise: He tried to bounce me to oblivion. The sum of the parts equaled a hole. Who killed Busy? Why? The Italians had Jones. Where? Keep kicking the cans, the rats would come.

The gardener, dead, buried, filed. The Cordell brothers, one dead, the other laying threats like nickel bets. The only connection between the two cases: The Cordell brothers worked for the syndicate—they kidnapped Jones. Dead, filed, buried, stop wasting the energy. Drive.

Wednesday morning no Sunday party: No guards met me at the gate. I drove up to the mansion, parked the car and staggered to the door. I knocked with an open palm, fell against Jerome as he opened the door. The butler was stout, he dragged me inside, into the sitting room and propped me on a love seat.

I lost consciousness, woke up to Virginia Prescott slapping my face. Her cool hand stung. Sheila stood behind her, panic spread across her face like thick makeup. Both women wore flowered sundresses, wide-brimmed white hats in their hands.

"Gus, Gus!" screamed Sheila.

"Quiet down," said Virginia. "He's awake."

She leaned forward, looked into my eyes. I could smell her perfume, a floral blend that offset her demeanor. Pure pro: "I've got bad news, Gus," she said. "You look exhausted, but I'm afraid we can't let you sleep. You might've suffered a concussion. We've got to keep you awake for a few more hours. Jerome is bringing you some hot coffee—he's already called for Dr. Lund."

I nodded, leaned back into the couch. "What happened, Gus?" asked Sheila as she slid on the other side of me, stroked the good side of my face. Her mother rested a hand on my thigh, grabbed my wrist and feigned searching for a pulse.

The truth would do no good, I had fun with the lie. "Little old lady didn't want to give up her parking space," I said.

"C'mon, Gus. For real," said Sheila.

"For real," I muttered. "Have you seen the price of parking lately?"

"I'm sure it was work-related," said Virginia. She squeezed my wrist, hard. "Isn't that right, Gus?"

I nodded. "Case closed. No worries."

The women looked at each other, back at me. I fought to stay awake. Jerome brought in the coffee and a wet rag full of ice.

Sheila struck at the rag like a cobra snagging a snack. Her mother's hand actually touched the back of Sheila's as she followed her to the rag. Sheila pressed it against my eye, gently, stroked my other cheek with her hand. I smiled, soft, took her hand and moved it away. She looked stricken until I took the cup of coffee and drank.

"I haven't seen any of our security people beaten as such," said Virginia. Her voice was pure and strong, her enunciation as clean and far away from her past as her language could propel. "You really must consider letting us help you find a job. Police work obviously doesn't agree with you."

"Then it's par for the course, because nobody seems to agree with me anymore."

"Then why don't you agree to let us help you?"

"You're doing it right now. Listen, I'm not exactly tied to being a cop, although I guess I was most of the morning."

"You've a queer sense of humor, Gus," said Virginia.

"Listen to her, Gus," said Sheila. "You should try to get a job with one of the families around here. There's the Simmons—they made their money in advertising. He's always worried about someone he offended. Why, they'd hire you, lickety-split. And Mr. Tanner really liked you. I bet he'd hire you."

I looked out the window. It was sunny and clear—their manicured lawn was already green and lush. Flowers had started to bloom, and a young gardener clipped at weeds as he leaned into the bushes lining the mansion. His sleeves were rolled up, and I saw the bulldog tattoo on his left forearm; a Marine clipped their bushes.

"One of the few spring days I can remember. Seems like we go straight from winter to summer here."

"Yes, it's a lovely day for a beating," said Sheila. She frowned. "And you think I change subjects abruptly. Gus, I want you to find something else to do. Police work is too dangerous."

I agreed, searched for something to say. Saved by the bell: The door-bell rang, and Jerome ushered in a short, thin, gaunt man carrying a black bag.

"Dr. Lund," said Virginia, as she met him, grabbed an elbow and com-mandeered him into the room.

The doctor removed his spectacles, bent over me and looked into my eyes. "What have we here?" he asked.

"Parking mishap," I said.

"Right. Looks like someone parked a jeep on your head." He gently pried open my right eyelid, stared at my eye. "No real damage to the eyeball. You're lucky."

He had me look all directions, examined the eye, looked into my other eye. "Pupils aren't the same size. You've suffered a concussion. Upset stomach?"

"No."

"Dizziness, weakness in one arm?"

"Some."

Lund lectured: "A concussion occurs when the brain bounces against the skull. The cranial nerves are damaged and need time to repair. These cranial nerves control activities like speech, facial movement, hearing, consciousness. Do you have any memory loss?"

"I can't remember."

"That's his infamous wit, Doctor," said Virginia. She folded her arms across her chest and glared at me. "He's being quite serious, Gus. Do you have any memory loss?"

"Less than I'd like. No."

"Good," said Dr. Lund. "Any other injuries?"

I nodded. "A few scrapes."

"Ladies," he said, "why don't you excuse us and I'll give him a thorough exam." Sheila and Virginia looked at each other, made a pact with their halfhearted smiles, told us they'd be in the kitchen and left the room.

Dr. Lund had me strip down to my boxers, put a cold stethoscope to my chest. "Breathe deeply. Okay, again."

He went through the whole routine, touched the bruises, cleaned the cuts on my back. He plucked out the glass, rubbed alcohol onto the wounds, bandaged them with gauze. He reached into his bag and pulled out a bottle of pills and a jar, told me to get dressed.

"These are painkillers," he said as he held up the bottle. "Take one every six hours. If you need something else for headaches, take this—plain, old everyday Bromo-Seltzer. Just follow the directions. Good stuff."

"Gene Tierney ever stops pitching Royal Crown Cola, you've got yourself a new gig."

He sighed. "Now, you need to get plenty of rest. Are you staying here?"

"I stay here, I don't think I'll get much rest."

"We'll see about that. Now, if your headaches increase or you get severely dizzy, have them call me. Usually no surgery is required, even with a severe concussion, but you need to be careful. You may feel frustrated, worried, overwhelmed. That's natural."

"I'll say it is. That's the way I feel every day."

Fake smile: "Any other questions?"

Nagging thought. None of my business, but I couldn't help it: "What's cerebral palsy?"

He curled a lip, raised an eyebrow. "What's that got to do with the price of tea in China?"

"Curious. You know anything about it?"

"Quite a bit, as a matter of fact. I have a cousin with CP. I see her frequently."

"Well?"

He sat down in an overstuffed chair, stretched his legs, took off his spectacles and dangled them. "Cerebral palsy comes in different degrees and conditions. We mostly associate it with quadriplegia, but that isn't to say..."

I cut him off: "English?"

"It's caused by an injury to the brain that controls the muscles, and it differs in severity. Some people with mild cerebral palsy can stand, walk and carry out normal functions with just a bit more difficulty. In other cases, they might not be able to stand, walk or carry out other physical tasks. It also affects their speech and other motor skills."

"Can you look at a kid and figure out how severe it is?"

"No. It's determined by what part of the brain was damaged and how severely. Some are quadriplegic, which means that all four limbs are affected. Others are hemiplegic, which means that one half of the body is affected and others are diplegic, which typically means that the problems lie more in the legs."

"Causes?"

"An injury to the brain before, during or shortly after birth. You're not a candidate, if that's what's worrying you."

"No. What typically causes the injury?"

"The mother may have medical problems like diabetes or high blood pressure. Maybe an infection. Maybe the baby doesn't get enough oxygen, or the mother takes a fall or is hurt in an accident. Impossible to tell. You can't pinpoint the cause of a child's CP. No opportunity for detective work there."

"Treatment?"

"Gaiting—mimicking movements; stretching; all sorts of therapy—physical, speech and language, occupational."

"Expensive?"

"Can be. Some decent programs out there. I think it's best to send them to special programs, keep them among their own."

I didn't like the sound of that. "Does it screw up their learning process, retard it?"

"No. But they spend a lot of thought and energy just trying to live."

Five days in the water; the doc didn't get it. We're all just trying to survive. I thanked him for his time, stood up, caught icy, glaring Virginia in the doorway.

She ushered the doc out, came back with her tongue snapping. "Dr. Lund did us a favor coming over here. You didn't need to waste his time with silly questions."

Sheila came up behind her. "Really, mother! Gus has been hurt. Leave him alone."

Virginia's bosom heaved, her jaw muscles clenched. Seething, but quiet, controlled: "You don't understand politics, young lady. The doctor did us a favor by coming over here. The least we can do is to try to limit the abuse of his time."

"Well, I think you're making too big of a deal out of nothing," said Sheila.

"And he doesn't come cheap," said Virginia. She turned to me, rearranged her expression like a Jap actor switching masks. "I'm sorry if I'm a bit short, Gus. You're welcome to stay in the guest house until you're feeling better."

"I'd love a quick nap, if you're sure you don't mind," I said. "And I can pay the doctor's bill."

"She doesn't mind," said Sheila as she took me by the hand and led me out of the room. "But I'll have to keep an eye on you." She turned and looked at her mother. "Because of the concussion and all, and don't worry about the bill. We can afford it, right, Mother?"

"Of course," said Virginia. She followed us out of the room. I heard her pick up the phone as we stepped out the back door and walked to the guest house.

"It's nearly eleven," said Sheila as she opened the door to the guest house and led me to the bedroom. I sat down on the bed, kicked off my shoes and lay down. "I'm going over to the Blanchards' for a bridge lesson. Why don't I wake you when I get back. I can ask Mother to look in on you while I'm gone."

My stomach fluttered. "I'll drop you. I just need an hour or so here and then I've got to get home."

"That's ridiculous!" she shouted as she sat down on the bed and slapped the mattress. Her dark hair spilled forward; her eyes lit with anger. "You're in no shape to be charging out of here."

"I'll be fine. I've got things to do tonight." The child, the girl—an unforeseen draw.

"You're impossible, Gus. What is it that's so important?"

"I don't know."

"What do you mean, you don't know? What have you got to do tonight?"

I stroked her hair. "It's the case I'm working on. I can't tell you about it. I shouldn't have come out here today. I don't know why I did."

She leaned forward, kissed me gently, caressed my cheek. "You know exactly why you came here, Gus. We're taking up right where we left off."

I didn't tell her that she left off with another man; I was someone different. I didn't tell her that I could never be close to someone like her— rich, spoiled, insulated. I didn't tell her that vague suspicions were starting to scare me. I told her I needed to be up by one and fell back onto the pillow, swallowed a pain pill, dry. Sheila curled up next to me and held me while I slept.

TWO HOURS LATER, Sheila nudged me awake. I felt worse than when I'd conked out—a quick look in the mirror showed yellow eyes streaked with red and lines that looked like they'd been scratched into my gray, clay face with a dull knife. Twenty-nine years old going on fifty.

While Sheila cleaned up, I sat down in the living room, lay back on the couch. Nat Prescott sauntered in, holding a drink and a cigarette. He wore knee-high, black boots, riding pants and a tan cotton shirt. A riding cap had tousled his long hair, and the sun had given his leathery skin a yellowish pink hue. I thought he looked like a Brit without a fox-hunt. I had to force myself to stop from yelling, "Tallyho!"

"God, what a magnificent warm day! Early afternoon rides are the best, Gus. The great beast galloping, cool wind in your face. And nothing like scotch and a smoke to follow it up." He took a swig of the scotch and a puff on the cigarette. "I peeked in on you while you napped. Jiminy, what must've happened to you." He shuddered like he'd sniffed rotten meat.

"Over and done with. Sorry to have shown up here. I guess I just needed to get out of the city for a while."

He sat down next to me. "Drink?"

"No, I've got things to do. But I'll consider it a rain-out so we can reschedule."

"We can reschedule any day; it's my ritual. Makes my wife a bit more tolerable. She's a hellcat, all right. Think long and hard before you get married, Gus. When they say, ''til death do us part,' it's meant as a warning." He chuckled. "Say, Gus, we're having a little political fund-raiser here on Friday night. If you're feeling up to it by then, would you like to work security?"

"With the goons you had for that last little soiree? No thanks."

"I'm afraid I've already arranged it with them, but in the future, if you like, I'll ask you first."

I thought about it. "Let's see. I've got an appointment with a spiritu-alist soon, so, depending on what she says, I might take you up on that."

"Having your fortune told?" he asked.

"No, actually, I'm making predictions for someone else. Who's your fund-raiser for?"

"The Republican Party. Why?"

"What do you think of Arvis Hypoole's shot at mayor?"

He set his drink on the coffee table, drew on the cigarette. "You never cease to amaze me, Gus. I had no idea you were interested in politics. Arvis Hypoole? I think he's got the pedigree, the reputation and a decent shot. Why do you ask?"

"Just heard a rumor about him running. Didn't know much about the man and figured you might."

"Well, I'm just glad you're getting interested in politics. It might not offer the same type of action you're used to, but it becomes pretty intox-icating." He swallowed his last drop of scotch, stood up and walked to the wet bar.

"Why are you so pro-Republican?" I asked.

"Well, if you want me to tell you that it's because of specific social issues or their agenda, I can't do that. It's pure business with me. We got along fine with previous administrations, but Mayor Kelly has proven uncooperative. Our construction company hasn't received a decent gov-ernment bid in years." He noted my reaction, waved his hand. "No, no, no. We're not in any trouble at all. Frankly, we do well without the City business, but I believe we're on the verge of a real construction boom."

"Good for you, eh?"

"I hope so," he said as he placed two fingers next to his glass, poured the scotch. He looked up at me, made a face like a kid looking for an extra-wide slice of cake, smiled and poured a third finger. "Little pick-me-up after that long ride. No reason to say anything to the Prescott women, though. They worry about me too much." He took a quick swig. "Anyway, what was I saying? Oh yes, the construction boom." He sat back down next to me, crossed his legs. "Do you know why we won the war?"

"I'd say I've got a pretty good idea."

"Oh heavens, I mean aside from our heroic forces. God knows, you men made a huge difference. But you know what I think it was? Mass production. We were able to produce planes, jeeps, equipment, supplies, ammunition, everything, so quickly that the Axis forces couldn't keep up."

"They said Hitler couldn't sleep because he counted jeeps rather than sheep."

"Anyway...I think the war is going to turn out to be remarkably profitable for all of us. There's going to be a real opportunity for those who seize it."

"Yeah, it's a real bonanza." Suddenly his scotch looked like piss and the laughter in his eyes looked like it was charged by a fool's grin. I searched for an out, found it when I saw the gardener working on bushes out back. "I'm going to stretch my legs, Mr. Prescott. Tell Sheila I'm in the backyard."

He stood up. "Why don't you stop by the party anyway, Gus? We might just interest you in joining the Republican Party. We could always use a war hero in our ranks."

I smiled. I didn't tell him the only campaigning I'd ever done was when I was a kid. Sam had me hand out palm cards at the voting booths—voters got his picks written neat. I didn't tell him the only vote I'd ever placed was after tossing Mayor Kelly's right-hand man through that window—I elected the Marines over the cooler. I didn't tell him that we didn't fight the war to line pocketbooks. I told him if the party matched the last one, I'd be there. I stepped out the back door as he went for more scotch.

THE BACK DOOR OPENED into a courtyard with a fountain at its center. A stone Cupid bent at its knees, a bow in one hand, the other reaching over its back for an arrow from its quiver. Brick walls marked the perimeter, large potted plants stood at the entrance. Lilac bushes guarded the house, and purple and white lilacs blossomed—their scent filled the air. The gardener was on his knees, bent over a bush, when I approached.

"Whatcha workin' on, leatherneck?" I asked.

He looked up, mopped the sweat from his brow. His light-blue denim shirt and jeans were soiled; dirt clung to his hands. He wore his blonde hair in a crew cut and sported a young man's smile. "Marine?" he asked.

I nodded. "And a friend of the family, I guess."

He stood up, wiped a hand on his jeans, laughed. "Don't think it's worth shaking. I'm Dan Garrett."

"Gus Carson. Pleased to meet you."

"You just getting some air, or is there something I can do for you, Mr. Carson?"

I smiled. He had that "it's good to be alive" attitude that so many had. "Little of both, I guess, Dan. Just escaping too much war talk."

He shook his head. "I know what you mean. They expect us to want to talk about it. I sure don't. I'd rather talk about the Cubs or the weather, or anything else."

"Hard to weather the Cubs this year."

He laughed. "Aah, they ain't so bad. Set the bar a little high last year, I guess. You know, I was gonna ask you who you were out here seein', but with that shiner, I ain't so sure it's anyone."

"Just my way of getting more rest—keeping one eye shut all day."

"Then you're gonna get plenty of rest, 'cause that eye's gonna be closed for quite a while."

I bent over a lilac bush, took a deep sniff. "You'd have asked me before the war what a lilac smelled like, I couldn't have told you," I said. "Now it's probably the most wonderful scent I've ever smelled."

He smiled. "Couldn't agree more. I came back, worked for Prescott Construction for a while, ran a jackhammer. I couldn't stand it, the noise, breaking up the concrete, chunks and dust flyin' everywhere. Just couldn't take it."

"So you just wandered over to the mansion and asked if you could become their gardener?"

He grinned, sheepish. "Nah, that was Mrs. Prescott. She saw me at the construction site a few times, struck up a conversation." He fidgeted. "I guess I mentioned to her that I worked in my old man's nursery growing up. Next thing you know, she came by and asked me to work around their yard."

"Not a bad gig, either," I said.

"Hell," he said. "They needed the help. During the war, they turned that garden out back into a Victory Garden. I helped 'em turn it back."

"What do you mean?" I asked.

He mopped his brow with a handkerchief again, returned it to his back pocket. "Lots of families did it. They converted their flower garden into a vegetable garden, kind of their war effort. They had beans, radishes, potatoes, rhubarb, the works."

"Not a bad way to help out, I guess," I said. "But I can't see the Prescotts hurting for food. Virginia will never let those cupboards go bare."

"Guess not," he said. He focused on me, measuring me. "Who did you say was your friend?"

"I see a bit of the daughter, if that's what you mean."

He looked relieved. "That's what I was getting at. I'd never do it now, but brother, if Mrs. Prescott wasn't married, I'd be on her like hair on Mussolini's ass. Man is she something."

"She's something, all right."

"Hey, I see that side, too. I mean to tell you, I don't have these flowers and this yard looking tip-top by Saturday night, I can kiss this job good-bye. Believe you me, I hear she runs through help faster than the Nazis ran through U-boats."

I saw Sheila open the back door. "How long you been here, anyway?" I asked.

"Just a few days."

Sheila stepped out, walked toward me.

"What happened to the last guy?"

"Fired, I guess."

Sheila said, "Come on," as she looped her arm through mine. "I don't want to be late."

I turned around, walked backward, kept up with her pace. "Dan," I said. "Ever meet him?"

"No," he said as he bent back over the bush, grabbed a pail of water. "Just some colored guy."

SHEILA DROVE AS I GAZED OUT at Lake Michigan. The sky had started to turn gray and the waves grew, but Ava Gardner could've surfed by naked and I wouldn't have noticed. Fatigue, the pain pill, questions had me as confused as a Mormon at a crap table. "So you didn't know the last gardener at all?"

"No," said Sheila. Despite the graying sky, she wore dark sunglasses, and the flowered scarf tied over her hair was for the look and not protection from any rain. It was my machine, but she played driver. "Why on earth would I get to know the help? I know Clarice, the cook, but that's because she's been with us since I was born. Those people are employees, not friends."

"How are they paid?"

"What do you mean?" she asked.

"Check, cash, what?"

"By check, I'm sure. Why on earth are you so interested in this?"

She made a right turn, slowed down like she was losing the Indianapolis 500. I gripped the armrest tight. "Humor me. If I wanted to find out who the last gardener was, how could I do it?"

"Well…" she said, like was telling a child how to open a door. "You could just ask my mother. She hires all of the staff and she's especially careful with the gardeners. April showers may bring May flowers, but Mother's gardeners grow the garden."

"Why don't you ask her when you get home? What time do you think that will be?"

"Mrs. Blanchard is going to teach me to play bridge. I can't imagine it will take too long, but I'll probably be there most of the afternoon."

"Why don't I call you around five thirty?"

She looked at me out of the corner of her eye, returned her gaze to the road. "Why don't you pick me up? We could get steaks—one for each of us and one for your ghastly eye."

"Working tonight. I'll call you at five thirty. Try to ask her like it's not out of the ordinary. Just say you were talking to the new guy and he wanted to know who worked there before him."

"You're being quite mysterious about this, Gus. What are you up to?"

A fairy whisper: "I've just got to find out how he grew such lovely roses."

"Very funny," she said as she slowed and turned into a huge circle drive. She coasted toward the front door, parked and leaned across the seat. She kissed me, quick, on the cheek. "I'll ask Mother. Call me at five thirty."

We both got out of the car. I walked around to the driver's side, and Sheila went to the front door, grabbed the heavy knocker and knocked. Someone let Sheila inside, and she waved as I opened the car door. I was about to get into the car when I noticed the light-green Plymouth parked on the street in front of the house next door.

There were probably hundreds or even thousands of light-green Plymouths on the streets of Chicago, but not many in Lake Forest and not many that had the same taillight broken as the one owned by Martha Lewis. I walked closer, noted the tag number, repeated it while I walked back to the Blanchards' house and knocked on the front door. Gloria Blanchard opened the door, nearly shrieked when she saw me.

"Oh, you poor thing, come in," she said as she placed a hand on her chest. "My goodness, Sheila called me this morning and told me you'd been hurt, but you look just awful."

"And the eye looks bad, too, right?" I stepped past her, into the foyer and took in the house. It wasn't on the scale of the Prescotts', but that was like saying that Billy Conn wasn't on the same scale as Joe Louis. Smaller just meant smaller, not a drop in quality.

"Well, at least you didn't have the sense of humor beaten out of you. What on earth happened?"

"Tried to pry the scotch from Nat Prescott this morning. Bad idea."

She laughed, and it echoed in the foyer and suddenly I felt uncomfortable. Echoes belonged in prison and government buildings, and I didn't like either one of 'em.

"Well, we're just setting down to tea and bridge, but why don't you come in and meet the girls?"

"I'd better not. Dr. Lund's already been out this way once today, and if those ladies get a load of my kisser, he might have to make another trip."

"Well..." she said. She lobbed it like a tennis ball.

"Well, I just wanted to say hello and, say, I saw a light-green Plymouth in front of your neighbors' house. Is it theirs?"

"Heavens no," she said. "Is there some kind of problem?"

"No, it just doesn't fit out here and I figured I'd ask."

"I believe it belongs to the cleaning woman," she said.

"Colored woman?" I asked.

"Of course," she said. "She cleans a few of the houses in the area. She's terribly sweet and she could certainly use the money."

"Why's that?"

"She's got a crippled child at home."

A pain shot through my head, crowbar bad. "How long has she worked here?"

"A few months. Ann Saunders recommended her and she's been excellent." She raised a brow. "Why are you so interested in this?"

I didn't tell her that a bookie I knew told me once that the odds on coincidence were two million to one. I didn't tell her that I was starting to smell a fix. I didn't tell her that I might've killed the Prescotts' gardener and was staking out her cleaning woman's house—I would have looked stark raving mad. I told her that I was just curious. I told her I'd see her again soon and walked out the door.

IT WAS NEARLY THREE O'CLOCK by the time I reached the city—three hours until I had to be back in front of the Lewis house. I knew if I tried for a quick nap I'd end up sleeping through my shift, so I opted for more of Harry's coffee. I hadn't missed that much sleep since my stint in the ocean.

Harry's wasn't too busy—a fact that I liked but Harry probably didn't. I smiled as I looked at the corner table—Big Mike, two friends and a table full of dead soldiers. Big Mike caught my eye, pointed a dead soldier toward the bar. He looked back at me, offered a silent nod. I looked at the bar and saw two suited dagos talking to the bartender, Frank.

They looked like two grapes on a vine. Three-piece suits, shoes shiny enough to slip under a girl's dress for a sneak peek, wide loud ties and black hair slicked back with enough grease to help each squeeze his head into a mouse hole. Odds said Carpacci; Frank said, "Hi, Steve."

I sat down next to the two men. They were nearly identical, mid-twenties with hand-me-down sneers. The one farthest from me was taller, the one seated next to me a bit wider. The wide one looked at me like a dogcatcher eyeing a mutt. "What's your name, big fella?" His voice was low and smooth.

"Bartender called me Steve, but he must be mixing me up with someone else. I'm Harvey Edwards. Jukebox business."

The tall one stood up, quick. The wide one leaned forward, casually picked at his teeth with a toothpick. "Some kind of wise guy, eh? Look of your eye, guy would figure you'd have learned to watch your mouth. Your name Carson?"

"Depends who's asking. If you know Albert Carpacci, then I'm Carson. You don't, maybe I'm Dick Tracy."

The tall one moved around the other, stopped in front of me. "We don't like wise guys or busybodies. You keep talking to my brother like that, I'll wipe the playground up with you."

Frank the bartender moved to the far end of the bar. I felt the sweat pop up on the back of my neck, my gut tightened automatic. I was about to stand up when the fat man stepped out of the bathroom.

If he ate a two-pound steak, he probably could've tipped the scales at the three-century mark, and he was at least six inches short of six feet. His dark moustache and thin beard made him look like he'd tried to stuff a cone full of mud into his mouth. He was dressed in a cream-colored suit with a white hat, and a black topcoat was slung over his shoulders. He held a walking cane in one hand, and it hung near his leg, like a saber, as he pulled up his zipper. A few years and a shitload of pounds ago, he looked just like his sons, who now both stood, glaring at me.

"What's going on?" the fat man asked.

"What's going on appears to be a domestic quarrel," I said. "Your sons are fighting over who gets whipped first."

"He's a wise ass, Pop," said the wide one.

"He's a busybody, Pop," said the tall one.

The man tapped the wide one on the shoulder, moved him away from the barstool. He moved his hand on top of the cane, for balance, as he stepped in front of the stool, turned and sat down. He took his hat off, placed it on the bar and ran a hand over his thinning black hair. I hoped he didn't offer it—that kind of grease would stick for a lifetime.

"You must be this Carson I keep hearing about," he said. His voice carried an Italian accent, but it wasn't pronounced.

I nodded. "And you're Albert Carpacci?"

"Yes. These are two of my boys, Alfredo and Constantin." Alfredo was the wide one. "Mr. Carson," he said, "you've been bothering us. Why?"

"It's Officer Carson, and you can tell me where they're holding Ed Jones."

The three men looked at each other, laughed. Alfredo pushed a bowl of salted nuts down the bar. "Nuts to you. We don't know no Ed Jones."

"Maybe your employer does. Ask Momo about him. You guys get ready to release him, give me a call."

Albert Carpacci raised his cane, flagged down Frank. "I'd like a cup of coffee, please, black. Carson, you want something?"

"Yeah," I said, turning toward Frank. "Tell Ernie to give me the same thing he did yesterday."

If I'd been a relative, we'd have had a nice little family reunion started. As it was, I was tired and sore and ready for this whole thing to end. "Listen, I know what you guys are up to. You're planning on taking over policy. Well, guess what? I don't care. All I want is Ed Jones. Guy I'm working for seems to think he's worth something, so he is to me. You turn over Ed Jones, I lay off."

Albert Carpacci set his cane down on the bar, accepted a cup of coffee from Frank, tasted it. "Aah, that's excellent," he said. "Hard to get a good cup of coffee anymore."

"What do you say?"

"What do I say?" repeated the fat man. "What I say is that you're out of your mind. You seem to think we're involved with gangsters. We're not. My boys and I run a legitimate business. I don't appreciate you going to the manufacturers and suggesting otherwise, and I certainly don't appreciate your little performance at the Chelsea. I also don't appreciate your bothering my customers, like Harry here."

"You'll be lucky if the Chelsea ever opens again. I tie you to the Josie, you'd go away with Marvin the Magnificent." I rested my hands on my knees, leaned forward. "Listen, I don't get Jones, my talking to your customers is going to be the least of your worries. Tell Momo I'll have an APB put on his ass for Jones and Busy Jackson. I'll tell every bootblack, schoolkid and housewife that you guys are forcing your way into policy. No players, no games. I'll spread it around the department that you're the one that tipped me off about Momo. See how busy I'll be."

The ceramic cup nearly burst in his hand. He took one last swallow, gazed at the bar. His boys both took a step toward me. He stopped them with a hand in the air. "No, boys." He stood up, pursed his lips, slipped the topcoat over his shoulders. "Someone has misled you, Carson. You're way off track. Yesterday you threatened my attorney and today you threaten me. When did the police start making threats and accusations? I can't speak for this Momo that you keep talking about, but I can speak for my family. If you start making good on those threats, you'll leave me no choice but to contact, uh, your superiors." He looked at the tall one. "Constantin, bring up the car." The tall one sneered at me and left.

I stood up. "It's hard for me to fall for this reputable business act when your sons' guns show under their jackets like they're growing tits.

I haven't seen many people pull a gun when a record's scratched, but with the crap you push, they probably should."

Alfredo put his hand on his father's shoulder, squeezed it hard. "Give me five minutes with this punk, Pop."

"Five minutes is two Bix Bennett songs," I said. "That's too many. I'm gonna have to drive you through the floor in about thirty seconds or I'll go nuts."

Albert Carpacci stepped between me and his son, threw me a sad look. "For a man who looks like he's been run over by an ice wagon, you talk tough. Why've you got a hard-on for us, Carson? What did we ever do to you?"

"Nothing. I got nothing for you. I just need Jones."

"I've told you, we don't have anything to do with it."

"And the little birds keep telling me you're lying."

He shrugged his shoulders. "No need to call me names. You don't believe me, you don't believe me. Nothing I can do about that. Where're you out of, Carson?"

"Wabash Avenue."

"Aaah," he said. "Wabash Avenue. Explains everything." He unbuttoned his coat, reached into a pants pocket and pulled out a wad of cash. He licked his thumb, ripped off five Andrew Jacksons. "You should've said something earlier. What do you say to a yard?"

"I say come to papa," I said as I held out my hand. He handed me the bills, closed his hand around mine.

"So we'll consider this matter over, eh?" he asked. I nodded. "See," he said to Alfredo, "just a little misunderstanding. Now Carson's gonna lay off of us, maybe do us a little favor in the future. Isn't that right, Carson?"

"I don't know what you're yipping about," I said. "I thought you were just paying for your coffee."

He jerked his hand off mine—the bills floated to the ground. His son picked them up as the fat man stared at me, bit his lip. "My boys were right. You are a wisecracker. I've never liked wisecrackers."

"Must be the only kind of crackers you don't like," I said as I glanced at his belly.

Alfredo was quick, but he'd never raced a bulldozer. He tried to throw a punch at me, but Big Mike grabbed him by the back of the neck, slammed him against the bar. I reached into his jacket, pulled out a .45 Special, stuffed it into the front of my pants.

Big Mike grunted as Alfredo swung his fists, kicked back like a mule. "Want me to snap this one in half, Gus?"

"Time for you boys to leave," I said to Albert Carpacci. He hadn't moved. "You know how to get hold of me. And this guy doesn't know you guys from the Dodgers, so leave him out of it."

The fat man tipped his head; his eyes wrote my obituary: You fucked with the wrong guys, too many times. Big Mike threw Alfredo toward the exit, he sprawled, caught his balance, banged his face on the door. "You're dead, Carson!" he screamed as he got up and wiped a jacket sleeve over his mouth. "You are so fucking dead!"

"Recurring theme," I said.

Big Mike's friends laughed as Alfredo jerked open the door and ran outside. The old man followed him, backed out the door, never took his eyes off of me.

I ran to the back room, grabbed the sawed-off shotgun from behind Harry's office door, ran back to the front door just in time to see them pull away. Alfredo screamed at me from the back seat.

I turned to Big Mike. "Thanks, Big Mike, but that wasn't too smart."

He offered an impish grin as he threw an arm around me, grabbed a bottle of beer off the bar. "Brother," he said, "after Normandy, you think I'm gonna let some dirty hoods tangle with my friend? You've had three good eyes all afternoon—two of mine and one of yours."

"Those aren't the kind of men you tangle with. They come for you when you sleep."

"Then you sure don't have anything to worry about. Doesn't look like you've slept since Moses passed gas."

He was right. I sat on a barstool, pushed the shotgun and .45 across the bar to Frank. Big Mike sat down next to me. "What's going on, Gus?"

"Work problem."

"Then you're in the wrong line of work."

"People keep telling me that," I said. Ernie came out from the kitchen, set a brown paper bag full of sandwiches on the bar, handed me a thermos full of coffee. I handed him a quarter, paid Frank for the sandwiches.

"That shiner part of your work problem?" asked Big Mike.

"Guess you could say that. Thanks for watching my back."

"Not a problem."

I stood up, grabbed the paper bag and thermos, shook Big Mike's hand. "Watch yourself, big fella," I said. "The dumber they are, the quicker the temper."

He nodded. "I'll keep that in mind. You be careful, now, Gus. You ever want a construction job, let me know. It's a lot less dangerous than what you're doing."

He was right, I thought, as I left the bar. I felt like an ironworker, perched at the top of a tall building, leaning out on an I beam. And everyone wanted to push me off.

I NEARLY FORGOT ABOUT SHEILA—pulled over and grabbed a pay phone. She answered on the first ring, I glanced at my watch and saw that it was five thirty on the nose. She spoke in a whisper. "Gus?"

"Yeah, what did you find out?"

"Nothing. Mother didn't remember anything about him."

"Baloney. The new gardener says your mother watches that garden like men watch her. She's lying."

"Please. That's my mother you're talking about."

"I realize that. What did she say, exactly?"

"Well, she got really quiet, then asked me why I wanted to know. I told her that you'd been talking to the new gardener and had just asked a simple question. She said there was a simple answer—she didn't remember the man's name or know anything about him."

"What else?" I asked.

"I didn't push it. It was all so queer. If I would've pushed it, I don't know what I'd have said if she asked me why I kept on about it."

"Well, you tried. I appreciate it."

"What's going on?"

"I wish I knew. Forget about it. Don't bring it up again."

"Don't worry. I won't," she said.

"Thanks anyway."

The volume grew in her voice. "When am I going to see you again?"

"Soon. My assignment's done this weekend. I'll have more time then."

"Well, don't forget about the party, Friday night."

"I doubt if I can make it. This is supposed to go on through Saturday."

I could picture the pout: "Well, I can certainly see where your priorities lie. Try to get out of it, Gus. It won't be any fun unless you're there."

I told her I'd try to make it. I hung up the phone, jumped back in my car just in time to hear Tom Mix start on the radio—5:45 p.m. sharp. I listened to the cowboy show, thought about Sheila's statement—"I can certainly see where your priorities lie"—a lie all right, but from her or her mother. A strong invitation to the party—an easy place to gauge me. Offered up by Sheila with the scent of Virginia. Hard to resist.

I drove toward Bronzeville, tried to see through the lies.

## '46, Chicago

I BARELY SAW MCGUIRE'S TAILLIGHTS DISAPPEAR as I pulled in front of Martha Lewis's house, and I was only there a few minutes before I decided to go inside. I knocked on the door as the evening sky started to drop a shade. Her mother answered and shook her head when she saw me.

"You's the type keeps putting your hand on a hot stove, ain't ya?"

I saw Martha in the background, holding her daughter. "I just want to talk with your daughter for a while, if that's all right with her."

Martha's voice popped up in the background. "Fine, Mama."

Her mother stepped out of the way and ushered me inside. "At least take off that mask before you see the child," she said, chuckling.

Martha sat on the couch, stroking her daughter's hair. She wore a beige skirt, white cotton blouse and beige jacket. I saw stains splattered across the bottom of the blouse and guessed that was the outfit she wore to work. Her mother wandered back toward the kitchen. A moment later, she peeked out, a mixing bowl in her arms. She pushed a spoon around in the bowl, watched me like a guard dog at the impound yard.

"Hello, Officer," said Martha.

I waved a hand. "Just Gus. How was your day?"

"Obviously better than yours," she said. "What happened to your eye?"

"I was in Lake Forest today, kept feeling a pain in my eye whenever I drank my tea. Finally I took the spoon out of my cup before I blinded myself."

"Very funny. Were you really in Lake Forest today?"

"Yep. Small world. I saw your car in front of the Saunders's house."

She dropped her gaze, caressed her daughter's cheek. "That is a coincidence. What were you doing out there?"

"Visiting. Not really my neck of the woods. How did you get a job out there?"

"Referral. They pay better in Lake Forest. What really happened to your eye?"

"Poked it in the wrong place, got poked, no big deal. So who was your referral?"

She balanced the infant on her knee, bobbed her up and down. The child's head fell gently to and fro; a smile crept over her face. Her big brown eyes glistened, and each time she dropped, she made soft sounds as the air escaped her lungs. "Why are you so interested?"

"Because things aren't making sense. Before I was asked to watch you, I killed a man after he committed two cold-blooded murders. There was no sense behind what he did, and now too many coincidences are popping up. I think he worked as a gardener for a family out in Lake Forest and today I saw you at a house next door to one of their friends. Something's not right. Who was your referral?"

"Mrs. Saunders recommended me to the Franks, if that's what you mean. But I clean for a lot of people. The Blanchards use me half of the day, but I spend a couple of afternoons a week at the Franks' and the Saunders', and I work at other homes on the weekends. I don't know any of the gardeners. Why don't you tell me what's going on?"

Against all the rules, common sense. I needed to work it out, and telling someone might help. I'd started to believe that Ed Jones would never turn up—he might not even exist. I started to take my jacket off, looked at her for approval. She nodded. I stood up, slid the jacket off. I saw her mother set a glass pan on the kitchen counter, pull out a long match and strike it. I cringed as she bent over to light the oven. The flame caught. I breathed a sigh of relief—I hated gas stoves. "See, I was at this joint on Friday night. I heard a couple of gunshots, went out in the hall and saw this colored guy making for the stairs. He fired at me, so I had to shoot him. I went down the hall and found a man and a woman dead. The woman worked there. The man was an attorney. The department's calling it robbery, but that's a load of bull. Nothing was taken. I think the colored guy was this gardener. What I don't get was, why would a gardener kill this attorney?"

"What's that got to do with me?"

"It's like I said: The gardener worked in Lake Forest and so do you. You work for the same group of people. So a guy hires me to watch you on account of this Jones getting kidnapped and his feeling that Jones might come here. So there's a connection between you and Jones and this gardener and attorney...and it's me. I kill the gardener, I watch you. Do you see where I'm going with this?"

"No."

"Hell, I don't either, and that's what's bugging me."

"Who's the man that hired you?" she asked.

"I'd better not say."

"That scares me. Why would someone think of me?"

"He thinks you're Jones's girlfriend, thinks he'd run here."

"Do you think that?"

"I don't know."

She lifted her daughter off her knee, crawled to the floor. "I've got to work with Grace, Officer. Do you have anything else?"

I did. I didn't. I wanted to stay. "I'd like to talk to you some more. I don't mind if you don't. I can help."

"No, thank you. I can manage. It's important for her to work every night. What else do you want to know?"

She stood on her knees, lifted her daughter in front of her so that she mimicked a standing position. She held her around the chest, under her arms and tried to turn her slowly so that a leg would swing out and mimic a walking movement. I got down on my knees next to her and reached for the child. "Let's do it like this," I said as I pulled the child toward me. "I'll hold like this and you lift her legs, one at a time, like she's walking."

Mild surprise colored Martha's gaze as she looked into my eyes. She started to say something, stopped and gently grasped one of her daughter's legs. She lifted it, slowly, by the knee. As she pulled the leg forward and the child's foot fell to the carpet, I moved her slightly forward. Soon we were in rhythm and the three of us moved slowly around the room.

"This is gaiting, isn't it?" I asked.

"Yes," she said. "It's like training her how to walk. Hopefully, something, sometime, will click."

"What other stuff do you do for her?"

"Mama reads to her during the day, tries to coax her into talking. The doctor said she'll never talk, but I don't believe that. She already tries. We're also trying to teach her to feed herself. Sometimes she doesn't chew right and food gets caught in her throat. Scares me to death. Mama grabs her and turns her upside down, pats her on the back. It's awful."

"Why don't you help her with her speech? You speak perfectly. And, no offense, but your mother didn't teach you."

"I met with a social worker when I was younger. She pushed me to learn very proper English, to enunciate clearly....My mother works hard with my daughter. I can't do everything."

"Her father help out?"

She stopped, shook her head. "I told you once, that's none of your business. If you're done, you can leave anytime." She scooped the girl into her arms, crawled over to the medicine ball, set the girl on top and began to roll it around.

"Look, I'm sorry. It's my job. Best advice I ever got is also the worst advice I ever got: Be curious."

"Is that why you've been checking into cerebral palsy?"

I felt a cold fist in my stomach. "That's what I mean. I just asked a doctor a few questions."

She looked away from me, put her palms on her daughter's lower back, rolled her around with the ball. Her voice got quiet. "What are you doing here? Why are you showing us so much attention? You could just sit in your car, bide your time until your friend comes back in the morning."

"I don't know. I guess I just don't buy this crap about Ed Jones and I want to get to the bottom of it." I shook my head. "Ever get the feeling that some things in life aren't random, things happen for a reason?"

Her nostrils flared. "No, I don't think things happen for a reason. My daughter doesn't deserve all this. She's going to have to work a hundred times harder than most people. That's not fair. And you know something? My mother didn't deserve it when my father left her, and she sure didn't deserve some of the things she went through with me. And I didn't deserve…"

"What?"

She bit her upper lip. Her eyes went blank. "Nothing."

"Look, I'm not trying to pry. I guess I'm just thinking out loud. I didn't phrase that right. See, I'm not talking about some religious thing here. I'm not saying that God's up there pulling strings or that things are laid out for us or that anybody deserves what happens to 'em. It just feels like somebody's…"

"What?"

"Aah, I don't know."

"Who's somebody?"

"I don't know who I mean. You know, when I was in the war, I…" I stopped.

"Go on."

"No, I probably…I just…"

"What is it?"

"Well, when I was in the war, somebody was always giving orders. Everything that happened, even though there wasn't always a good reason, happened because somebody gave an order. There was no coincidence. Guys are killed because somebody ordered 'em to be at a certain place at a certain time and somebody on the other side ordered their guys to be at that same certain place at that same certain time. And it's not coincidence, because *somebody* knew they'd all be at that same certain place at that same certain time. See, people don't just die in a war, they're killed. And right now..."

"What?"

"Well, it's not just right now. I mean, I'm trying so hard, but it just feels like..."

Her voice was as soft as spring rain. "What?"

I looked at the brown-skinned woman with the bright eyes. I watched her gently roll her daughter on the medicine ball. I looked around the room, wondered how the hell I'd gotten there, wondered what the hell was happening to me. I smelled meatloaf baking in the kitchen, heard her mother hum as she moved about.

I couldn't... "That meatloaf smells good. You know, before the war, seems like everybody ate steak; now they eat meatloaf."

She chuckled. "That's because a one-pound porterhouse steak was twelve ration points and a pound of ground beef was only seven. Don't try to change subjects on me, Officer. What were you going to say?"

"Nothing," I said.

"Now who's holding out," she said. "You want me to open up, but you can't do it yourself."

I threw up a weak smile. I was so tired. My train of thought derailed. My grip on the balloon slipped. It leaked out. "Before I joined the Marines, I was a pretty bad guy. I never knew my father, and my mom killed herself when I was a kid. She'd had it pretty bad, but I'll never know why she did it—just jumped into the Chicago River and didn't come up until she floated up."

"That's horrible."

"Yeah. Then this cop and his wife took me in. She died a few years later and it was just me and him. He was never meant to be any kind of father; I'm sure it was his wife's idea to bring me home. But he taught me. He taught me everything I'd ever need to know about graft and corruption, torture, brutality, hate. The guy taught me that we're all out for ourselves and that you'd better take it from the other guy before he takes it from you. He ended up in prison and I ended up in the Marines. And you know what? I found something out. I found out he was wrong."

"Of course he was. He sounds like a horrible man."

"He was, is, in a way. But in his own way he always looked after me. I'd rather die than end up like him, but I kind of owe him something."

"What happened in the war that changed your mind?"

"Things. You know, the last thing I had to do was bring this prisoner back to the States for trial. We were in the bowels of this ship and I never told any of the rest of the crew what he'd done. They figured it wasn't that bad, I guess, 'cause they brought both of us food every day. They looked after us just like we were shipmates. And then, well, I ended up seeing things that change a man forever."

"What things?"

She cradled her daughter in her arms, walked over to the couch and sat down. She looked at me, kept looking at me as I fell silent. I moved to the other side of the room, sat on the floor, pulled my legs up in front of me and wrapped my arms around my knees. I didn't...hold back. I told her everything.

I TALKED FOR HOURS. I didn't stop when her mother came into the room, plucked Grace from her mother's arms, put the child to bed. I didn't stop when Martha took out the blanket and the pillow, set them on the couch for me to use. I didn't stop until she went to bed at nearly midnight. Exhaustion, relief, cradled me in their arms: I drifted to sleep in seconds flat.

## THURSDAY, MAY 16

M ARTHA SHOOK ME AWAKE just before six. She was already dressed for work, coffee boiled on the stove. She handed me a cup.

"Better drink up fast. Your partner's going to be here shortly."

"Not my... never mind. Sorry I got so mushy last night."

"You went through a lot. Sometimes you've just got to get stuff off your chest."

"Anyway, I appreciate the ear. Listen, I'll talk to my employer today, tell him I think this is a waste of time, get us off your back."

She smiled, thanked me. I drained the cup, stood up, ran a hand through my hair and grabbed my jacket. She walked with me to my car, started back for her house, turned and came back to the car. I rolled down the window. "What's up?"

"You know, you can tell your employer that Ed Jones isn't going to come here," she said.

"You seem pretty sure."

"I am. I know he'll never come here."

"Why's that?"

"Because," she said, "I've never met the man."

My head spun. "Whatta ya mean?" I asked, loud.

"That was just something we made up to keep people from bothering us. I've never even met Ed Jones."

She walked back inside as I started up the engine, fought confusion. I moved forward, pulled a U-turn and saw McGuire sitting in his car. His glare testified: He'd seen me leave the girl's house, talk with her. He knew I'd made contact. Hypoole would know soon. I might've blown five hundred dollars.

I KNEW MCGUIRE WOULD RACE TO A PHONE like a kid ratting out his older brother. I decided to take Hypoole head on. I drove to his house so I could look him in the eye.

I laughed out loud as I knocked on the front door. I don't know why I hadn't noticed it before, but a flyer for a World War II Liberty Loan War Bond was still plastered in the front-room window. I looked up to see if his Christmas lights were still up, when the front door opened. Six thirty in the morning, and Arvis Hypoole answered the door himself, a frail old man in a checkered flannel bathrobe tied tight at the waist. He seemed surprised to see me, beckoned me inside.

"My land, Gus, what happened to your eye?" he asked as he led me to the breakfast nook, offered me a seat at a table. He sat down opposite, me; the sun peeked in, must've bothered his eyes. He let the blinds fall, returned the room to its preferred state: lit like a cave.

"Accident. I just came by to see if you had anything to talk to me about," I said.

"Me, no, should I?" His question seemed legit; either McGuire hadn't called or Hypoole could bluff his way into the next DeMille movie.

"Guess not," I said. "I just figured you'd be itching for info."

"Of course I am. Anything to report?"

"Not really. No sign of Jones. I talked to Hogan yesterday. The family says they've heard zippo from the kidnappers. No way of telling whether that's true or not. But we're making progress."

"How so?"

"Truth is, I'm rattling those cans I told you about. Yesterday I got snagged by Lincoln Johnson. He's another Negro policy guy. One of his guys got it and he thought it was me. It got pretty bad. That's where this eye came from, and *I* got the best of it. Then, yesterday afternoon, I ran into some of the Syndicate's boys. Remember the Carpacci guy I told you about?"

"The jukebox man?"

"Yeah. I met him and his sons yesterday, laid it on the line. They'll squeal to Giancana and Accardo today. They'll probably contact me, or they just might pay me a little visit. The bad thing is, the only thing I've got to barter with is threats. I told 'em I'd put an APB out on Momo, keep hassling them. These guys eat threats like garlic—doesn't really mean a whole hell of a lot."

"Suppose we offer to pay some kind of ransom?"

"His brother's got a pile of money, too. If they haven't asked for a ransom yet, they probably won't. My bet is that either Jones is already dead or they've contacted the family and the family has decided to keep the cops out. Neither one would surprise me."

"Then what do you suggest we do?" he asked.

"We've still got a couple more days left. I'll talk to the attorney again. He must've felt some pressure; he called Carpacci and told him I'd been by. I'm also gonna contact this Lincoln Johnson. I'll let him know that if he helps us find Jones, the courts'll go easy on him."

"How will you contact him?"

"His sister's some kind of spiritualist just off Wentworth Avenue. You know, she reads palms, fortunes, probably a crystal friggin' ball."

"Do you think he'll play along?"

"No. I'm going by there just the same. Frankly, Mr. Hypoole, I'm beginning to think this whole thing is one big dead end."

"Well, keep plugging," said Hypoole. "You've only got two more days."

"So what if I don't find the guy? What if it's just a wild goose chase, what then?"

"Chief Hogan will still go to bat for you. He's assured me of that. And then there's this." He pulled a clean, crisp Ben Franklin from his robe pocket. "I saw you drive up, figured you might be spread a little thin. This is a one-hundred-dollar advance against the thousand that I'll pay you if you find Jones. If you don't, keep it anyway."

"Our deal was five hundred. Why'd you decide to up it?"

"Looking at your face, it's been a bit more difficult than I'd imagined. You might try a little of the same with the attorney." His voice drifted off, suggestion powerful on his breath. "And I agreed with your earlier warning; I haven't told anyone you're working for me. I'd appreciate it if you'd keep quiet about it, too."

"Sure," I said. "I haven't told anyone and I won't."

Hypoole stood up. "Gus, you've been up all night, but I'd like to hear about this in more detail. Can you spare me another twenty minutes or so?"

"Sure."

"Then how about a cup of coffee?"

"Fine," I said.

"Black okay?" he asked as he left the room.

"Sure," I yelled after him.

He came back moments later with two steaming cups of coffee, set them on the table, went back into the kitchen and returned with a crystal pitcher filled with orange juice and two glasses. He set one of the glasses in front of me and filled it with orange juice. "Go ahead, try it," he said. He urged me on like he was selling a bottle of homemade cure-all.

"What gives?" I asked.

"You're about to taste progress."

I sipped some of the juice. "It's good," I said.

"Yes," he said, obviously impressed. "And it was also frozen, made from concentrated orange juice. Now, all you have to do is just add water. It just came on the market. I think it's going to make some people a lot of money."

"Wow," I said. "What'll they think of next?"

He shrugged. "Hopefully some kind of substitute for cream," he said. "A young man like you doesn't have to worry about stomach trouble, but people like me wouldn't mind something else to soften the blow of that morning coffee."

His statement caught me like the sound a guitar string makes when it breaks, but I didn't know why. A few good hours of hard sleep, but I was still half out of it. I'd be half out of it for at least two more days. I'd be half out of it until I could lock the door to my apartment, caulk it shut, plug my ears with cotton, smash all the lightbulbs and sleep for a week.

Hypoole leaned back into his chair, surveyed his glass of juice, finished drinking it. "Lost in thought?"

"Just lost," I said.

"Things seem complicated?"

"Kind of. Just a lot of things that don't make sense on a lot of fronts."

"This case?"

"No. That's pretty straightforward—nothing going on. Personal stuff."

"Have to do with your lady friend?" he asked.

"Told you the other day, I'm just sampling the goods."

"Yes, I'd forgotten. What is it then?"

I thought about telling him that I'd talked to Martha Lewis, suggest we drop the surveillance. Something still nagged me; I filed it away, played it cool. "Nothing. Back to the case. What do you want to know?"

He wanted to know everything. He quizzed me for an hour, asked me for details. I was surprised he didn't take notes. He wanted names, times...He was fascinated by my story of the warehouse, puzzled by my talk with the Carpaccis. He'd probably rarely seen a jukebox, didn't realize the money the racket made. He'd probably never been in a real bar—people like Big Mike were characters in a movie to him. He probably didn't know what it was like to struggle to pay the bills, put food on the table. He probably didn't understand why people would tear the last pennies from their pockets to play a game called policy.

I tried to tell him. I told him everything. I told him nothing.

IT WAS NINE O'CLOCK IN THE MORNING when I finally got home. I figured I'd grab a couple more hours of sleep—I figured wrong. The Williams kids were playing in the hall. The boys shot marbles on the landing; the girls played with their dolls on the stairs. I could smell the boiling diapers and knew Mrs. Williams had shooed the kids into the hall while she cleaned. At least the kids were quiet—like a jazz band playing their last gig at the Chez Paree. I'd get as much sleep as a smecker cold-turkeying junk.

I boiled more coffee while I sat down in my easy chair and breezed through the newspaper I'd picked up on my drive home. Japan won most of the space on the front page—former President Hoover warned that we'd better send six hundred thousand tons of food or occupation forces would be endangered by civil unrest. I figured Albert Carpacci could cover most of that by skipping a snack. Good news for cold feet: Japanese silk was coming in, so silk stockings were going back on the market, to the tune of two dollars and fifty cents a pair. My toes sighed.

I read the latest excerpt of "The Laughing Detective," skimmed the comics and sports. A dozen fights were listed in the "Fight Decisions" column—par for a Wednesday night. Out of habit, I checked to see if there were any good fights at the Marigold Garden on Friday night. There were plenty, and there was also an ad for the Frank Sinatra show at the Chicago Theater. That reminded me of girls, and girls reminded me of Sheila, and that reminded me of the Prescotts' party—a party I'd have to miss if I couldn't find Ed Jones. I was about to fill a cup with java when the phone rang.

"Carson."

I recognized the heavy breathing before I even heard the voice. "Want to know where you can find the shine?" asked Sam.

"Like you want that pardon."

"Then listen up, be at this phone tonight, say eight o'clock. I should have some information for you."

I thought about Martha: If I didn't show at six, McGuire would know something was up. "No good, how 'bout five?"

"I ain't your prom date. Seven's the earliest I can do. I gotta lay out some favors for this."

"What's it cost me?"

"Pasqua."

"No deal."

"Motherfucker."

"You could be talking 'bout your wife there."

"Fuck you. Pasqua or no deal."

"Can't do it. Why do you think you can find out something in there that I can't find out here?"

"'Cause you changed. Me and you had this case, you would've beat it outta somebody days ago. I've got somebody on it."

"Care to let me in?" I asked.

"Tonight. Whatta ya say? Pasqua?"

"No. Something else."

There was a pause on the line. I knew Sam was trying to stop from beating the phone against the wall. I could hear metal doors clang shut in the background, a voice come over a bullhorn yelling for lockdown. I pushed him, gently: "You shouldn't worry about Pasqua. You got that pardon coming, remember?"

"Only thing's for sure in this world is that we're all maggot meal. Just think about it. Be at your Goddamned phone at seven." He hung up.

I hung up, glanced at my watch—nearly ten. A lot to do before six; I changed clothes, threw on a pair of khakis, a tan cotton shirt and a shoulder holster. I grabbed my .38 and a brown leather bombardier's jacket and hit the road. Twenty minutes later I turned off Wentworth Avenue and looked for 230 West 47th.

I found the address, parked my car and looked at the building for a moment before I got out. It was a two-story jobber and Madame Gail's Religious House took up the ground floor. Madame Gail had her name painted on the storefront window in letters two feet high, and I assumed it was her that stared at me through the word "Spiritualist." She wore a hard scowl along with her black dress, and judging from the height of the sign, she couldn't have stood more than five feet tall.

I ignored the scowl as I walked toward the building, opened the door and stepped inside. A bell rang. "Madame Gail?" I asked.

The room was filled with candles, and incense burned strong enough to knock out the foulest cigar smoke. Pictures of Christ covered the walls, each with a red price tag taped to the bottom right-hand corner, and Jesus figurines stood throughout the room like toy soldiers invading the store. The short, angry woman stepped from in front of the window. She wore all black, and it accentuated her hourglass figure; unfortunately for her, it was only the bottom half of the hourglass. She motioned me toward the back room.

"I'm Madame Gail. I've been expecting you." Her voice was high, shrill and loud, the kind of voice that came from a woman who figured louder was better: Volume controlled belief. She threw back a black curtain and stepped across the hardwood floor into the back room. I followed.

The back room was a stockroom: It looked like a Jesus convention—
various figurines stood on the shelves. Jesus came in brown or white,
two inches to two feet high, arms open or folded across his lap. I figured
if I looked hard enough, I'd find Jesus dressed in a cop's uniform—a
perfect gift for Sam.

"See me in your crystal ball?" I asked.

"No. I don't tolerate heathen worship. You are Officer Carson, aren't
you?"

"Yeah."

"My brother said you might be stopping by." She sat down at a card table,
offered me a folding chair. I unfolded it and sat across from her. She lowered
her eyes, picked up a small box off the floor and pulled out a handful of
blank price tags. She started to talk again, used a pencil to write prices on
the tags. There didn't seem to be any rhyme or reason to the numbers she
wrote—Jesus would sell anywhere from five cents to five dollars.

"My brother has a message for you," she said.

"I've got one for him, too."

"He says he's sorry," she said. "He's forgotten the incident and he
hopes you have."

"Not likely," I said. "And if they weren't dead, his friends wouldn't
forget it either."

"No one died."

My heart leaped. "No one?"

"That's what I said. One of 'em got his neck cut, won't talk again, but
he probably deserved it."

"I'll bet he'd have something to say about that."

She slid her chair across the floor, picked up a box, slid back to the
table. She reached into the box and picked up a handful of Jesus figurines, started looping price tags around their necks. "Bound to happen.
Lord says it's gonna happen, it's gonna happen. It's all written for us."

"Then what's written for me?"

"You'll just have to wait and see," she said. "Lord works in strange and mysterious ways."

"So does your brother. He tell you what happened?"

She looked up. "He tells me everything and he tells me nothin'. Only voice I listen to is the Lord's."

"Then ask the Lord why your brother sent an apology. First he tried to kill me, now he wants to apologize."

She shrugged. "Lord says men make mistakes. Forgive and forget."

I didn't buy it. "No can do. Why the apology?"

"He was wrong about you. You didn't have nothing to do with Busy Jackson."

"The Lord tell him that?"

She spread her arms wide, like she was gesturing at a congregation. "It's in His hands now."

"Then somebody's getting fingerprinted, and since I don't have a direct line to the Lord, it's gonna be your brother."

She picked apart tag strings, looked up at me. "Just let it be. They didn't mean you no harm."

"No harm my ass."

"Watch your language in here. This is a house of the Lord."

"A for-profit house. Talk or I'll have your brother pulled in and I'll send a squad car over here, tell 'em you're running numbers out of Jesus' back room."

She shook a finger at me like she was trying to get something off the end of it. "You're a heathen! Jesus don't tolerate gambling!"

"Stow it. Tell me about your brother."

"I told you, he said forget it."

"I'm not forgetting."

She sighed, buried her eyes in the box. "He knows you didn't kill Busy."

"Who did?"

"It's been taken care of."

"Gonna have to sell a lot of candles to bail your brother out of jail."

She lifted her gaze out of the box, glared at me. "Don't you threaten me. God has a way of dealing with people like you."

"He's already dealt with me, sister. Now, you tell me who killed Busy Jackson or I'll start dealing with you."

She paused, set a handful of price tags on the table. "Roleen."

"What?"

"She found out Busy cheated her, went after him with a rolling pin. Hear she nearly knocked his head off."

"I'll be a son of a bitch."

"Watch yo language!" she yelled, but the bite was gone from her bark.

"Can it, sister. What'd they do with her?"

"Put her on a train to Wisconsin."

"Didn't want the law to take care of it, eh?"

"I don't know nothin' 'bout that. All I know is what I was told and I just told you. Now why don't you get on outta here with all your heathen talk."

I stood up. "Awful cranky, aren't you?"

"I'm just tired of you white folk hasslin' me. That damn brother of mine's gonna have to stop using me like a answering service. The sum bitch."

"Watch your language; the owner gets offended easily."

"Screw you."

I fished. "What do you mean about using you like an answering service?"

"He told me you might come by and then some old white man called here, asking where he could find him."

"When was this?"

"About an hour ago."

"What did he sound like?"

She squinted at me, barked. "What'd I just say? He sounded like some old white man. Sounded like he had something caught in his throat."

"What did you tell him?"

She slid her chair back from the table, put her forearms on the table and struggled to her feet. "Told him the same thing I'm fixing to tell you. I ain't no answering service no more, so leave me alone."

"You didn't tell him where he could find your brother?"

"Hell no. He coulda been the police."

I stepped back, halfway through the curtains, fished a nickel out of my pocket, threw it on the table.

"What's that for?" she asked.

"Buy yourself a bar of soap," I said as I parted the curtain. "You've got a filthy fucking mouth."


THE SUN PEEKED OUT FROM BEHIND THE CLOUDS like a firefly sticking his ass out of a can of gray paint. May in Chicago: Winter flirted with summer, but they never screwed. I drove north of the Loop, parked near the lake, walked south: I needed the time to stretch my legs and sort out the mess.

South down Michigan Avenue, I crossed the bridge over the Chicago River, walked across the esplanade, cut over toward State Street.

Playback: Bunny to Busy Jackson to Lincoln Johnson. Johnson says the Italians. Johnson's right. No doubt in my mind that the Italians had Jones: He was either dead, buried or would be released to the tune of a shitload of cash.

Busy Jackson's dead: Dishonesty wasn't the best policy. His boss tried to take me out—revenge for Busy. Wrong guy, wrong time. I had one good eye on him.

The gardener, dead, buried, filed. Filed wrong: I'd killed the socialites' gardener, watched over their maid. The only connections between the two cases: the Cordell brothers and me. Now Arvis Hypoole was checking up on me. Hypoole, the Cordells, something bothered me, but I couldn't put my finger on it.

Connections, connections, what were the connections? Arvis Hypoole: mayoral candidate; Ed Jones, policy racketeer, Good Samaritan. The connection was bullshit: Someone leaked it to Arvis Hypoole—but the maid didn't know Ed Jones, she'd lied about it. Questions: Who did she tell, who told Hypoole? Why did she lie? Why would the gardener kill Don Cordell?

The connections ran together as I walked south down Wabash, underneath the elevated train. The train screeched and clanged above me, I pitied anyone who had to listen to it all day. I found Cordell's office building, went inside and stepped into the elevator. The elevator operator looked at me funny. "What floor?" he asked.

"Attorney named Cordell."

"That would be nine," he said as he closed the gate, latched it shut and started the lift. I stepped to the back of the car and he sat on a stool. We stared at each other for a moment. He was a tiny man, and his uniform consisted of a dark jacket with yellow cuffs and a yellow collar, tan slacks and a black bow tie. He returned my gaze, worked on a piece of gum.

"How 'bout those Cubs?" I asked.

He continued chewing the gum. "How 'bout 'em. They stink like yesterday's stool."

"They're not that bad."

"Not bad? Hell, the Red Sox just had a streak of fifteen wins in a row, 'til the Yankees clipped 'em. Know what? That's practically more wins than the Cubs have all year."

"Still early."

"Yeah, I guess you're right. I'm still burned about last year." He held his right hand in the air, thumb and forefinger extended—half an inch apart. "That close to a World Series title. That close. Never know when you'll get that close again."

"You said it, brother," I said as he stopped the car on the ninth floor, maneuvered the car up and down until we were flush with the floor and he let me out. "See you in a few."

"In a few," he said as he closed the door.

I looked up and down the hallway. A dull paint and dull carpet set the tone for the nondescript building. I walked toward one end, saw names printed on the office doors—enough Esquires, Attorneys at Law, and firms with three names to make me want to gag. I found an office marked "Cordell and Cordell" and stepped inside.

A cute brunette sat behind a counter and played receptionist—her tight red sweater must've been her resumé. She looked up from her typewriter as I entered, frowned and asked if she could help me. The frown was a shame: I'd have liked to see her smile.

"Yeah," I said. "I need to see Burt Cordell."

"Is he expecting you?" she said. She gave me a skeptical once-over.

"No, he's not," I said. "But tell him it's Carson from the firm of Carpacci, Johnson and Jackson."

She stood up. "Oh, yes, Mr. Carson, right away." She scampered off, came back a moment later. She shook her head. "Very funny," she said as she sat back down, returned to her typing. "He'll be with you when he can."

"And when will that be?"

"Whenever. He said if you can't wait, you can leave."

I smiled, opened the door and stepped inside. The receptionist leaped up, yelled at me: "Hey, you can't go in there."

I ignored her, followed the sound of Cordell's voice down the hall to the last office and stepped inside. The receptionist followed me inside, shaking. "He just barged on in, Mr. Cordell."

Burt Cordell sat at his desk. He hung up the telephone, fixed his bloodshot eyes on me. His desk was covered with papers—no picture of the family. No plaques or citations hung from the white walls, and no trophies or pictures sat on the credenza. It was the office of a man who didn't want attention.

Cordell waved his hand at the receptionist. "Beat it, Margaret, nothing you could do."

I sat down in one of the two brown leather chairs in front of his desk, leaned back, crossed my legs. Cordell bit his upper lip, snarled: "You're a regular fucking comedian, aren't you?"

"Cut to the chase. I saw your clients yesterday."

"I know. You didn't make any friends. The boys want to dump you."

"So what? I'll tell you the same thing I told the old man: I want Ed Jones."

He rubbed his red eyes. "And I'll tell you the same thing they told you: They don't know Jones and don't have anything to do with him."

"What about Momo?"

"What about him? Listen, Carson, I did some more checking on you. You ain't got a friend on the force and you're going around making threats? That's not smart. You're not being a bright boy. We've got more friends on the force than you do."

"So you got a few friends." I shrugged. "That's not gonna stop me from screwing with the numbers racket. I'll tell you what I told your clients: I just want Jones. I get Jones, I'll leave you boys alone. Simple as that. Now where is he?"

He curled his thick lips, leaned back in his chair. "I've got nothing for you, Carson. You can't get anything from me because I don't know anything. I already told you my theory on the Negro."

"Then why did you go running to your clients? What spooked you?"

"Someone starts talking about my clients, they want to know about it."

"Giancana your client? Accardo?"

His eyes narrowed. "Time to time."

"And did you tell them anything about me?"

"Attorney–client privilege."

"Bullshit. I *want* you to tell them about me."

"You are one crazy fuck, Carson. Why don't you leave this to the *real* cops, the FBI?"

"Money talks."

"Who're you working for?"

I smirked. "Cop–client privilege."

"Then I can't help you."

"Sure you can. And someday, maybe I can help you. See, if my client gets Ed Jones, there may be a shake-up in city hall. That happens, there'll be favors to be doled out."

He snickered. "We've got plenty of Chinamen downtown, Carson, so that doesn't help. Besides, that's an old trick in Chicago."

"What do you mean?" I asked.

"Trying to push policy into politics. Cermak took over, he closed down all the games, told 'em that if they didn't start paying, they'd stay closed. Democrats built up a nice little machine with the money from policy, the slots…"

He kept on talking, but bells went off in my head. Everybody knew Mayor Kelly stood waist-high in shit—pinning it to him it was the Republicans' best shot at winning the mayoral race. The Italians weren't the only ones that wanted policy—so did Hypoole. He needed it. He'd throw his list—the "twenty-seven martyrs" to the press, take all the accolades, while Kelly raced to smash the wheels. Then he'd cir-culate word through the Negro community that if the Republicans took office, it was business as usual—the rackets would reopen. That's why he'd quizzed me like a game-show contestant, called Lincoln Johnson's sister. Hell, that was probably why he wanted Ed Jones—not to parade him in front of the Grand Jury, but to gain his cooperation. I felt the pressure inside my head release like a blown tire; I'd figured it out.

His voice trailed off, "You think I rep tough guys? You shoulda seen the guys our old man repped. Nothing tougher than a crooked pol."

I snatched him off memory lane: "Who killed your brother?"

"What?"

"Who killed your brother? You know."

"You think if I knew who killed my brother, I'd let them get away with it?" He slapped the desk, hard. His voice rose. "You know my clients— you think *they* would let anyone get away with it? You're something else, Carson. You're really something else."

"Save it," I said. "You know, we sat in that diner, that waitress mistook you for your brother. Ever think about the reverse of that? What if the guy that killed him thought he was you?"

A non-strategic pause: "Th...that's bunk. The man that killed my brother was a petty thief. The motive was robbery. He didn't know him."

"Speaking of bunk...You know as well as I do it's ridiculous to think that a man would follow your brother into a brothel to rob him. Let's say he was following him, he'd either get him before he went in or wait outside. He sure as hell wouldn't go inside to do the job. No, the man who killed your brother had a reason, and the reason he botched it up is because he was the wrong man for the job—an amateur, probably hired by amateurs."

"You're delusional."

"Am I? Guy in your brother's shoes makes a mistake with a client, they fix it fast and they fix it clean. This was far from clean...so far it was stupid. Only two things motivate like that, and that's hate and money, and I don't buy hate. You told me you and your brother didn't deal with Negroes, well, I'll buy that, so that just leaves money, but who and why? What have the two of you been working on?"

He rose from his desk, tucked his shirt back into his pants. Sweat stains grew so far under his arms they nearly reached his belt. "This has gone far enough," he said. "First you bother me about my clients, and now you dredge up my brother's murder. I'm walking out this door, Carson. I'm walking out this door, grabbing a cab and going over to the Wabash Station to have a nice chat with Captain Griffin."

"Give him my regards," I said as he slipped into a topcoat. I glared at him, fought the urge. A few shots to the kidneys, force a knuckle sandwich down his throat and he'd talk. The old Gus would've finished it all right there: I sat on my hands to keep from jumping him.

He walked out the door, I stood up, followed him. We passed by the receptionist. "I'll be back in an hour," he said.

I grinned at her. "Want me to wait for you after work?"

"I never..." she said.

"Keep that frown on your kisser and you never will," I said as I followed Cordell out the door.

We walked down the hall, stopped in front of the elevator. Cordell hit the call button and we waited. "You know something, Cordell, and you're not doing anything about it. Your conscience bill you by the hour?"

He stared straight ahead. "The only thing I know is that you just turned your suspension into a retirement plan with no benefits."

"Who queered the investigation into your brother's murder, Cordell? Was it you?"

"I don't know what you're talking about."

"Sure you do," I said. "Two flunkeys were put on the case, and one took vacation right away. Nothing happened. Even a lawyer deserves better than that."

His face went from red to purple. The elevator door opened, and the operator straightened when he saw the look on Cordell's face. I smiled at him as we entered the car. "This guy's a huge Cubs fan," I said. I jerked a thumb at Cordell.

"That so, Mr. Cordell?" asked the operator. "I didn't know that."

"Shut up and get this thing down," said Cordell. He dug his hands into his pockets, stared straight ahead. The operator's face went flush—he bit his lower lip like it was made of granite.

"Yeah, a huge Cubs fan," I said. "I'll bet he and his brother bet on the games, loser had to buy lunch." The operator stared at me like a foreigner witnessing his first Halloween. "His brother just died, you know."

"I...I heard that," said the operator. "I already told Mr. Cordell how sorry I was about that."

"Hear how it happened?" I asked. He shook his head. "Bad meatloaf."

The operator stopped the car on the ground floor, opened the door. Cordell raced out, tripped. "Shit!" he yelled as he lumbered across the lobby.

The operator smiled, closed the door and leveled out the elevator. We'd been four inches below the floor. He grinned: "That true about the meatloaf?"

I didn't answer. I stepped out of the elevator, walked across the lobby, lost in thought. It had dawned on me as I'd ribbed Cordell in the elevator. Only one way to be sure—I stepped outside and walked back to The Kitchen.

I SAW THE HEAVYSET, RED-HAIRED WAITRESS as soon as I entered The Kitchen. I looked at the hostess, pointed at the waitress: "Her table, okay?"

The hostess said, "Sure," and led me to a booth near the back of the restaurant. It was only thirty minutes shy of the noon hour and the place was filled, so I didn't complain when I rested my arms on the table and felt them stick when I shifted. Somebody's ginger ale had turned the table into flypaper.

The waitress finished taking an order at another table and scurried over to my booth. "Can I bring you something to drink?" she asked. Bustling around had turned her heavy cheeks a rosy hue.

"Glass of water with a wash cloth," I said.

"Oh, is the table dirty?" she asked. I nodded. "I'll be right back."

"Thanks, Lou Ann," I said as she walked away. I watched her push the swinging doors and start into the back room, look over her shoulder to see if she knew me. A minute later she came out with a glass of water and a damp cloth.

She wiped the table clean, set down my water. "Do I know you?" she asked.

"You might not remember me, but I'll bet you remember the guy I was here with the other day," I said. "Guy who ribbed you about your killer meatloaf."

"Oh yeah," she said. She put her hands on her hips. "He a friend of yours?"

"Not even slightly."

"Good," she said. "What a jerk. Was he telling the truth about his brother?"

"Yep. Not about the meatloaf. That's what I wanted to ask you about. You remember you mistook him for his brother, said his brother had been in here with another man?"

She nodded. I continued: "Remember anything about the other man, the guy you said couldn't drink his milk?"

"Sure," she said. "Said he was allergic to milk. Some old guy. Sixties, skinny, bald on top."

"Big ears, thick gray eyebrows?"

"Sounds about right."

"They seem like friends?"

"What do you mean?" she asked.

"I mean, did it seem like they had a pleasant conversation?"

"I don't know. The old guy sat through the other guy's second helping of meatloaf, so I guess they were friendly enough."

"Anything else?"

"No. I left them alone. I think they were planning a party or something."

"What makes you say that?" I asked.

"On account of they had a list of names with 'em."

"Whatta ya mean?"

"The one guy, he had a list of names. He had to move it when I brought out their food—just a list of names, like you make when you're having a party."

"How many names?"

She shrugged her shoulders. "I brought them their food, I didn't mail out the invitations."

"Roughly."

"Roughly? I don't know, twenty, thirty."

"So the old guy had a list of twenty or thirty names with him?" I shook my head, pondered it.

"No, no, no," said the waitress as she reached behind me, took a pot of coffee off of a table at another booth. "Not the old guy, the one guy. You know, the brother. He was the one with the list."

Another gut punch. "Are you sure?"

She nodded.

"How can you be so certain? Why do you remember 'em so well?"

"I'll tell you why. I'm certain because the one guy must've been kind of like his brother—he rolled up that list and wagged it in the old guy's face. And why do I remember 'em so well? Mister, have you ever tried our meatloaf? Nobody has two helpings."

I ordered it, ate it. She was right.

I THOUGHT ABOUT ARVIS HYPOOLE as I made my way north up Wabash, cut east on Wacker Drive. I figured Hypoole knew Don Cordell; Cordell knew Hypoole was the key to the Republicans. I figured a power-hunger-fueled confrontation at The Kitchen: Cordell had pulled his list of transferees, told Hypoole he was going to expose them, offered the Republicans a chance to get on the inside. Out with the Democrats and the Negroes, in with the Republicans and the Syndicate. The cash would still flow—the Republican administration could offer protection. Hypoole to me, re: his stoolie: "He is unable to offer any more information." His stoolie: Don Cordell, dead.

My bet: Cordell told Hypoole that Ed Jones was going to be kidnapped, his clients were taking over policy. Cordell's follow-up: "Mayor Kelly is going down; we've got a list of cops hard on policy that ended up transferred." Did Hypoole have him killed—for the list? Was that enough? Odds favored no, but the connection was tight. I felt my bad side rise up to interrogate Hypoole. I thought hard as I stepped across Michigan Avenue onto the east sidewalk, started across the bridge.

I ran possible Hypoole/Cordell connections, scenarios, played them out. I figured they knew each other, some way, somehow. But why did Cordell assume Hypoole would cooperate? What did he have on him? Approaching Hypoole seemed like a gamble, and experience told me that mob attorneys didn't gamble. Too few clues, too many bold-faced liars. It was getting close to the time to confront Hypoole, even if it meant losing the thousand dollars. I decided I'd run it past Sam during our call, nearly missed the background noise: Tires squealed, a car jumped a curb. I heard screams, turned and saw the black Packard plow up the sidewalk.

People dove out of the way, the Packard clipped a couple, sent them sprawling onto the sidewalk. The driver gunned the engine—the grill of the car looked like a sneer as it rushed toward me. I sprinted forward, faked a move left. The car turned street-side, came back at me. My options came at me full speed: I sprang, caught the rail with my right foot, brushed it with my left. I heard the car scrape the concrete barrier as I dove into my mother's cold embrace.

THE RIVER TOOK THE BREATH OUT OF ME: I swam hard toward the bank. I came up on the south bank, dragged myself out of the water, ran to Lower Wacker Drive. A man looked out of his fish shack, cackled as I went by: "Ugliest mermaid I've ever seen." I ran across the street, found the staircase. I climbed back up to Michigan Avenue, saw a crowd of people peering over the edge of the bridge: They must not have seen me make it out of the water. I flagged down a hack, climbed in. "Holy Mother of God," he said as I jumped into the back seat, shook like I was filled with an electric current.

I gave him my address, stammered, "St...st...step on it."

He peeled one hand off the steering wheel, shook an arm free of his jacket, repeated the move and tossed it into the back seat. "Put this on, Mac," he said.

I took off my wet bombardier's jacket, pulled his around me, felt warm air fill the cab: He'd cranked the heater for me. "What the hell happened to you?" he asked.

I looked out the window, wondered the same thing. "Guess I just got too close to the rail," I said.

"Right."

He figured right: We were silent the rest of the way. I had him stop two blocks from my place, reached inside my jacket for my wallet and found out I was out of cash. "Wait here and I'll be back in fifteen minutes," I said. "I'll leave you my jacket. I've just got to get into my place and grab some cash."

"Nothing doing," he said. "Ride's on the house."

"You don't need to do that," I said. "I'll just run in, grab some cash and come back."

"Mister," he said as he reached back for his jacket, "I'm no Good Samaritan. Your condition and you don't want me parking in front of your place? I don't want to hang around."

I couldn't blame him. I asked him his name, told him I'd send some cash to the cab station. He shook his head. "Me and you never met," he said as I got out of the cab. He burned rubber as he sped away.

The second day in a row I sneaked up on my own apartment building. I looked out from behind a building across the street, didn't see any black Packard. I slipped between two buildings, jogged across the street and came up the rear alley: no Packard anywhere. I moved around front, jostled the door handle—it was locked. I fished for my keys, thanked God when I found 'em, let myself inside. The door to my unit was locked—another small miracle. I unlocked it, stepped in, locked it behind me and took off my clothes like a stripper backstage.

I turned on the shower and cranked the water hot. I stepped in and let the water nearly scald me—it pooled around my feet, brought feeling back to my toes. I stayed in the shower for nearly ten minutes. When I finally got out, my skin had wrinkled like an old sailor's.

Beaten, nearly run over, drowned—the rats were out in full force. I figured the Carpaccis for the Packard, pictured wide-body Alfredo in the driver's seat. No telling how long it would take them to track me down, I dressed quickly, hit the road—sped north toward Lake Forest.

TRAFFIC WAS FINE, I had plenty of time to get there and back before my seven o'clock call with Sam. It was a gray, windy, fifty degree day, and Lake Michigan lashed like a tub full of water as a fat woman struggled out. The wind pushed against my car—I knew how the car felt. Plenty of progress, but I was still a few bottles short of a case. I still didn't figure the gardener. A few minutes at his home had told me he wouldn't need to be pushed hard—that sort of poverty bred desperation, and there were plenty of candidates ready to play on it.

I turned right, toward the Prescotts', thought better of it and pulled a U-turn. The bridge game would be in full progress, I could use Sheila as an excuse, maybe catch a glimpse of Martha, talk to Gloria Blanchard.

I drove by the Blanchards', circled back. No light-green Plymouths; Martha must've been working somewhere else. I pulled into the Blanchards' driveway, parked, walked up to the front door and knocked. A colored woman answered the door, took my name and left. Minutes later, Gloria Blanchard strode up to the front door. "Gus, how nice," she said. "Come in. Twice in two days—well, it's nice to see your eye is healing."

I stepped inside, noted her blouse and green skirt—women and bridge called for a different dress code than poker and guys. I smiled as she asked me why I was there.

"I knew Sheila was here, figured I'd just say a quick hello. You know, I've been working so much lately that I've barely seen her. You wouldn't refuse a thirsty man a cool drink, now would you?"

"I think that cool drink's losing her shirt," she said. "Let's give her a quick break."

She left the foyer, walked into the living room. Five tables were set up, four women sat at each. Pots of tea and platters of cookies were scattered through the room, and although it was no Sinatra concert shriek, they did ooh and aah when I followed Gloria into the room.

"Gus, what're you doing here?" asked Sheila. She stood up quick—

she had that virgin gambler's anxious look written all over her face. Too loud: "But it's so wonderful to see you."

"In the neighborhood," I said. I looked around the room at the women—gray, white and brown-dyed hair, polished nails, full makeup, bright spring outfits and enough jewelry to start a run on the market. A closer look: more booze in the glasses than tea, more lipstick-stained cigarette butts than a dance hall, society women fighting the shakes and old age. Gloria Blanchard handed me a rum punch, offered me a cookie. I took the punch, turned down the cookie.

"Gus," said Sheila, grabbing my arm and walking between the tables. "Let me introduce you around. This is Margo Baxter."

"How do you do?"

"And this is Gertrude Doolittle."

"Pleased to meet you."

It continued for five minutes. Every time Sheila told me one of the women's names, it printed in my head like a typewriter key slapping a letter on a white page. I got twenty names—a few meant something to me.

"Mrs. Saunders," I said to a gray-haired woman in a floral dress. She fluttered her thick eyelashes as I spoke. "Didn't you recommend the Negro cleaning woman to the Blanchards?"

"Why, yes, I did," she said. "Such a lovely girl."

"And how did you come by her services?" I asked.

A voice shot up from the back of the room. Edna Franks: "That's easy. I introduced her to Beatrice."

"And I introduced her to you."

"And I introduced her to you."

It went around the room quicker than a glad-hander, finally stopped at Margo Baxter. The short, plump woman wore the worst brown dye job I'd ever seen and her eyes drifted. Half a glass of rum punch sat in front of her, scared for its life. "I guess she started with me," said Mrs.

Baxter. She laughed, looked at the other women. They all chuckled. "I guess I talked about her at bridge club and now she's working all over!" She pressed her hand against her chest and looked at Sheila. "Good heavens, if Sheila keeps playing bridge with us, maybe the girl will work for her some day!"

The women laughed heartily. I didn't.

"And how did you meet her?" I asked.

"Oh, well, she worked for friends of my husband."

"And who were they?"

She got quiet, took a slug from her drink. "I'm not sure I remember."

"I remember," said Gloria Blanchard. The room was silent, someone shuffled a deck of cards as the rest of the women looked at their drinks. "You told me she was recommended by Mildred."

"I guess that's right," said Mrs. Baxter. She scooped up her hand of cards, pretended to get lost in them.

I knew the answer, asked anyway: "Mildred?"

"Mildred Hypoole," said Gloria Blanchard.

The women reacted to the name Hypoole like it was coated with castor oil. Their silence told me he'd never get the women's vote.

"She was an original member of our bridge club," continued Mrs. Blanchard.

"Then you must've started this bridge club before forty-two," I said.

A few smiles sprang up, a couple of the women shouted, "Yes," before it dawned on them. Gloria Blanchard spoke for 'em: "How did you know she died in forty-two?"

"I've had some business with her husband."

Gloria Blanchard changed the subject quicker than a phys ed major at a science fair. "I hate to hurry you along, Gus, but we've got a lot of cards to play."

The rest of the women concurred, said good-bye to me and resumed their games. Sheila told the women at the table that she'd walk me out. We left the room and I heard the buzz start before we stepped off the carpet.

"Listen to that," I said as a murmur rose in the background. "It must be spring when you can hear the unmistakable call of the yellow-bellied gossiper."

"Very funny," said Sheila. "If I didn't know better, I'd almost say you came out here just to ask about that maid."

"But you know better."

"Of course. Say, Gus, don't forget Mother's dreadful party tomorrow night. If you can get away, I'd love it if you could make it. You'd turn a horrid evening into a wonderful one." She wrapped her hands behind her back, looked up at me and beamed.

I reached for the door and opened it. The cool air rushed inside. "I'll see what I can do," I said. "Things are changing every minute."

"It'd be wonderful, Gus," said Sheila as she pecked me on the cheek. "Call me."

I told her I'd call her. I fired up my machine, drove back downtown, ignored the signs. I already knew the way—they all pointed to Arvis Hypoole.

I MADE IT TO MARTHA LEWIS'S HOUSE just before six o'clock. Art McGuire sat in his car, stone-faced when I drove by. I parked and got out, walked up to his car as he rolled down his window. "What the fuck were you doing in there yesterday, trying to screw up our deal?"

I rapped my fingers on the roof of his car, leaned down. "You tell Hypoole?"

"I look stupid?" he screamed. "The man's connected in the department and you want to screw this up! I want the damn money and I want the perks. Now, what the fuck were you doing in there?"

I laughed. "I was getting ready to take a leak when her mom came out. They know who we are, that's no secret. She could see what I was up to, told me to use their john. Probably trying to score some points."

He looked out the windshield, back at me. "Huh. You looked awful friendly with the girl."

"Professional courtesy. I just told her we heard she may be in some trouble, were watching the house."

"She buy that malarkey?"

"Would you?"

"Well, don't let it happen again," he said. "This Hypoole's the cat's meow as far as I'm concerned. Him on our side, the sky's the limit."

"Nothing to worry about," I said. He rolled up the window and drove off. I watched him, saw him jerk his head to look in the rearview mirror. I went back to my car, turned on the radio, leaned back in the seat and waited. Twenty minutes later, McGuire drove by, held a thumb and forefinger in an okay sign, turned around and drove off.

I waited another twenty minutes before I went up to the house. Forty minutes before Sam's call, but I needed facts. I knocked on the door, smiled when Martha opened it. "I didn't think you'd be back, Officer." She looked happy to see me, prettier than I remembered.

She opened it wide, I stepped inside. "Appearances. The other guy out there didn't see me tonight, he would've gone straight to my employer."

"And who's that?"

"I think you know exactly who it is."

Her mother walked in, carrying Grace. The infant was excited; bursts of sound escaped from her, her cheeks bunched up, eyes shone. "That's my little Gracey," said the grandmother as she moved the infant up and down. "Who's my little girl? Who's my girl?" She stopped when she saw me. Her smiled turned sour, turned sweet again. "Ain't you had yo fill of us yet?" she asked. She let out a belly laugh and carried the child into the kitchen.

"That is one pretty little girl," I said.

"Thank you," said Martha.

"And your daughter's not bad either."

She laughed. "Mama heard you say that, she'd have you out doing the rumba."

"I don't know a rumba from a foxhole," I said.

She laughed again. "You mean fox trot."

"That either. I'd love to learn all about it, but I've got a hot date with a telephone operator tonight—a collect call from a guy who only gets one a month, so let's get back to the q and a. It seems we've shared an employer. You used to work for him, I do now: Arvis Hypoole."

I watched her face, not a hint of emotion surfaced. That might be good in poker games and at the altar, but in real life you bring up a familiar name, everybody shows emotion. I tried her again. "I had a nice chat today with some gray-haired card addicts. Seems you've worked your way around Lake Forest, but you started with Margo Baxter. Now Mrs. Baxter seemed to think she was introduced to you by a friend of her husband, but upon further questioning, the truth came out. She met you through Mildred Hypoole."

"So?"

"So Hypoole hired me and he's got me watching you. You told me the other night that you've never met Ed Jones and now I find out that you do know Hypoole. It didn't take much for me to figure out that you told Hypoole you know Ed Jones. What I want to know is, when and why?"

"When and why what?"

"When did you tell Hypoole you know Ed Jones and why?"

"I didn't tell him." She sat down on the couch. I sat in the easy chair, opposite her. "I guess he must've overheard me talking to somebody one day. Or maybe his wife said something."

"How did you know the wife?"

"She was the social worker I told you about the other night. I met her through a church group. She ran a literacy program and took a fancy to me. That's all. There's nothing sinister there."

"It's not that neat," I said. I pushed my palms against my eyes, rubbed and winced: My right eye was still swollen and sore. "I kill a man, a gardener—I think he worked for some wealthy socialites in Lake Forest. Hypoole hires me to find Ed Jones, watch you. You know him and you work in Lake Forest. It isn't just some coincidence. Now why would Hypoole be so absolutely certain that Ed Jones would show up here if he only overheard you talking to somebody? He wouldn't." I lifted a brow, waited.

She crossed her legs, folded her arms across her chest, reared her head back. "There's nothing to tell, Officer. My mother and I are two single women with a crippled child. We told some people that we know Ed Jones as a form of protection. This man is revered in our community and if anyone thought we knew him, they'd leave us alone."

"Protection from who?"

"Anyone, people."

"Who?"

"You know, just people. Men who wanted to mess with me, thugs that saw easy targets. Just people."

"How do you afford the house?"

"What?"

"This house, how do you afford it? I figured you knew Jones, he helped you with it, but you say no. Well, how do you afford it?"

She held her mouth open, too wide—mock horror. "I don't believe you! We let you come in here out of the kindness of our hearts and you're questioning me like a criminal. How do I afford this house? I'll tell you. I scrub floors all day long. I get down on my knees, scrub their damn floors, scrub their toilets. I *do* wash their windows. I *do* clean their clothes. I play the meek and mild maid all day long while the white women who couldn't survive a day without their husbands condescend to me and tell me how lovely I am because they don't want to have to clean their damn toilets themselves. I'm silent when their kids track mud across the floor I just scrubbed, and I'm silent when they scold me when their husbands are around because they want to show their husbands that they can talk loud, too. And I'm silent when their husbands look at me and..."

"And?"

She fought for composure, curled her fingers into a fist and slammed her hand onto the couch. "And I'm sick of it!"

"Sick of what?"

"Everything! I'm just so damn sick of it."

I needed to press: "You still didn't tell me how you bought the house."

"Get out!" she screamed. "We let you into our home, I let you bleed your heart to me and now this? Get out!"

The perfect opportunity; a few more jabs and I'd have her on the edge, drag out some answers. I opened my mouth and we both heard the scream.

I was two steps in front of Martha when I heard her mother yell again, pain in her voice: "Gracey!!" I hit the kitchen, saw the grandmother holding the child upside down, shaking her like she was trying to get the last grain out of a wet bag of coffee. A high chair lay on the floor, an empty cup beside it, milk had sprayed the wall.

I grabbed the child, turned from the grandmother. "I was just sitting for a minute; all she had was some collard greens!" The old woman screamed again as I lifted the child upright, spilled her forward. I repeated the move, saw the child's eyes bug, go frantic. She wasn't getting any air, whatever was lodged in her throat hadn't moved. I flipped her over again, pushed on her stomach. It didn't work. Martha yelled, grabbed at the child. I spun the infant toward me, pressed my lips to hers, blew like I was trying to fill a dirigible. I pulled back and the girl spat out a mouthful of gunk.

Martha grabbed the girl from me, sat down at the kitchen table, set the child's head on her shoulder and patted her back. She started to cry, softly. Her mother joined in. "I'm sorry, baby," said the grandmother. "I'm so sorry. I just sat down for a minute and I looked around she was blue. Oh God, what did we do to deserve this? Why us, Lord, why us?"

I slumped against the wall, jostled a picture of Christ, moved away and straightened it. I wanted to tell the old woman that she asked the wrong question. Five days in the water, all of my shipmates dead. I bobbed, fought shark-filled panic attacks, froze at night, burned during the day. But I survived. "Why me?" Wrong question. I figured it out when they told me Sollie the Jew was gone. "Why me"? No, no, no. "Why not me?"

I left the room so the two women could cry in private.

MARTHA CAME OUT A FEW MOMENTS LATER, her eyes puffy, cheeks streaked with tears. I sat on the couch, elbows on my knees, head tucked against my chest. She walked across the room, stopped in front of the radio. She switched it on: Perry Como sang "Prisoner of Love." She stood in front of the console for a moment, let the music wash over her like a warm shower. Her head dropped to her chest, eyes closed. Her shoulders moved slowly with the tune. Como's voice started to fade, a commercial came on for Lucky Strike cigarettes. She turned the volume down, stepped over to the sofa and sat down next to me.

"I'm sorry, Off... Gus. Thank you."

"I'm the one who's sorry," I said. "I'm sorry you've got to go through that, and I'm sorry I pushed you."

She reached over, patted my hand. The brown skin of her hand contrasted with mine. "Mama just overreacted. It gets like that sometimes. Our nerves get worn to a frazzle."

"I know," I said. "I played on that and I shouldn't have. I've just got this gnawing feeling in my gut that something's really wrong here and that I'm being played for a fool."

She stroked my hand, looked up at me. "I guess I haven't made it any easier. I knew you were working for Arvis Hypoole the minute you pulled up front."

"How?"

"I just knew."

"Then tell me about it. It's important." She froze, looked straight ahead. I continued. "When I got back from the war, I swore I'd never kill another man. Just this week I've killed one man and wounded others and I don't know why. Somebody's playing me for a fool, and they're turning me back into the man I left in the ocean."

She pulled back to the corner of the couch, looked out the front window toward my car. She sat silent, furrowed her brow, fought her demons. Minutes, seconds, later, she started, quiet: "One day Mrs. Hypoole came to our church to give a talk about the value of reading. Now, this was a church in the heart of Bronzeville, and a lot of the people in that audience couldn't read, but after a while, the catcalls fell silent and the people just listened to her read. She chose a selection from *Tom Sawyer*, and when she read the part about whitewashing the fence, even the men in the audience laughed so hard they fought tears. Then she read a bit from *A Tale of Two Cities*, and then she read a little bit from *The Man in the Iron Mask*, and it wasn't just that she was reading from great books. It was the fact that this white woman would come to our church, alone, and take the time to talk with us. And then she said, 'The Good Book isn't the only good book. Reading is the only way to get ahead in life.'

"Well, I sat in that front row, with my mother, and even though I was only fourteen years old, I knew she was right. I saw my mama, who could barely read, work her fingers to the bone at the Ben Franklin Store—yes, I told you the truth about that. But I didn't want that. I wanted more for myself. So when Mrs. Hypoole started teaching a class after church on Sundays, I stayed. Pretty soon, she would come pick me up after school. She'd take me home and work with me on my reading and just talk to me. She was a very special woman."

I interrupted. "How the hell did she ever end up with a man like Hypoole?"

"I don't know. I imagine that when she was young, she didn't get a lot of attention from boys. She was smart and funny, but not what boys would consider attractive. She said one time that Arvis was the smartest man she'd ever met, so I always figured that's what she saw in him."

"So you knew him, even in those days?"

"Yes. He'd come home early, sometimes, and I'd still be there. Mrs. Hypoole would always tell him to find something to do until we finished the lesson, and then they'd both drive me home."

"And when was that?"

"Started in thirty-six, when I was fourteen."

"So you were twenty years old when she died, in forty-two. Was she still working with you?"

"Of course not. I was taking night classes at the university. Mrs. Hypoole hired me during the day to clean their house. Believe me, she never thought twice about that: She believed in hard work and didn't care what you had to do. She told me she grew up on a farm, and the only time she wasn't doing chores was when she was studying, so she certainly didn't pity me having to clean her house for some money."

"And then she died."

She sighed. "And then she died. She'd been sick for a while, but it was still a terrible shock. The only time I came out of my room was when Mama and I took the bus to take Mister Hypoole a casserole and to go to the funeral."

"What about Hypoole? How did he take it?"

"How did he take it? He changed. He changed."

"How?"

She looked down into her lap. "He got bad."

"What do you mean?"

"He became a different person. Like nobody I'd ever seen before. But part of me knew that I *had* seen him before—he was always bad, just held it back when his wife was alive."

"And..."

"And... it got bad."

"And it got bad enough that he found you a job with the Baxters..."

She didn't move. Her eyes welled with tears. She pulled back farther into the couch, like a ghost had appeared in the room. On cue, Perry Como came back on the radio, barely audible, broke into "Surrender."

I went on, softly: "... and he had Margo Baxter recommend you to her friends, who recommended you to their friends..."

She sobbed.

"... so that you'd make plenty of money..."

She began to rock, sob harder.

"... because he wanted you to be comfortable..."

She put her hands over her face, bawled hard.

"... and he knew you wouldn't take charity..."

Her hands spread over her eyes like a mask. She gulped for air.

"... and he needed to buy your silence..."

"No!" she screamed, wailed.

"... so he bought you this house, so that you wouldn't talk, could live here in solitude, because..."

She screamed, threw her hand across my mouth, fell against my shoulder, heaving, sobbing. She fought for air, struggled to talk. She told me everything.

I HIGHTAILED IT HOME, skipped driving around the block to check for a stakeout. I heard the phone ring as I blew through the door. I grabbed it, out of breath.

"Jesus Christ!" yelled Sam. "I thought I told you seven o'clock. I've been on the line for ten fucking minutes!"

"I got detained."

"You cost me three cartons of cigarettes. I want 'em back."

"Done. What've you got to tell me?"

"Wrong, kid. What have you got to tell me?"

"Pasqua?"

"Yeah."

"No."

"Goddamn it! I need that taken care of. What's your problem?"

"My problem? I don't want to end up next to you."

"Bullshit. You know you could do it or get it done. I heard about you, saw it when you came here. You turned yellow."

I gritted my teeth. "You don't know the first thing about it."

"Course I do. You had it rough during the war, and now you can't stand the sight of blood, ain't that it?"

"Like I said, you don't know the first thing about it. You never served."

Sam growled: "What's that supposed to mean?"

"You never served. You don't know what it's like. That's it."

"So I don't know yellow when I see it?"

"You can't even spell it."

"Fuck you."

I jabbed. "Remember that night at Clubber Jones's place?"

"Of course," he said.

"Well, so do I. I remember I went in that door first, you stayed back, your .38 drawn. Odds are, if I wasn't there, you'd have never gone in."

"You're out of your fucking mind. I let you take him 'cause I knew I'd kill the nigger if I went in first."

"You like to think so."

"You were standing here, I'd beat you like a stepchild."

"You already did that."

"What the fuck do you want with me?" he yelled.

I paused, made him wait. The prison phone call gave me the edge; Sam wouldn't hang up if I insulted his dead wife. "You told me you could find out about Ed Jones."

Surly, proud: "And I did."

"And?"

"And what're you gonna do for me?"

"I do it. I play building manager for you, check on your accounts, collect your rent."

"Not enough. Why should I help you, you won't help me?"

"You owe me."

"I owe you?" he growled.

"That's right."

"I raised you. How the hell can I owe you?"

"'Cause you made me your son and that's a hell I wouldn't wish on anyone. You give me Jones or I'm through dealing with you. Through collecting for you, pushing for you and watching things for you. You get that pardon, you ain't gonna have nothing left to come back to."

A long pause. I heard him breathe in the distance; he must've held the phone a foot away from his face to stop from screaming. He pulled it back, menacing, restrained: "Now you listen to me, you ungrateful son of a bitch. I'm gonna give you this Jones on a fucking platter. It cost me plenty so you owe me. You understand that? You owe me."

A deal with the devil, I couldn't stop myself. "Done. What do you know?"

"They've had him locked up in a room, mouth gagged, eyes taped, the usual, but he's okay. They got through to the brother, he's bringing them a bundle. Say, a quarter million in ransom."

"Jesus."

"It goes down like this: Sixty-second and Gillette, ten o'clock tomorrow morning. They meet the brother and the money, dump Jones."

"You figure it straight?"

"I figure they worked something out with Jones. We have got one golden opportunity, *son.*"

"How do you figure?"

"You grab the money, clip 'em all. You get caught, you were just doing your job. You don't, we split it sixty/forty—me."

"Not gonna happen."

"I knew it, you turned yellow. I ain't too worried about it. I figured you'd have to have at least three guys and you ain't got anyone. All right, play it straight. Guy like you doesn't have enough pals to play it right, so play it straight. Even you should be able to get some backup from the department."

"How'd you find all this out?"

"Not everybody's yellow."

I cringed. "Meaning?"

"Meaning my brother Tom's got no problem with it."

"What'd he do?"

"He visited that attorney you told me about, Cordell."

"Jesus, when?"

"Few hours ago. You owe me big."

"Sam, I saw Cordell this morning, threatened him. I'll be the first one fingered."

"Got an alibi?"

I thought fast, went through my day. Most would cover for me; I prayed it had happened before I visited Martha. Gloria Blanchard, Sheila, Margo Baxter, they made great alibi; a Negro from the South Side amounted to more suspicion. "Maybe. What time did he do it?"

"How the fuck would I know? I didn't have him punch a time card."

"Cordell's gonna talk to the police. I've got to find out what time Tom was there."

"Not a problem. Cordell's not telling anybody."

"Oh, fuck; body bag?"

"Nah, but his mouth's gonna have to be wired shut. Seems he tried to eat a phone."

"And Tom believed him?" I asked.

"Said he whimpered like a little girl, begged him to stop. Tom told him Jones wasn't there, he'd be back."

"He's there, I'll drop a hundred dollars at the charity of your choice."

"You told me you were getting five C-notes. Make it two-fifty."

No need to share my raise. "All right, two-fifty."

"And my favorite charity is me. Drop it at Billy's pool hall: tell him to add it to my package."

"Consider it done."

"Far from done. You owe me big."

"Right."

"I gotta hang up. You watch your ass. Cordell might not be able to talk, but Carpacci and his boys find out he's in the hospital, they're liable to blame you, and they don't ask about alibis."

"Thanks for the concern."

"Concern, shit. You get my two-fifty, dump it with Billy."

I hung up, thought through the conversation. The Brodys were persuasive; no reason to doubt either one. I figured Tom Brody saw something—he wouldn't have passed the info on to Sam if there was a shot for him to score big. There was something else out there, something that scared off one of the meanest cops around. I figured play it smart: Call it in, get kudos and some backup. I figured play it cool: Watch it unfold, grab Jones, turn him over to Hypoole, collect on the favors. I figured it the only way I could: Grab Jones, throw him to the Grand Jury, take Hypoole down like a rabid dog.

SAM WAS RIGHT ON THE MONEY—I knew the Carpaccis would come after me. Problem: nowhere to go, no one to turn to. Sam was in jail; I couldn't put Sheila's family at risk. I decided to sack at home, prepare for the worst.

My watch read a quarter 'til eight—fourteen hours until they'd release Jones. Time to think. Martha Lewis clarified it all for me. I ran it through my mind. Case number one: the kidnapping. Arvis Hypoole, would-be Republican mayor, fields a call one day from an attorney/friend, Don Cordell. Cordell tells him that the Syndicate is taking over the numbers racket—they're kidnapping the biggest Negro policy leader. Hypoole hears the name Ed Jones. He's got a jones for Jones. Cordell tells him to meet him at the Kitchen. The lunch meeting: Cordell springs it: He's got a list of twenty-seven men that have been transferred because they wouldn't play ball with the policy leaders. Cordell tells him that he's going to go public with the list—it'll bring down the Democrats. He wants in with the Republicans; policy cash will flow to them, they protect the rackets in return.

Hypoole sees through it. He's got his own plan: Grab Jones, parade him in front of the Grand Jury, expose the Democrats. But the Syndicate was useless to him—they couldn't deliver the votes. Note to the

Negroes, "Vote Republican and you'll get back policy." Hypoole's problems: how to get rid of Cordell, Jones.

Case number two: Don Cordell/the gardener. Hypoole plays the need to get the list from Cordell, silence him. He calls in an old favor, tells 'em it's for the good of the Party. Prescott isn't too hard to convince; no City contracts might force them to sell the estate. And since she'd been born into a dry well and married deep water, Virginia Prescott simply wouldn't allow that to happen. So she calls in the gardener, uses money or a threat, convinces him to kill Cordell.

But they didn't count on me. Or did they? No way to know I'd be at Mona's, I figured coincidence. But only at first. Hypoole got word that I'd killed the gardener, had me checked out. My record sold him an old bill of goods—I was violent, would play ball. *He* got me suspended— that's why they hadn't bothered to confiscate my badge or gun. So Hypoole had me look for Jones, show him around the policy rackets. And now I could finger Jones's release—where and when.

I figured that was it, in a nutshell. At least, that's what Hypoole wanted everyone to think. But I knew there was a dry, shriveled-up nut inside that shell, and I planned on plucking it out and shoving it down his dry, shriveled-up throat.

Exhaustion overtook me. My eyelids felt like they were made of concrete. I had to get some shut-eye; ten a.m. approached like a speeding train. Nowhere to turn. Nowhere to go. The Syndicate wanted me, the cops didn't. Hypoole had enough control in the department to get me suspended; he could squash any attempt I made to get help, get out. I was in it up to my neck.

I stepped into the hallway, locked the front door, walked back into my apartment and bolted it shut. I opened the door to the closet that sat just inside the front door, on the near side of the living room. It was cluttered with coats; boxes filled the shelf. I reached up, pulled one down, pulled out the pearl-handled revolver, checked it for bullets and stuffed it in my pants. I peeled off my jacket, hung it up. A box on the shelf yelled at me; I reached up, took it down, opened it.

My kapok jacket had held me in its warm embrace for five days, barely survived the ocean. It was in worse shape than me. It was old. It was moldy. It was dirty. It was the most beautiful jacket in the world. I put it on, stared into the closet. Seconds later, the lights out, I stepped into the closet, turned the closet light off with the tug of a string, pulled the door shut and sat down.

Dark, quiet—the ocean at night. Hot, rugged—the ocean during the day. The sharks, the Syndicate, the policy rackets, dirty cops, crooked politicians…it all ran together as I slumped against some old boots, filled my hands with the revolver and my .38 and tried to rest.

I heard the Williams kids from upstairs. They screamed as they played; my ceiling shook as they jumped up and down. I pictured them jumping off the couch like soldiers parachuting from a plane. Their screams reeked of joy, terror, hope. They drifted away as I leaned back into the old boots and, for the first time in hours, slept.

I HEARD THE RUSTLE AT MY DOOR and came awake with a start. No background noise: the adjacent unit was vacant; upstairs, the Williams kids were asleep. It must've been late. I listened close: Something scratched at the door. Muffled whispers came to me like the scent of bad perfume—slight but strong. Suddenly something thumped against the door. It got louder and louder, and I heard the doorjamb splinter as the door sprang open. Two pairs of feet shuffled into the room. A crack of light snuck under the door and into the closet. No, no, no.

Two men, a hushed conversation; I recognized the voices. "I'll check the bedroom," whispered Constantin Carpacci. His heavy shoes thudded off.

I heard Alfredo move quickly around the room, step into the kitchen. Constantin yelled from the bedroom, "He's not here!"

I heard trudging above me; someone in the Williams apartment was awake. Footsteps hurried down the stairs. Don't, don't, don't. Don't make me kill them.

Alvin Williams hit the landing, yelled, "What's going on in here?"

No, no, no, no.

A shot rang out. I sat up like I'd been stabbed in the gut with a bayonet. I heard a crash, scream and another shot. "What the fuck did you do that for?" yelled Constantin.

Alfredo, too calm: "He was coming at me."

"Let's get the fuck out of here!"

"One last look-see," said Alfredo.

I heard him stop in front of the closet door. He fumbled with the handle, started to pull it open. I curled my feet up under me, threw my arms straight. Damn, damn, damn! A creak, then he pulled the door wide. I shoved the pearl-handled revolver into his stomach and shot him back through the doorway.

Screams, Alfredo's death belch, Constantin, me. I pushed off the wall behind me, came to my feet, stepped into the front room with both guns blazing. Alfredo crumpled to the floor in front of me. Shocked, Constantin caught one in the throat. The next shot took the back of his head off like a pumpkin going Halloween. His sawed-off shotgun barked into the ceiling as he fell back, dead, and hit the floor.

I stepped over Alfredo, rushed over to Alvin Williams. He was as dead as the other two. I threw off the kapok jacket, grabbed my trench coat from the closet, hit the door hard.

I WAS JUICED AS AN ELECTRIC CHAIR ON EXECUTION NIGHT. My heart tried to beat its way through my chest as I leaped into my machine, turned on the ignition, popped the clutch, threw it into gear and sped away.

Nowhere to turn, nowhere to go. I looked at my watch: three in the morning. Squad cars would be coming—I'd heard Mrs. Williams scream as I ran out the door. Seven hours 'til Jones was released; I needed somewhere to hide. Martha Lewis? No, with a capital *N*. The Prescotts'? I was saving that visit. Nowhere to turn, nowhere to go, like a streetwalker on a rainy night. Streetwalker...it hit me like a cold woman's slap.

I rounded the corner, took it slow and easy, moved across the city like I didn't have a care in the world. I saw the house, eased my car down the back alley, backed it in, parked two doors down and walked across the gangway. I jostled the screen door, tore it open, put my shoulder into the back door and pushed my way through.

It was dark and cold. Com Ed must've turned off the electricity, I thought, as I strolled through the kitchen, front room and into the entryway. I pulled a match from my pocket, struck it, found a candle and lit it. I looked at the landing, remembered Vaughn White, thought about how it had all started here, six days before, at Mona's.

There's something sad about an empty brothel, something sadder about a full one. The cops had shut Mona's down, something Mona didn't appreciate but I sure did. I needed a few hours of sleep, if that's what they still called it. I doubted it'd come, but I needed to hide, so it was worth a shot. I walked up the stairs, passed the room where I'd been, shuffled across the dusty floor toward the room where they'd died. I shoved the candle into the room, watched it come to life as quickly as life had left it.

The mattress had been changed, but there were dark stains on the walls and the floor. The dank odor of blood filled the room, and the wind banged against the shuttered windows like ghosts protesting my presence. I stepped across the stained floor, sat down on the bed. I rested the candle on the nightstand, flipped my shoes onto the bed, fell back and stared at the ceiling. I thought about the dead prostie, Don Cordell. I thought about Lucas Tanner's son, Alvin Williams, the Carpaccis. I thought about the Prescotts, Martha Lewis and her daughter. I thought about Arvis Hypoole. I thought that even if someone was to visit Mona's that night, they'd avoid this room like it had been quarantined. I thought it was perfect for a man who should've died in the ocean.

## FRIDAY, MAY 17

I MADE MY WAY TO HYPOOLE'S pre-six a.m. Squad cars passed me twice; neither stopped me. Chief Hogan had probably kiboshed any warrants, held the department at bay. It was no small feat—my hours were numbered.

The house was still dark as I pushed through the gate, approached it and rapped on the door. Arvis Hypoole answered the door quickly, wide awake. He wore the same checkered flannel robe and slippers; he tied the robe after he opened the door. "Why aren't you in front of the Lewis house?"

I stepped past him. He closed the door and we walked toward the breakfast nook. "No need," I said. "I got word last night that Jones is being released this morning."

"I'll bet you did."

"What's that supposed to mean?"

He sat down at the small table, offered me a chair and poured me a cup of coffee. He filled his cup and set the pot back on a coaster. "It means that I got two calls from Chief Hogan last night. He said you paid our attorney friend a little visit."

No need to squelch: "So?"

"I guess I should say 'Welcome back,' Gus. I was beginning to think you might not be the right man for the job."

"You said two calls."

"I did. He also told me that three men were killed in your apartment earlier this morning."

"Tag two of them for me. They killed my neighbor from upstairs."

"Chief Hogan covered for you, but it won't last long. He said you've got bodies to answer for."

"All on your behalf. I'm gonna need you and the chief to back me when I go in."

"And we will."

"All justifiable. The Negroes kidnapped and attacked me, and none of them died, and the Carpaccis killed my neighbor."

"Sounds reasonable to me. The attorney might be a little harder to explain."

"He won't press charges. A guy in his position wants attention like a reformer wants a drink."

Hypoole picked up his cup and took a sip of coffee. His bony hand shook slightly as he held the cup to his mouth, blew on the drink. He gazed at me, lids half shut, tried to cover his eagerness. "So tell me, what's the situation with Mr. Jones's release?"

"It was the Syndicate, just like we figured. They contacted the brother and he's bringing the ransom."

"Funny, Chief Hogan didn't tell me that."

"Cops wouldn't know. I figure they told the brother if he blew the whistle, Jones was dead."

"When?"

"This morning, ten o'clock."

"Where?"

"Sixty-second and Gillette."

He stood up, slowly, pulled the blinds, looked out the window as the sun continued to rise. The streaming light gave his gray features a bit of color, caused him to squint. He undid the knot in his robe, retied it, tighter. "This is a bit more complicated than you know."

"Kind of like taking apart an engine, eh? You start to take it apart, you realize that there's a hell of a lot more to it than nuts and bolts."

He continued to look out the window, clapped his hands in front of his face, held them like he was saying a prayer. "Precisely. This isn't just about Mr. Jones. It's about the future of our city, our country. Now that the war is over, there's going to be rapid change, and we need an administration that's able to lead us through it."

I rested my hands on the table, played with my coffee cup. "Save it. I know about policy and your election plans. You ask me, it's for the birds."

He turned around, puzzled. "What do you mean, you know?"

"I know you plan on throwing your list of 'martyrs' in front of the papers, embarrassing the mayor and using that to pry the Democrats from office. I know you're going to tell Ed Jones or Lincoln Johnson or the Pied Piper to tell the Negroes that if they vote Republican, you'll let them have policy back. I know it was awfully convenient that Cordell died."

His eyes narrowed. He stepped toward me, placed one of his cold hands on my shoulder, looked into my eyes. "You're smarter than I thought, Gus. There will always be a place for you in the administration. There's no limit to how far you'll climb in the police department. Say, chief of police, captain..."

"I was thinking more along the lines of something sooner. Say, something cold and hard and green."

"One thousand dollars when you deliver Jones."

"But you don't want me to deliver Jones."

His hand jumped, remained on my shoulder. "Why would you say that?"

I held back. "Because you can get Lincoln Johnson now. The only reason you needed Jones was to walk you through the rackets, spread the word through the Negro community."

He pulled his hand off my shoulder. Relief washed over his face like aftershave. "That's correct. Nearly."

"You said 'Correct. Nearly.' How near?"

"This is an extremely important election for us. The Negroes vote strongly Democrat in the presidential election, but it's much narrower in Chicago. Here, Negroes only vote a little over fifty percent Democrat. It's close enough that with a little shove, we can push them Republican."

"How near?"

He walked back in front of the window, turned to face me. "If we take office here, there's no telling how many Negro votes we might be able to swing away from Truman in forty-eight."

Almost a shout: "How near?"

"And I think Truman is quite vulnerable. You see, if we..."

I shouted: "How near?!"

Sunlight streamed over him, caused me to squint. He set it on the table like he was ordering carryout. "We need you to kill them, Gus."

Expected, but still a fist to the solar plexus. "Who's them?"

"Ed Jones, the mobsters that deliver him."

"Why?"

"The Negroes need to be convinced that the Democrats aren't with them. First, one of the linchpins of their community will be killed; then, when the list is exposed, the Democrats will be forced to shut down policy."

"Why the goons?"

"To send the Syndicate a message. Once we take office, things will change."

"But the money'll still be green. They pay protection to the administration just like their clients pay them. You just want them to know who's in charge."

"Precisely."

I let him think I ate it. "What's in it for me?"

"Well..." he let it dangle like a big, fat worm. "There is the matter of that ransom money."

"Too hard. Chances of me getting the goons fall between slim and none. They'll grab a bag of money and push Jones out the door faster than a jilted girlfriend. I can't promise anything about the goons."

"But you can take care of Jones and his brother?"

"How much?"

"Two thousand?"

"I can make more than that selling rabbits on South Parkway," I said.

"How much do you want?"

"Forty thousand, cash."

He put his hand to his heart. "Forty thousand dollars?"

"It ain't alimony, drop the staged surprise. You think you can buy those votes any cheaper?"

"I'll have to see." He left the room, headed for the stairs. I figured the wall safe I'd seen in his room. Five minutes later he came back, jaw clenched.

"I can manage it. Both brothers dead or there's no deal. If one of them lives, it'll do me no good."

"I thought you said it was just for the shove. Lincoln Johnson can spread the word for you."

His eyes went cold; he dropped the friend act. "Don't you worry about my reasons. For forty thousand dollars, I want both of them killed. If the brother doesn't show up, find him and kill him. One of them doesn't die, you don't get paid."

"And what if I say no?"

"You've lost that option. If you say no, neither Chief Hogan nor I will stand up in your defense. You've killed three men and beaten a respectable attorney nearly to death. You just might get the opportunity to join that friend of yours in Terre Haute."

I drummed my fingers on the table, stared at him, let him sweat. I finished my coffee, gestured for another cup. "Pour it yourself," he said.

I laughed, poured myself another cup of coffee. "You've got a hell of an edge when that mask comes off."

His turn: "Say yes, Carson."

"Then again, I might too if I was cooped up in this musty old house, all by myself."

"Say yes!"

"You know, you should really hire a maid to do some cleaning in here. Those blinds open up it looks like someone's dusted the whole joint for fingerprints."

"Say yes!"

"But I wouldn't want to see all of the prints around here. Some of them just might set off my temper."

"Say yes!"

"And that's not always a good thing."

"Damn you! Say yes!"

"And speaking of tempers…"

He slammed his hand on the table, dust jumped, coffee slopped out of my cup. "I said, say yes!"

"Yes."

THREE AND A HALF HOURS TO GO and the law still wasn't on my back. Time had an advantage: It was running out, but I couldn't. Hypoole had me trapped. He'd laid it out, nice and neat, let me wander into it like a duck hunter stumbling into bear season. I knew what lay ahead, figured the odds dropping and not in my favor. No guarantee that I'd make it out alive. But I had to see it through. Or Ed Jones was dead.

And if Ed Jones died, so would Martha.

I PULLED IN FRONT OF A STOP AND TRADE FOOD SHOP, bought a pad of paper, a pen and an envelope. I drove south, found a safe alley, parked behind a dilapidated garage and wrote it all down.

I filled page after page, minutes fell off the clock as I wrote, but I didn't cut it short. I said everything. Time to deliver it. One last responsibility, one last confession. I took off quick, cruised south, saw the rotting tenement home in the distance and turned onto Switzer.

I COULDN'T SWEAR IT WAS THE SAME TWO WOMEN I'd seen a few days prior, standing on the back porch, two stories high, but they looked the same. Their tattered dresses matted against their dark skin as the wind blew in their faces, and a mist started to fall. Their eyes were vacant, nearly black, and neither one spoke to me this time, as if they remembered me, expected me to know where I was going. The wind whipped harder and a screen door blew open, banged against the building. A trash can fell in the back alley and a stray cat shrieked. I pulled my jacket tight, jogged toward the building, let myself inside and moved toward Lydia White's unit.

Someone had already come in out of the rain and the dirty hall floor bore footprints; the wall held a small handprint. The ceiling creaked as people upstairs walked, and when I started down the hall, I heard a door slam.

A handwritten sign was taped to the door of Lydia White's unit. It said, NOT FOR RENT. YET. STAY OUT. I stared at it for a moment, then rapped on the door.

Nobody answered my rap, so I knocked again, harder. Still no one answered, but I heard someone shuffling around inside, so I leaned against the wall opposite the door, lit a cigarette and waited. Moments later the door opened and a small boy started out, an armful of toys clutched to his chest.

"Oh," he yelled when he saw me. He stopped in the doorway, startled by my presence. He wore a pair of tiny overalls over a red-and-white-striped shirt, and his tiny brown leather shoes were scuffed and untied. He barely stood up to my waist, and his eyes were wide and his mouth seemed set to blow a bubble. He couldn't have been more than seven years old, and I recognized him as the boy that had been lying in bed reading the comic book when I'd first visited. He was Vaughn White's son.

I stamped my cigarette out on the floor, looked down at him. "It's all right. I came to talk to your mother for a moment." I fingered the envelope in my pocket. "I brought her something."

He dropped his head, looked up at me through his brows. "Ain't you that police officer?" he asked in a small, high voice.

I nodded. "Yes, I am, and your name is Donnie, right?"

He nodded.

"Well, Donnie," I said. "I need to talk to your mother for a few minutes."

He stepped into the hall, pulled the door shut behind him. A toy soldier fell from his arms, and I reached down, scooped it up and handed it back to him. He took it from me tentatively and stepped back. "She can't," he said.

"Is she gone?" I asked.

He nodded his head, slowly.

"When is she coming back?"

"Don't know," he said. His eyes started to well up with tears. "You ain't gonna tell nobody, is you? Don't tell nobody I came back. I just left some o' mah toys."

I squatted down, leaned forward and rubbed my hand over his short, bristly hair. "Hey, now, little man, do I look like I'm gonna rat you out?"

He shook his head.

"Well, that's good, 'cause I'm not. But what do you mean that you're coming back for your toys; are you moving?"

He nodded his head again, slow, like an oil drill on its last legs. He kept nodding, and I took the forefinger of my right hand, pressed it against his forehead to get him to stop. He stopped nodding, smiled slightly. "Where you moving?" I asked.

He looked down the hall. "Cecil's family."

"Cecil's family?" I asked. My heart started to pound. "Where did your mommy go?"

"Don't know," he said.

I dropped to one knee, looked him straight in the eyes, tried to stay calm. "Did your mommy get hurt?"

He nodded, again.

"What happened to her?"

His lips moved slow, his voice fell soft. "Mommy cut herself. I found her, called the neighbors."

"Did an ambulance come?" I asked.

"Ambuhlence came and Mr. Crabbe from the building came and told me they was gonna take me away, but Cecil's mom said I was gonna stay with them for a while."

"Is Cecil's mom home right now?" I asked.

He shook his head. "No."

"And that's why you came back for your toys?"

"Yes." His eyes started to well up with tears again.

I reached over, scooped him up in my arms. "Come on, little man, let's go back down to Cecil's. And don't you worry, I won't tell anyone I saw you."

"Promise?"

"Promise," I said.

"Here it is," he said, as we reached the end of the hall. I set him down in front of the door, patted him on the back.

"You go back on inside, little man," I said. He opened the door and stepped halfway inside, then leaned out, hand on the doorknob and stared up at me. "And everything's going to be all right," I promised.

He smiled, closed the door. I heard him yell, "Cecil!" as I walked back down the hall. I reached the White's unit, slowly opened the door, quietly stepped inside. It was nearly like it was the last time I'd seen it... save the dank odor that I'd recognized all my life.

THE RAIN STARTED TO FALL, HARDER, as I drove north. The rage started to brew in me like coffee boiling on a stove. I fed it with the things I'd wanted to tell the little boy. I wanted to tell him that I'd killed his father but it was an accident. I wanted to tell him that I'd figured out why his father and I had been set up, that I'd make people pay. I wanted to tell him that when he woke up in the middle of the night, wondered why his mother had taken her life, that it wasn't his fault. I wanted to tell him that it had taken me a lifetime to figure that out. But I knew it didn't matter what I told him—he'd still wake up, still blame himself. He'd pay for others' sins for the rest of his life.

I PULLED IN FRONT OF HARRY'S around eight thirty, found the key in the crack at the base of the streetlight and let myself inside. It was dark, but not so dark that I couldn't find my way to the back room. I slipped in, grabbed the sawed-off shotgun and went to his desk. The bottom drawer was the jackpot; I yanked out a handful of shells, beelined out.

I replaced the key in the crack on the sidewalk, opened the car door and sat down. The envelope sat in the passenger seat, undelivered. Lydia

White couldn't read it, go public; the department would trash it. It was useless. I grabbed a match from the ashtray, struck it with a thumbnail, lit the envelope on fire and tossed it out the window.

Vaughn White, Alvin Williams, Lydia White, Donnie White. Victims calling for vengeance. Civilians, issuing me an order. A letter wouldn't suffice. I had to survive.


IT WAS NINE THIRTY by the time I hit 62nd and Gillette—thirty minutes to come up with a plan. I glided by the corner, pulled a U-turn, drove around the block. The rain continued to fall; I ignored my wipers and scoped the place out. Brick buildings lined the streets; foot traffic was nil, but cars lined up three deep at the intersection. The sidewalks grew sloppy; someone had dropped a bag full of leaflets—"Congressman William L. Dawson" matted the pavement.

I figured the drop-off for the north side of the street—that left them heading west, a quicker route out of town. The ten a.m. drop-off I admired; although the streets were more crowded and it would be harder to spot a stakeout, it would also be harder to pin them in. Pedestrians, civilian traffic couldn't be controlled. Any ambushers had to deal with additional obstacles. I figured the kidnappers would tail their own getaway car—insurance against surprise. I figured Jones's brother had been instructed to drop a bag, hightail it until he heard from Jones. I figured I was being set up like a rich, married dope.

There was a tavern on the south side of the street, fight posters in its window. It was dark, so I figured it was empty. Next to it was a beauty salon; I could see colored women in chairs, beauticians tugging at their hair. A young woman leaned over one of the customers, filed at her nails. None of them looked out the window; gossip and laughter held their attention.

I cruised west, circled the block, again. No sign of Jones's brother, nothing out of the ordinary. I shot up a side street, drove north one block, slipped between two cars and parked. Instinct took over; I decided to walk it, risk the tough getaway.

The rain continued in a steady torrent. I pulled on my trench coat, grabbed a fedora from the back seat and pulled it low over my eyes. I loaded my .38 and the shotgun, tucked the .38 in my pants and held the sawed-off inside my coat. I walked south and thought.

I figured only four other people knew Hypoole's secret and one of them, Don Cordell, was dead. My role in *that* scene was a fluke, but Hypoole had dragged me into the rest of it because he needed a man with a tie. I wore the tie. It was the kind of tie that tightened around your neck like a noose and never came off. I knew the Prescotts; they could keep an eye on me. I'd killed the gardener—that tagged me as a killer. I had the reputation that would make it easy for them to brand me as a rogue cop gone worse. I stepped into an alley, walked close to the brick building, watched for the sign that my intuition was right.

The alley was just short of the intersection set for the drop-off, behind a row of brick buildings. It was a hundred yards long and full of trash cans. A fire escape ran down the back of each building, water gushed off the landings, pooled at the bases. Mud slid out of the alley, pushed up against the overhead doors. A trash bin had been backed up to the door nearest me. I inched my way around it, slipped into the next doorway, peered down the alley. A man at its end could peek out into the street, see the tavern, beauty salon, entire intersection. It also offered cover and a quick escape route. I thought it was the perfect spot for an ambush. So did Carl Jameson.

Jameson had his back to me, stared straight out into the street, but I couldn't mistake his stocky build. It fit; he was soaked—must've been there for a while. I figured he'd called Hogan, pronto, after Mona's. The Jones kidnapping on the horizon—Hypoole and Hogan needed a stooge,

I'd fit the bill. It played out just like they'd planned. Jameson, his partners, would kill Jones and the Italians…and me. They'd blame it on the rogue cop gone worse—a mountain of bodies would testify against me, posthumous. The verdict: guilty—vengeful, crazy, dead Gus Carson. I stepped softly into the next doorway, pulled the sawed-off from my coat.

I glanced at my watch—five minutes 'til ten—fought for a plan. I figured Jameson and maybe two others; more added too much attention. His plan was purely non–department-sanctioned, although I could see him beaming for medals if it played out. I figured one shooter crisscross at the opposite corner, one more in a car. The car would be parked west of the intersection, able to block off the getaway route.

Traffic rolled by, Jameson finished a smoke, threw it onto the ground. He tugged his own sawed-off from his jacket, checked it, stepped away from the building and peered into the street. He started, waved a hand toward the opposite corner. I figured the ransom had been dropped; he signaled his crony.

He stepped out toward the street, looked east, then west, threw his hands in the air and shrugged his shoulders. I figured he was looking for me. He stepped back into the alley and peered 'round the corner. A horse-drawn wagon moved past the alley, headed east. The driver concentrated on the road, his head hung low, like a bored cabbie. I saw Bunny standing in the back; the wagon was probably filled with the dead rabbits he sold in the city. He bent over, pulled a rabbit up by its feet, looped a rope around them.

I started counting my breaths like the waves. I felt the sharks below me; rain fell like the ocean mist. The squeal of tires filled the air, Jameson stepped out toward the street. I ran through the alley, filled my hands with the heat, yelled his name: "Jameson!"

He turned, shocked. When he saw me, he snarled. "You dumb fuck!" He lifted his sawed-off, fired at me. Brick exploded over my head. I fired back, still running, belt-high: I nearly took off his head with one load. He crumpled to the ground, his rifle skittered across the alley. I sprinted out of the alley, saw the horse buck, high. Its front feet hit the ground and it made a mad dash. Bunny spilled out the back of the wagon, a string of rabbits followed—one fell on his chest. A man in a dark suit scampered toward a black Olds. He held a pistol straight up, a lumpy bag tucked under his arm; he was one of the kidnappers. He'd grabbed the ransom money—Jameson wasn't alive to stop him. The rear passenger door flew open, a man fell out, rolled in the street. The kidnapper with the bag stepped over him, dove into the car as gunfire erupted from the corner.

Tires spun in the water, caught concrete and the Olds took off. A man in a black trench coat ran across the street, toward the Olds. I caught his build, saw his face. I lost my breath, felt my hand shake: Sam, but not Sam. Sam's brother Tom. Tom drew a rifle, sent a shot toward the car. It missed high, took out a shop window. The Olds fishtailed, flew down the street as he turned his attention toward me.

I dove behind a parked car, heard a round crash into the cement. I peered under the car, saw a colored man scurrying toward it. Another bullet scarred the street in front of him. I fell into a crouch, peered over the trunk of the car, aimed my sawed-off.

Tom saw me. "Wrong place, wrong time, Carson," he yelled as he raised his rifle. He fired, hit the trunk, blasted the sawed-off out of my hands. I fell flat on the street, pulled my .38. I threw my hand under the car, squeezed off shots, quick. The bullets caught the street and his ankles, blew out his feet. He hit the cement, bellowed in pain. He rolled over, faced me as I peered 'round the car. His face, masked in pain, red with rage as he clawed for his rifle, tried to come to his knees. His face, Sam's face: I pulled the trigger, erased it. His rifle belched as he fell back; its load filled the air like buckshot fired at birds already gone south.

I looked up the street, watched as a car tore out after the Olds two blocks away. The two cars ran the next intersection and disappeared. I heard footsteps fade, turned and saw Bunny racing down the street, his rabbits skipped behind him like tin cans tied to a honeymooner's bumper.

My heart pounded, I couldn't seem to get enough air. I pointed my .38 toward Tom Brody, held it on him like a castigating finger. A noise to my right caught my attention and I stepped around the car, saw the colored man scrape his heels across the cement as he moved back. His back thudded against the driver's door, his eyes wide as dinner plates.

"Ed Jones?" I asked.

He nodded.

"Go home."

I jogged back through the alley toward my car.

MY HANDS SWEATED SO MUCH that I could barely hold the steering wheel. I rolled the window down, sucked in the cool, moist air. Rain shot through the open window, spat against my trench coat. I looked through the windshield, tried to play cool.

Two blocks away I saw the squad car in my rearview mirror. Its lights came on and its siren yipped. I turned down the next side street, pulled over to the curb, grabbed the shotgun and slipped it under the seat. I tucked the .38 in my pants as the cop stepped from his car. He came up on me slow and easy, like a nervous child approaching a cage at the zoo.

"Getting a little wet there, eh, Gussie boy," said Tony Carvone. He gestured toward my window; his rain slicker glistened. A stream of water spilled off his hat as he leaned in the window.

"Reminds me of the ocean," I said.

He rested his hands on the hood. "Memories you don't need," he said. "You've got a problem, Gussie."

"What's that?"

"Hogan just put out an APB on you."

If the car tailing the kidnappers was full of cops and they'd seen me, I was done. Straight on: "What for?"

"Seems they found some bodies in your apartment. He said you've gone over, gone Sam."

"You believe that?"

"If I believed that, would I be talking to you like my sister?"

"What're you gonna do?"

He stepped back. "Step out of the car, Gussie."

Anyone else…I tied the belt tight 'round my trench coat, shut off the ignition, stepped out of the car. Rain pelted me, I lowered my head, let the brim of my hat shield my face. "What now?"

"Give me your keys," said Carvone.

I handed him my keys, started to turn, prepared to be cuffed. He grabbed my shoulder, spun me around. He put a set of keys in my hand, pointed down the street. "Two blocks over, Nathan Avenue, number two-thirty-eight. My brother's red Chrysler's in back. Anyone stops you, you stole it. We go back, so tell 'em you swiped the keys a long time ago."

"Why?"

"I don't believe 'em."

"It may cost you," I said.

"Cost me? Are you kidding? My brother died on the *Arizona*. He didn't die for fucks like Hogan."

He grabbed my hand, tightened my fingers around the keys. "Get going."

"I get outta this, I'll let you know where I dump the car."

"Don't bother," he said as he turned and walked back toward the squad car. "He don't need it anymore."

IT TOOK REAL EFFORT to stop from speeding to Hypoole's, fly through every light. But I knew that if I was pulled over again, I wouldn't be so lucky. I thanked God it had been Carvone that stopped me, drove careful and slow.

I parked in front of Hypoole's house, went straight to the front door. I banked on shock, was rewarded with the look on his face when he answered my knock. Surprise showed on his kisser like it was the first time he'd seen his girlfriend without makeup, but he composed himself, asked me to come inside.

He was dressed for the day—a brown tweed suit, black wingtips, white cotton shirt and a red tie. I figured it was his press conference outfit.

"Surprised to see me?" I asked.

He ignored it. "Come in, quickly. What happened?"

We walked through the foyer, into the living room. He sat in a blue high-back chair, motioned toward the couch. I sat down. "There were a few problems."

"Did they release Jones?" he asked.

"Yep."

His voice rose: "And?"

"No."

"His brother?"

"No."

His face went crimson: "Unacceptable! What happened?"

"You tell me."

"What?"

"It was a setup. It's gonna cost you."

He stood up, threw his hands in the air. "What are you talking about?" He stepped behind the chair, put his hands on its back.

"Playtime's over, Hypoole. I'm onto you. You sent Jameson to take me out. Well, he screwed up. No hard feelings. I want my cash."

"You're out of your mind. What happened?"

"You figured you'd brand me rogue cop, clean up the whole mess by letting it fall on me. You figured if Jameson killed me, my story would go with me. Well, you figured wrong."

"Gus, I am telling you, you're out of your mind. You're stark raving mad if you think I sent Jameson anywhere."

"Am I? Guess I forgot to tell you that I've been onto you for a long time. Oh, at first I thought it was all about the Negroes and the Democrats and the Republicans and votes and policy. I figured you conned Virginia Prescott into finding someone to kill Cordell. Hell, for all I know, she volunteered. I figure she's part of your steering committee."

Softly: "You're mad."

"You're damn right I'm mad! I'm mad that I ever went to Mona's. If I hadn't been there when the gardener killed Cordell, I probably never would've gotten involved in this mess. But I was, so you pulled me in, played on my hate for Mayor Kelly, offered me a nice sum of cash. You had me usher you through the policy rackets like a tour guide. You had me find out about Ed Jones, tried to get me to kill him. But I didn't follow your orders to a tee. I could've killed him as easy as stepping on a June bug."

He stamped a foot. "You fool! Why didn't you?"

"It's May."

"What? Listen, I don't know what you think you're onto, Carson, but you're out of line. You've failed, so kindly get your wet clothes off of my couch and leave."

I stood up. He came around the chair, started for the door. "I don't need you to show me the way out."

"Good."

"Because I'm not going anywhere." I opened my trench coat, pulled out my .38. "Hit the stairs. You're donating that forty thousand dollars to my own little fund-raiser."

"The hell with you," he said. He stepped forward and I cracked him on the back of the head with the butt of the gun. He fell forward, caught himself on the banister. When he turned around, fear showed on his face like it been stamped there with a tanning lamp.

"Get moving," I said.

He started up the stairs. I followed. "You're making the mistake of your life, here, Gus."

"A minute ago it was Carson. I guess a conk on the head turns you real civil."

We reached the second floor, walked down the hallway toward his bedroom. The wood floor creaked beneath our shoes. The wind and rain battered the side of the house and as we passed the study, the arched window screamed. Hypoole jumped as it strained against a sudden gust of wind.

I pushed him down the hall, through the door of the master bedroom. I looked at the painting of Mildred Hypoole on the wall, pointed to it with the .38. "Peel her mug off the wall and open that safe."

He walked to the wall, removed the painting and spun the dial. His long, bony fingers shook as he tried to locate the numbers. He failed, tried again and opened it. "Whatever happened out there's got to you. You're not yourself, Gus. We should sit down, talk this thing out."

"We're gonna talk all right," I said. "And it's not going to be that crap you tried to feed me this morning." I pushed past him, peered into the safe. The bills were stacked neat, some coins and a piece of paper sat in the front. I grabbed the paper, glanced at Hypoole's infamous list.

Suddenly Hypoole moved behind me; I caught him out of the corner of my eye. I started to turn as he grabbed the portrait of his wife and swung it at me. I threw up my left arm to block it, tore straight through the canvas. I yanked my arm out of Mildred Hypoole's face as Hypoole dove across the bed.

He was agile for an old guy and he rolled off the other side of the bed, pulled a single-shot derringer from underneath a pillow. He didn't hesitate, squeezed off a shot.

The bullet tore through my left shoulder, spun me around. I banked off the wall, fell to the floor. Hypoole rushed over, kicked me in the face, grabbed at my gun. I yanked his hands away from the gun, drew up on my knees, grabbed him around the waist. I lifted him, tossed him against the dresser. The mirror shattered as he landed on the dresser, then slumped to the floor. I stumbled over, slapped the side of his face with my gun. He let out a burst of air, went prone.

I stepped over, reached into the safe, grabbed the rest of the bills and threw them on the bed. Blood filled my sleeve, my ears rang, shoulder throbbed. "We're going to talk, all right," I said. "We're gonna talk about how you used everybody in your sick, twisted scheme. We're gonna talk about how you convinced everyone that the high, mighty Arvis Hypoole needed to take down the policy rackets so he could become mayor. We're gonna talk about how you told Virginia Prescott that if Cordell went to the press with that list of cops that had been transferred, you'd lose your moment in the sun, the election!"

"It's true," he stammered. "This is much more important than one man."

"One man," I yelled. "One old, sick, twisted man! You probably sold it to yourself that it was some kind of war, casualties could be expected! You probably convinced yourself that you really were doing it for the election, for the country!"

"I was!" he screamed. "The Negro vote could put us over the top, and the only way to get it was closing the policy rackets and then promising them the new administration would return it. Can't you see? If Don

Cordell showed that list to the papers, we wouldn't get any credit. It would allow the Democrats to clean their own house. Then, even if they closed down policy, they'd have so much status with the white community that even the Negro vote couldn't help us. The Democrats are more vulnerable now than they'll ever be! This is our only chance!"

His voice grew stronger; his confidence returned. He palmed the wall like a spider, stood up. "Think about it, Gus. With Ed Jones out of the way, Lincoln Johnson would've become the leader in the rackets. He promised me the Negro vote! We can win the election!"

"But Jones is alive."

"For now!" he screamed. "You can still find him. There's forty thousand dollars there. Find him and kill him and it's yours! Do you think I would've stashed that much money in my safe if I didn't expect you to succeed?"

"Yep."

"You're wrong!"

"You never expected me to succeed, because you never expected me to live. Maybe that money's for Jameson, but if it is, I can promise you he's never gonna collect."

"W ... what happened?"

"Jameson's dead. So's the flunky he brought with him. Their tail followed the Italians, but I doubt if he caught 'em. And Ed Jones is probably home by now, safe and sound."

"But you can still find him. You'll kill him ... I know what kind of man you are."

"You're about to find out," I said as I stepped toward him.

"But ... our deal, the money ... ?"

"Consider that money your first real charitable donation." I palmed his face, pushed him onto the bed. He landed on his back, scurried back toward the headboard. I fell down next to him, leaned on top of him, put the .38 under his chin. "Tell me about the girl!" I screamed.

"What?"

"Martha Lewis, tell me!"

He started to slobber, shake his head like he'd stepped on a live wire. "I don't know what you're talking about. She's Jones' girlfriend…he might go there…she's a threat."

"She's not his girlfriend, you stupid fool. She just told you that to scare you away. She didn't realize it would put her in so much danger."

"But you…"

"I talked to her! I forgot your order and talked to her. She's a scared young lady with a crippled child to raise. She's got a lifetime of hard work ahead of her, but your money's gonna make it a little easier. You think you know me? That's a laugh. But I know what kind of man you are."

"W…what?"

"I know!" I screamed.

"Th…there's nothing to know. You can't possibly…"

"I know," I screamed, again. I grabbed his necktie, pulled it so hard that his face filled with blood; he struggled to breathe. "You raped her! Your wife brought her into your home to try and help her, but she delivered her to the devil. Then your poor, sympathetic, stupid wife had the audacity to let you outlive her. And you raped the girl! You raped her!!"

"No!" he shrieked. His eyes froze in terror. "A pack of lies. You've got it all wrong!"

"You raped her and she had your child, and when you found out, you put her up in that house so she wouldn't talk! She was just a scared girl with nowhere to go, so she lied about knowing Ed Jones, to keep you away. But it didn't work. You thought Jones knew, too. So you worked up this story about policy to sell to your cronies, me. You may have believed your own plan, but you really wanted to silence anyone that knew your dirty secret."

He shrank back. "The girl...th...that's not true. Someone's lying. And Jones, the votes...that was Virginia's idea. I didn't know anything about policy. You've got to believe that. She's used us both."

"Save it for your lawy..." It hit hard. "That's it," I said. "It's that fucking simple. You went to Cordell about Martha. He was your lawyer."

"That's not..."

"Attorney–client privilege," I murmured, hearing Burt Cordell use the exact words. "You figured he'd never say a word." I shook my head. "He didn't have to. He knew he had something on you so he told you about the kidnapping, gave you the list, tried to work a deal with the Republicans. Out with the coloreds and the Democrats, in with the Republicans and the Syndicate! But all he really did was tell you the timing was perfect for you to carry out your damn scheme. He had no idea how far you'd go to protect your secret and win office. You threw cash and promises at every stupid greedy man you could find...Hogan, Jameson, McGuire...and...oh God, where's McGuire?"

"I don't...I don't know," he said. Bull: I yanked on his hair. "I don't know!"

I shoved the gun deeper under his chin, pushed his head against the headboard. Quiet, I seethed: "You tell me right now, or I swear to God, I'll kill you. Is he at the girl's?"

"I don't know."

I slammed the butt of the gun down on a kneecap, he shot back, rigid. "Aaah!"

"Is he?"

"I...d...don't know."

I did it again.

"Aaaaaaaagh! Aaaaagh. I don't..."

I lifted the gun. He stammered: "Yes, yes. The girl's house…noon. If he didn't hear from me, that meant Jones was dead."

"And with Jones and Cordell both dead, you thought only one person, or one family, knew your secret!"

His mouth opened and closed like a fish out of water: "Gus," he stammered as I pulled the gun away from his neck, "please, please, put the gun away. You're not rational. You're not yourself." He trembled, clawed at his face, fought hysteria. "Please Gus, please… I'm begging you, be a good boy."

"You don't know," I said as I forced the muzzle into his mouth, stifled a sob, "how hard I've tried."

I shot his brains into the wall, filled a pillowcase with the cash, hit the stairs running.

Blood spilled down my arm, chest, like a flooding gutter. I dumped the money in the back seat, wadded the pillowcase into a ball, stuffed it inside my shirt, pressed it against the wound and buttoned the shirt tight. I'd lost a lot of blood—I weaved the Chrysler through the streets like a Friday-night drunk.

My tires scraped curbs; I sideswiped a delivery truck. I concentrated on the road, willed myself to the Lewis house. The rain had stopped, but I sprayed the sidewalks as I took every corner hard.

Lies: Martha Lewis's and Hypoole's. Lives: too many to count. Lost in it all, I turned her corner and saw Art McGuire walk toward the house. No time: I hit the gas pedal, jumped the curb. McGuire turned, his eyes went wide, a scream tried to work its way out of his throat. I hit him straight on, launched him toward the house like he'd been shot ass-first out of a cannon.

I stumbled out of the car, staggered to the front door. Martha Lewis opened it and I fell into the front room. McGuire's legs had caught on the windowsill—he hung in the front room like one of Bunny's rabbits. Martha screamed as her mother bustled toward the kitchen. I heard her pick up the phone as Martha yelled at me. "What's happening? What's going on? Gus, you're hurt!"

I slumped against the wall, pulled my left hand up to my shoulder like I cradled a robin's egg. "He was going to kill you. I had to…"

"Kill me," she shrieked. "Why?"

"Hypoole. He thought you told Ed Jones about Grace. He wanted you all dead."

"Oh, my God!" she screamed.

I heard her mother on the phone; she yelled their address, pleaded with them to hurry—the cops would be there in minutes. My legs went out from under me, I slid to the floor like a drop of water down a window. "Gus," yelled Martha, "you're hurt! We've got to get you to a hospital."

"Can't. No time…" I said. "Got to get out of here…"

"Oh, God," she said. "What's happened?" She kneeled down next to me, ran a palm across my cheek.

"They're dead."

"Who?"

"Hypoole, the people that wanted to hurt you. But I've got money in the car. I can take you all away. We can go…"

"Go where?" she asked, as she ran a hand across my brow.

I looked at her like she'd asked me to spell the final word at a spelling bee and it was a word I used every day but on this day it stared me in the face like a foreigner. Where? Where? I struggled with consciousness, looked for the word.

She pried my hand away from my shoulder. "We've got to get you to a hospital."

"Can't," I said.

"We have to."

"No...we've got to go away."

The sadness in her eyes answered me. She reached down and squeezed my hand. "But they might come," I said, but I didn't believe it.

"Who? You said they're dead."

"I...they are. But, you've got to...You...need me."

Her mother ran into the room, screaming. "They's on the way."

"We've got to help him, Mama," said Martha.

I reached for my wallet, emptied it on the floor. I pushed a slip of paper toward Martha. She looked at it, nodded her understanding.

My mind reeled: the car, the money. Martha's eyes had said it all: They wouldn't go with me, wouldn't take the money. "There's a little boy..." I said. They started to babble. The room spun like a merry-go-round. Their faces blurred, voices faded. I felt Sollie the Jew cradle my head. "You're gonna make it, Gus."

He lied again: I slipped back under the water.


I RODE ACROSS THE ROOM LIKE A BODY SLUNG OVER A HORSE. A steel mouth opened, I fell inside. Fumes, jarred, we moved.

More voices, attention, concern. Lifted, I floated, fell back on cool white cotton. My coat, shirt disappeared. The burning in my shoulder got worse—someone screamed from inside me. The veins in my neck popped, sweat poured from me like I'd sprung a leak. The scream hurt my lungs, burned my throat. A bee stung my neck. Everything went black.


I WOKE IN A STRANGE ROOM. My shoulder, body ached. My vision was blurry and I was drug-tired. I reached for my shoulder, felt the tape and gauze. Someone had cleaned up the wound, sterilized it; I could smell the rubbing alcohol. I rolled onto my right elbow, gritted through the pain, sat up. I glanced at a window—the blinds were closed tight.

I looked 'round the room, saw my clothes strewn over a chair. A walnut dresser and matching mirror sat on the other side of the room. I looked on top of the dresser, saw a jar full of pennies, a pocketknife and a picture. I studied the picture as Lucas Tanner slowly opened the door and stepped inside the room.

"My son and me," he said as he stared at the picture. His leathery face went soft. "That's when he was fifteen."

He noticed my expression, smiled. "No, this wasn't his room. It's a guest room. I put that picture up 'cause I like talking about him. He and his mother never lived here. His mother died a long time ago—flu."

"What time is it?" I asked.

Tanner glanced at his watch. "It's about six o'clock in the evening. You been out for a few hours."

"How did I get here?" I winced. My shoulder hurt, head swam.

"Young Negro girl called me. She said you gave her my number right before you passed out, so she figured I was a friend. I told her she figured right."

"Did she bring me here?"

He chuckled, smoothed his thick white moustache. "No, that was something else. The girl told me what happened, so I told her to bring you over here. Not thirty minutes later this big old colored gal pulled up in a green Plymouth, opened up the trunk and there you was."

"Did she leave anything with me?"

"Nope," he said. "Just said to tell you everything was gonna be fine."

A weak smile worked its way onto my face. They would keep some money, help Donnie White. Some good out of the whole thing. "Where am I?"

"My house," he said. "Lake Forest."

I closed my eyes, bit my tongue. "You're gonna need some more shut-eye; I'll leave you alone," said Tanner.

"Not yet," I said. "Who fixed me up?"

He chuckled. "Doc Green. He's still payin' off his debt."

"Will he keep it quiet?"

He smiled. "I made sure of that."

"How?"

"Don't you worry 'bout that," he said. He sat down at the foot of the bed. "I'm guessin' you're in a lot of trouble. I been thinkin' 'bout headin' back to Kansas, Gus. Seems like it might be a good time for you to clear out of town, too."

"How much do you know?" I asked.

"The girl didn't tell me nothing, 'cept you'd been shot and didn't want to go to a hospital. That was all I needed to know."

"No, it's not," I said. "You're risking a lot having me here. I killed some men today. I killed some cops today."

"Jesus!" he hollered. "What the hell happened?"

"Two of 'em were going to kill me, one of 'em was going to kill the girl that called you."

He shook his head. "Three men, Gus. You are definitely up to your ass in a mound of manure."

"Four men."

"Who was the fourth gonna kill?" he asked.

"Anyone that got in his way."

I pushed the covers off, saw that I'd soaked the mattress with sweat. My skin was damp and the air felt cool and good. I looked him straight in the eye and told him what had happened. He nodded his head as I talked, told me I'd had no choice. I didn't tell him he was wrong—the old Gus should've stayed buried. I didn't tell him that part of me enjoyed it—killing Hypoole was just. I didn't tell him that when I'd killed Tom Brody I'd seen Sam. I told him I wasn't done. I told him there was one more person who had to pay. I told him to get me some coffee, find me some clothes. I told him I was heading back to the Prescotts'.

THE DRIVE FROM LUCAS TANNER'S HOUSE to the Prescott estate was a short one and the May sun had just set. I grinned as Tanner drove along the windy road. When I'd told him I was going to the Prescotts' party, he'd looked at me like I'd told him Hope and Crosby were breaking up. The expression on his face still caused me to smile.

I cracked my window to let the night air slap me awake. "Sorry," I muttered to Tanner. He grunted and kept driving.

The air whistled over the window, and the hum of the engine stalled any conversation. I took advantage of the lull and rehearsed. I knew that Virginia had hired White, but there was nothing to tie her to Cordell's murder. I needed proof or a confession, and I wanted both. I pictured her in my mind, listened to her answers, practiced my lie.

WE SLIPPED INTO A LINE OF CARS outside the gate to the estate, waited to gain entrance. Tanner leaned over, looked at me, stern. "You sure you want to go through with this, Gus?" he asked. "No tellin' who's gonna be here. Your face just might send a hundred people to the phone."

I shook my head. "Only a few people know about my involvement and the only ones I don't trust are in the department, and they're still trying to find out what happened. Nobody could i.d. me at Sixty-second Street. None of the rest of you will say anything, and Hypoole's not talking."

"Well," he said. "Radio already reported that Jones was released, there was a shoot-out."

"But they didn't mention my name?"

He shook his head.

I ran through it, tried to convince myself. "I'm not sure how much Chief Hogan or any of the department stooges know about Hypoole and his plan," I said. "Hogan didn't know anything about the girl. Hypoole never seemed to leave his place—I doubt they even know he's dead, yet. It wasn't my car they found at the Lewis house, and I'm sure Martha and her mother told them they didn't know the driver. So nothing I've done leads back here, and if it did, this would be the last place they'd think I'd go."

The car in front of us moved through the gate, and we rolled up and stopped in front of a tall, black-haired young man in a monkey suit. It was the same guard I'd seen at the first party, and the snub-nosed revolver still bulged from under his jacket. Floodlights had been set up atop the gate, and I squinted as the guard stuck his head near Tanner's window. He smiled at Tanner, glanced at me. "Good evening, gentlemen. Welcome back. I remember you both from the last party," he said. "But you'll have to forgive me. I don't remember your names."

I started to open my mouth, Tanner cut me off. "I'm Lucas Tanner and this is my son's friend Ted."

The guard looked at his list, checked off Tanner's name. "I don't see a guest next to your name, sir."

"That's right," said Tanner. "Wasn't sure Ted here would come back, but guess that little filly of a daughter got to him. Say, if you need to call on up to the house to check and make sure it's okay that he joins me, I'm sure Mrs. Prescott won't mind being pulled away from the party for a few minutes."

The guard chewed his lip, tapped the pen against the list. "No," he said suddenly, "I guess it's all right. Like I said, I remember you both from last time. Enjoy the party."

The gate opened, and we glided up the driveway, stopped the car in front of the valet. Tanner tossed him the keys. The valet remembered me too—he whistled softly when he saw Tanner's silver Rolls, gave me a wink. "And it's silver, too," said the wink.

Tanner hurried around the car, walked close to me. Some of my strength had come back—the wound had turned out to be only a deep graze, but my legs were still wobbly, weak. We matched strides as we walked to the front door, nodded at the doorman and went inside.

It was nearly eight o'clock and the party was in full swing, so no one met us at the door. VOTE HYPOOLE FOR MAYOR, shouted a fifteen-foot banner, and judging from the party murmur that filled the air, nobody seemed to notice that the guest of honor hadn't shown yet—a fact that I didn't mind though Virginia probably did.

Music filled the air, and a woman's voice suddenly hushed the crowd noise. The voice started to sing a song I'd heard Sinatra sing: "Someone to Watch Over Me." Tanner and I followed the sound, which came from the ballroom at the end of the north wing. As we entered the room, with a procession of guests, a waiter handed us each a glass of champagne and I took mine in one gulp, placed the empty glass on the tray and took another. "Don't worry," I said as I noted Tanner's expression. "This is it for me. The painkillers are just wearing off."

Another red, white and blue banner proclaiming, VOTE HYPOOLE FOR MAYOR was strung behind a makeshift stage that had been set up near the back wall in the center of the room. A twelve-piece band stood on top of the stage, but in place of the lead singer, who looked on admiringly, stood Sheila. Her lips were painted a dark red and they glistened as she belted out the lyrics. She wore a deep red dress and black gloves, and her black hair was tossed across her shoulders. I figured she'd gotten her Cadillac. I figured it was as much her coming-out party as Hypoole's. She lifted her chin high, belted out the tune. Zachary Bloodworth stood off to her left, beamed at her.

I grunted, looked around the room. I wasn't surprised at the number of guests I recognized—their names had been etched in my mind since the last party, their bridge game. Margo Baxter gulped wine, lipstick smeared her glass and face. Gloria Blanchard stood with her back to her husband, talking to no one at all. The Saunders and the Doolittles chatted quietly, their eyes on Sheila. Eunice Saunders and Edna Franks pretended to do the same as they hustled toward a buffet table that had been set up on one side of the room.

There had to be two hundred people in the ballroom, and they all clapped adoringly when Sheila finished the song. She beamed and yelled her thanks, then bowed and stepped off the stage. Bloodworth took one of her gloved hands, pulled her toward him and gave her a passionate kiss. She stood there, for a moment, let the kiss linger, then turned to face the crowd and saw me. I returned her gaze but couldn't offer up any emotion. It was like trying to work up something for an old bicycle after your sixteenth birthday. I smiled and tipped my head back. Her brow furrowed, she said something to Bloodworth, let go of his hand and started to work her way through the crowd, toward me.

"Don't look now," said Tanner, " but here comes trouble."

"I know what you mean," I said.

He tapped my shoulder and nodded off to my right. I turned and saw Virginia bulling her way through a crowd of men. She squeezed by Tanner, let out a deep breath and said, "Well, I'm surprised to see you here, Gus. I don't recall inviting you."

"Your husband did," I said as a waiter walked by with a tray full of appetizers. I grabbed something with shrimp and bacon and popped it into my mouth. "So did Sheila."

"They do a lot of things without thinking," she said. "Lucas, if you'll excuse us, I'd like to talk to Gus alone.

Tanner glanced at me as Virginia grabbed my arm and started to lead me out of the room. Sheila walked up; when she saw her mother's arm wrapped in mine and the look on my face, she gasped. "Gus, where are you going?"

"I don't know," I said. "Why not ask your mother?"

Virginia nearly spat at her. "This doesn't concern you. Go make your-self useful. Sing another song or mingle with the crowd."

Sheila's face melted. "Gus?"

"Later," I said. My shoulder throbbed and I could feel the anger stir in my gut. I wanted to keep it fresh.

Virginia and I strode out of the room like two picnickers determined to win the two-legged race. Her heels clicked as we rushed down the hall; the heavy thud of my steps echoed. We reached the end of the hall and she opened the door to the study, nearly pushed me inside.

I steadied myself against a wall, fought blood-loss fatigue by concen-trating, surveying the room. A large oak desk stood in the middle of the study, a cup of cold coffee and a stack of papers on top. A leather captain's chair sat behind it and two brown leather chairs sat in front, flanked by matching floor lamps. Bookcases lined the perimeter and were filled with books that were mostly for show. They were covered with more dust than an umpire in Oklahoma, and I wondered if anyone in their family had ever read anything more than the funny papers or the business page.

Virginia interrupted my quick inventory with a hushed scream. "What the hell is going on, Gus? I got a call from a Chief Hogan a little earlier saying that you'd been involved in a shoot-out and that we'd bet-ter watch out for you. I guess I should've told the men at the gate."

A lock of her blonde hair fell across her forehead; she brushed it away with her hand. Her face was flush and the color drew out her eyes. Her bosom heaved, and the light blue gown that she wore nearly burst from the pressure.

"I'll tell you what's going on," I said. I moved close, and she stepped back toward the door. "What's going on is that Arvis Hypoole has turned on you."

She ran a hand behind her, brushed against some books. "What do you mean?"

"I know all about it. Cordell and Hypoole and the policy rackets and the Republicans. I know Hypoole came to you, that you paid the colored guy that worked in your garden to kill Cordell. I know that Hypoole lied to you."

Her legs began to tremble, and she ran both hands behind her as I stepped closer. Her left hand brushed more books, then the wall and finally the doorknob. "I don't know what you're talking about," she said. The fear started to drop from her voice. Her eyes darted, and suddenly her hand moved off of the doorknob and onto the latch. She turned the latch and locked the door. "What do you mean Arvis lied to me?"

"Hypoole told you that Cordell had a list of the twenty-seven men that had been transferred because they were cracking down on policy. He told you that if Cordell took that list to the press then the Republicans' only shot at mayor was over. Well, he lied. Cordell wanted to work with the Republicans. He gave Hypoole that list. I saw it myself. It was in his safe."

Her eyes moved around the room. She focused on my chest, slowly looked up from my neck to my chin to my nose to my eyes. When I caught her gaze, it wasn't the gaze of a strong woman, but that of a frightened child in search of a friend. "What makes you think all of this, Gus? How could you think these things of me?" If I'd have looked hard enough, I probably could've seen a tear pool in her eye.

I snorted. "Hypoole told me. He told me everything. He's not coming here tonight. He's going to the police and saying that it was you and me that planned the whole damn thing. He's saying that you came to him after your gardener killed Cordell. He's saying that you concocted the whole scheme and that Chief Hogan will side with him. He's going to the police and tell them that you told me Vaughn White was going to be at Mona's and that you set me up to kill him after he'd killed Cordell." My voice got louder, I grabbed her shoulders. "Think about it! I knew your family, I killed Vaughn White, it fits perfectly!"

She shrieked, stammered. "But Gus. That's not the way it happened! Arvis came to me. Arvis said that..." She broke free from my grip, ran behind the desk. "You're lying!"

I stepped forward, slapped my palms on the desk. "I'm not lying! Hypoole had another game going. Did you know about the girl?"

She looked at me like I was crazy. "What girl? What're you talking about?"

"He raped the colored woman that cleaned for him, the one with the crippled daughter. She was so afraid of him that she made up this lie about knowing Ed Jones. And Hypoole panicked. He told his attorney what had happened. His attorney, Don Cordell." I paused to let it sink in. "That's the real reason he wanted Jones and Cordell killed. He thought they both knew about the rape and he knew if word got out about what he'd done, he could kiss the election good-bye. Can't you see? He fooled you! He used you."

She threw a hand across her throat, scratched the nape of her neck. The frightened child act was over. She was all business: "Oh, Gus, you almost had me. Oh, Gus. Arvis Hypoole rape a girl. Hardly."

"Hardly?" I screamed. "Hardly?" I tore off my jacket, ripped open the neck of the shirt Tanner had given me. "Then why did he shoot me? Can you tell me that? Why did Hypoole shoot me?"

She saw the crimson-stained gauze wrapped around my shoulder, saw the bits of flesh surrounding it. She lost her balance, grabbed at the desk. "Oh, my God," she muttered. She regained her balance; her hands trembled. "Where is he?"

"He's at the police station by now. We've got to figure our way out of this. The son of a bitch offered me money and I went along, but now we're in this together." I stepped around the back of the desk, grabbed her by her shoulders. "How can he tie you to this? How?"

She looked up at me, her eyes went steely. She searched my eyes for an answer. "I don't know. No one will believe him. Gus, I swear..."

I shook her shoulders. "How?"

"But he..."

"How?" I shook her harder. Her hand whipped across the desk, hit the coffee mug and sent it crashing into the wall. Coffee splashed on the wall and drapes.

"He can't!" she screamed, frantic. "It's his word against ours, and Gus, I swear, I'm on your side. I'll say that he's crazy, that I never knew Vaughn White. I'll stay with you! You've got to believe me."

I squeezed her shoulders harder, slammed her into the back wall. The leather captain's chair toppled over and Virginia gulped for air. "How?" I screamed. "Hypoole said he could prove you hired White. How can he do that?"

She gasped for air, mouthed the words, quiet. "The checks."

"What checks?"

"Paychecks. But they don't prove anything. They just prove that we employed him. It's just his word against ours. Oh, Gus," she said as she straightened up. "We've just got to stick together. We're from the same side, you and I. Arvis can't beat us. The word of a war hero and a socialite against the word of a washed-up old man? He can't beat us!"

I felt her hands on my hips. She ran her hands up my sides and across my back, gently over the bandages on my shoulder. "We'll beat him," she said. "And when we do, that security job is yours—here." She looked into my eyes, her eyes darting between mine like she was typing a plan into my head. "It's you and me, just like it always should have been."

She leaned forward and kissed me, softly, tenderly. I let it go on, let her slip her tongue into my mouth, push her body against mine. I pulled my head back, slightly.

"There's only one problem," I said.

"What's that?" she whispered.

"I was wrong about Hypoole."

"What do you mean, wrong?"

"He's dead," I said.

She reared back. "Dead?"

"Yeah, dead. Funny thing is, he used my gun. And my hand."

She tore loose, leaped back and then lunged forward. I turned to avoid the blow, but she drove her fists into my shoulder. The pain shot through me, it took me to my knees.

Virginia screamed, kicked me in the groin, then stamped a high heel into my shoulder. I slid to the floor, fought nausea, felt blood start to drain from my shoulder. She reached over me, tore open a drawer and pulled out a pistol. She stepped around me, stopped near the edge of the desk, just out of my reach. I rolled onto my side, looked up at her. "Why?" I asked. "Because you might not get some government contracts? Because you might have to divide your estate into a subdivision or quit buying a new car every year? What the hell?"

She pointed the gun at me. "I told you. Once you've had money, you won't ever go without again."

"But your husband has money!"

"My husband is a whimpering fool," she said. "If I didn't take over the business, he'd swallow the rest of our money with a shot of scotch and if I didn't take care of this, he never would've. I'm sorry, Gus, but it appears you killed White and Hypoole and whomever else and you just tried to kill me."

I rolled, hard, to my right, as I heard the gun go off. I heard the thud of a body as I came to my knees and scrambled around the end of the desk. I peered around the desk as the smoke cleared and saw the blood-stained wall and Virginia's arm. She was lying face down, blood gushed from her head and already formed a small pool. I grabbed the pistol from her hand and looked over the top of the desk.

"It's all right, Gus," said Nat Prescott, the door still open behind him. He was dressed in a tuxedo with a black bow tie and cowboy boots. A rifle hung, loosely, at his side and he rocked, slightly. He had the dazed and confused look of a man who'd just shot his wife, and his lower lip quivered. "I . . . I couldn't let her kill you. I . . . She'd gone on long enough. She was a horrible woman, Gus, mean and spiteful and a worthless mother. I made a terrible mistake bringing her into this home." He looked at her body, tapped the rifle against his boot. "You know, I think this would surprise her. And I don't need a shot of scotch with it."

"No!" I screamed. I scrambled to my feet and dove at him, but I was too late. Nat Prescott put the end of the rifle in his mouth and joined his wife.

THE MUSIC HAD DROWNED OUT the sound of the shots from reaching most of the party, but a few people quickly gathered in the hall. When I came out and they saw the look on my face and the blood-soaked bandages on my shoulder they screamed and ran toward the ballroom.

I moved toward the foyer, not sure of what I was going to do. I'd walked into the study to con Virginia into helping me convict her. Then I'd planned on turning myself in, testifying against her and Hypoole and playing it out. I'd get off for the Carpaccis, die for Hypoole. I figured it was fair. I figured I'd do anything to keep someone else out of the ocean.

People flooded the hall, ran toward the study, others rushed for the door. "What the hell happened?" people yelled. Someone peered into the study and screamed.

Lucas Tanner was one of the first ones out. He saw me, shielded me from the onslaught, moved me into the foyer. He grabbed a trench coat off the banister, slipped it over my shoulders. "Follow me," he said.

We followed the crowd out the door, past the security men that streamed inside. "Nobody leaves!" yelled the black-haired kid with the snub-nosed revolver. His colleagues tried to stop everyone in the driveway, yelled at the valets to stop retrieving cars. A young valet with red hair stopped in front of us. I recognized him from the Carpaccis' theater. "Few more bucks for the horse races, kid?"

He looked up at me, grinned. "You again. I didn't see anybody come out through the window."

I looked into the distance. "What's the chance of us getting our car?"

Tanner handed him a tag with our valet number. The kid jerked his head to the right. "You can follow directions, chances are good. Got a sawbuck, the chances are better."

Tanner tapped the wallet in his breast pocket. The kid smiled. "Good. Now follow me and just walk cool. See, none of these people get their own cars, so when the cops show up, they'll figure if the valets ain't brought the cars, nobody's left. Just walk nice and slow."

We walked along the house until we moved past the glare of the house lights and reached the sanctuary of the oaks. Then we made straight for the street, nice and slow, like three chums on a Saturday night stroll through town. We reached the street in just a few minutes. No one was around—all of the activity was centered at the house and front gate. The kid led us down the street until we found Tanner's car. Tanner handed the kid his money, then thought better.

"Son, how'd you like to make another sawbuck?" he asked.

The kid looked at him like he'd been asked if he enjoyed breathing. "What gives?"

Tanner handed him the keys and the kid nodded in understanding as we slipped into the back seat, fell low. The kid fired up the car and started to drive. "No," said Tanner. "The other way."

"That's toward the house," said the kid as he leaned toward the back seat.

"Trust me," said Tanner. "This ain't my first county fair."

"Your money, Mac," said the kid.

The noise of the sirens grew closer as we moved and I pictured the squad cars approaching the driveway as we attempted to pass. The kid slowed down, said, "Keep it quiet back there." We ground to a halt. The squad cars' lights flashed through our car and I heard the kid roll down the window. Tanner and I dropped our heads, like it would do any good.

"Problem, Officer?" asked the kid. He was cool and collected; twenty bucks made him our buddy.

I heard a man's voice. He was still a few yards away, but I could make out his shouts clearly. "Nobody passes here. Oh, Hank, it's just a damn valet. What's that? Okay. Sorry, kid, but you'll have to take this car back the other way and park it. Nobody gets their cars and nobody leaves, so park this at the end of the block and come on back."

"Sure thing, Officer," said the kid. He rolled up the window, pulled a slow U-turn and started to whistle as we slid down the street.

THE KID HAD TURNED OFF HIS LIGHTS near the end of the block, and we'd made it far enough away to drop him off and thank him. We stopped off at Tanner's briefly, gathered his things and hit the road. We were silent throughout the ride. We made it out of Lake Forest, and nobody paid us any more notice than the coal truck on its daily route.

I stared out the window while the radio played: A commercial for Danny Thomas's show at the Chez Paree. An interview with Chief Hogan about the crackdown on policy: "The release of Ed Jones in no way decelerates our crackdown on the policy rackets." A report on a group of orphans singing for homes—nearly two hundred Polish war orphans had gathered at Union Station and sang the national anthem, the only words of English they knew. I nearly bit through my tongue at the thought.

Tanner reached over and turned off the radio. "What the hell was all that really about, Gus?"

I didn't know how to answer. I didn't tell him that I'd saved Ed Jones but was certain that the blacks were still going to lose policy. I didn't tell him that even though I'd added to the names of the dead, they wouldn't keep me awake at night. I didn't tell him I was through paying for others' sins. I told him it was Chicago politics. I told him it was greed. I told him to wake me when we hit the airport. I swallowed more pain pills and slept the rest of the way.

I WOKE TO THE NOISE OF PROPELLERS. I was seated in the back seat of an airplane. Its engines hummed, the propellers turned. Lucas Tanner turned to me from the pilot's seat.

"Where the hell are we?" I asked. I had to scream over the noise from the engines and propellers.

"It's a Lockheed Electra 12A. Same kinda plane that Amelia Earhart flew, but don't worry—my luck's better than hers."

"No, I mean where?"

"Midway Airport."

"Jesus," I said. "For a minute I thought I'd slept all the way to Kansas."

"Not hardly," he said. He turned around, started to work the controls. The hum of the propellers grew louder, and we started to taxi down the runway. "Nothing to worry about, Gus. Just sit back, relax and enjoy the trip. You're gonna love Kansas City. It's your kind of town."

We gathered speed, shot down the runway. We lifted, rose, flew. I looked down as the buildings grew smaller, lights grew fainter in the distance. I forced myself to relax, stay calm. I didn't think about the cops that were after me, the Syndicate's new price on my head. I didn't think about the bodies in my wake—the Carpaccis, Jameson and McGuire, Tom Brody and Hypoole. I didn't think about the other victims—Lydia White, Nat Prescott, his wife. I didn't think about Sheila, Martha Lewis, her mother and daughter.

I thought about growing up without a mother, a father. I thought about those orphans, singing the anthem. I thought of Donnie White and the money I'd left with the Lewis family—for them, for him.

I thought about '46, Chicago. The lights disappeared in the distance. I left it all behind.

# Chicago Daily

SATURDAY, MAY 18, 1946

## MURDER ROCKS HIGH SOCIETY!

### Lake Forest Murder Attempt/Suicide
BY DALLY RICHARDSON

Wealthy construction magnate Nathaniel Prescott III shot his wife and then killed himself last night, ending one of high society's most baffling marriages. No motive has been established in the shooting, which took place at a party at which the son of influential Republican leader Eustace Hypoole was to have declared his candidacy for mayor.

Virginia Prescott was listed in critical condition at press time, after being shot in the face with a bullet from a hunting rifle. Doctors are hopeful that she will survive but are already certain that she has been brutally disfigured.

The shooting took place at the Prescott estate in Lake Forest, which is presumed to be the last of the great estates. Witnesses said that Mrs. Prescott left the party and adjourned to a study with an unidentified male guest. After a loud argument ensued, Nathaniel Prescott approached the study carrying a hunting rifle. Witnesses said that Prescott appeared to be under the influence of alcohol and, moments after opening the door to the study, shot his wife. The unidentified male is said to have fled the scene.

The 1927 marriage of Nathaniel Prescott and Virginia Glockenheimer stunned high society. Prescott was the scion of the wealthy Prescott Construction family, while Glockenheimer was a reputed B-girl with a lengthy arrest record.

*See Beauty Scarred for Life, page 2*

## COPS KILLED IN SHOOT-OUT!

### Two Killed
### as Policy Racketeer Released

Two Chicago police officers were killed at the scene of the release of kidnapped Negro policy racketeer Ed Jones. A police spokesman said that Officers Carl Jameson and Thomas Brody were killed by unknown gunmen as they attempted to arrest the kidnappers and rescue Jones yesterday morning.

The police spokesman said that Jones's brother George left a bag full of ransom money at the corner of 62nd and Gillette, as the kidnappers had demanded. Moments later, the kidnappers picked up the money and released Jones, only to be confronted by Jameson and Brody. Both officers were killed in the ensuing gunfight. Jones told the police that the shooter was short, stocky and Italian.

Brody was the brother of infamous Chicago cop "South Side" Sam Brody, who was convicted in 1943 for the murder of a federal judge.

*See Brody, page 3*

### Son of Famous Pol Murdered

The son of the late Republican leader Eustace Hypoole was shot and killed yesterday in what police are deeming a random burglary.

Eustace Hypoole was one of the city's most influential political leaders. In his heyday, he christened many a Republican mayor. It was thought that Eustace Hypoole's blessing was all that was needed to become the Republican candidate.

*See Eustace Hypoole, section 3, page 7*